Murder on Ashton-on-Tinch

THE BRITISH BOOK TOUR MYSTERIES | BOOK 7

EMMA DAKIN

Seattle, WA

CAMEL PRESS

A Camel Press book published by Epicenter Press

Epicenter Press
6524 NE 181st St. Suite 2
Kenmore, WA 98028.
For more information go to:
www.Camelpress.com
www.Coffeetownpress.com
www.Epicenterpress.com

Author website: www.emmadakinauthor.com

All rights reserved. No part of this book may be reproduced or transmitted in any form or by any means, electronic or mechanical, including photocopying, recording, or any information storage and retrieval system, without permission in writing from the publisher.

No generative AI was used in the conceptualization, planning, drafting, or creative writing of this work. No permission is given for the use of this material for AI training purposes.

This is a work of fiction. Names, characters, places, brands, media, and incidents are the product of the author's imagination or are used fictitiously.

Design by Rudy Ramos

Murder on Ashton -on-Tinch
Copyright © 2026 by Marion Crook

ISBN: 9781684922819 (trade paper)
ISBN: 9781684922826 (ebook)

LOC: 2025942369

DEDICATION

To all those people in Hampshire and Devon who lifted my suitcase on and off trains, carried it up and down stairs, stopped in their busy day to give me directions or explain the streets to me, and who always knew the best places to eat.

AUTHOR'S NOTE

This book takes place in Hampshire and Devon in the south-west of England. Ashton-on-Tinch, Hampshire, is an imaginary village located near the real town of Alton and village of Overton. Basingstoke is the nearest large town and the city of Winchester to the south is located about 20 miles (33 km). I spent time in that beautiful country among the friendly and informative residents.

While researching this book, I stayed at the Grand Hotel in Torquay, Devon, where Agatha Christie stayed and where the characters in this book stay. The tourists in this book also travel to Oxford. I could imagine them wandering over Oxford, on top of the Carfax Tower, in Blackwell's Book Store, and walking over the Magdalen Bridge because I have recently been to those places. I travelled into many of the byways and small towns they explored and ate at some of the restaurants. I couldn't manage the huge meals they enjoyed, but the menus were a poem.

There is a unit called the Major Crimes Team in the Scotland Yard Police, although they've never heard of Detective Inspector Mark Evans. Like many police forces, the Met (Scotland Yard) had staff shortages at the time I researched this book. I expect that hasn't changed.

When writing the book I set it in the time I do the research, and while communities change with time, they seem to change less in Britain than they do in many other places. Homes built centuries ago are still standing and still lived in as family homes. While the people who live in a village may be contemporary thinkers and comfortable in this digital age, they live among their past. Such proximity colors life, gives it continuity, and evokes connection to other villagers. Such an atmosphere is reflected in this book.

CHAPTER ONE

My Victorian brick and flint semi detached looked welcoming. The late dahlias splashed a corner of the garden with burnt orange; the rowan tree flashed bright red berries; Peter Brown's special bronze chrysanthemums decorated a sheltered spot near the door. While I shared the house with Mark, I still felt proprietorial, as if I'd somehow built it brick by brick. A fantasy. It's nineteenth century, and I am fifty-two years old not two hundred.

"Claire, *cariad*. Home, wonderful home!" Mark picked me up, whirled me around and carried me across the threshold. That was no mean feat as I am almost as tall as he is and no light-weight. All those muscles, though. Lovely. He set me down in the foyer and kissed me.

We'd had a brilliant holiday in Cornwall and were back in Ashton-on-Tinch. I'd savor the flashes of memory of walking along the shore, pub dinners in the evenings, and all those lovely B and Bs. I sighed. We were home now and needed to be ready to take up our lives again: me to shepherd American tourists to the sites of mystery novels and Mark to keep order as a Detective Inspector for the Hampshire Constabulary. He was currently on loan to the Major Crimes Investigative Team and could be posted anywhere at a moment's notice. It made for an unpredictable life. Holidays were rare, so we'd made the most of this one.

Mark gathered the mail that had accumulated on the floor before Gulliver could make confetti of it. My well-behaved dog has just developed a passion for paper. Mark dumped the letters on the kitchen table and put on the coffee. Gulliver, all twelve pounds of wriggling Cavalier King Charles spaniel, kept his eyes on the envelopes. By the time I'd put our luggage in our room, the coffee was ready—Seattle's Best, a luxury.

Gulliver had abandoned his efforts to wrest the envelopes from the table which he couldn't reach and settled underneath it. Mark pulled up chairs and spread the mail before us. I glanced around the kitchen, appreciating the cheerful yellow curtains, the wood paneling, the flagstone floors. I loved this house.

Mark glanced at his letters, then looked more closely. "This one is from a solicitor's office. I wonder what they want. 'Churston and Taylor'. Never heard of them."

"Where are they located?" A letter from a solicitor was a curiosity. It could be disastrous, like a notice of motion to sue you or a demand from the tax department. A solicitor's letter wasn't always good news, but it could be. I remembered the notification I'd received from my stepfather's solicitor informing me of the legacy that had changed my life.

"Surrey. It's from Surrey." He pulled a key from his pocket and slit open the envelope. I watched him, happy to just appreciate him: his curly black hair still abundant at fifty-four, his height a little taller than my five-foot eight, and his stocky Welsh physique. *Cariad.* He'd called me, his darling. Those Welsh endearments gladdened my heart. I was getting used to this feeling of warmth and appreciation that surged over me on occasions like this. I waited while he read the letter, enjoying the calm, the peace, the loving energy.

Mark had stopped reading and was exceptionally still. Every muscle seemed frozen. His face paled. He looked as though someone had hit him over the head with a griddle pan.

"What's wrong?" My lazy feeling of contentment evaporated. "Your family? Your mum? Your dad? They're all right?"

"*Oes*, as far as I know. Its's not about them." He bent to re-read the letter, looked up at me, chewed his lip, and started to speak, only to stop, then try again. I was starting to worry.

"This letter from Peter Churston of Churston and Taylor," he said.

"Yes," I encouraged.

"He..." Mark hesitated then took a deep breath and went on. "He tells me that Britanny Helen Wilson has died. Cancer. A quick and fatal cancer."

I'd never heard of her. "That's too bad. Did you know her well?" That was a foolish question. If he was getting a letter from her solicitor, he must have known her well.

Mark cleared his throat. "At one time, a little over ten years ago." I relaxed. Ten years ago, I was making unsound relationship decisions. He might have been doing the same.

"Is her death a shock to you?" Did he still have feelings for her?

"Well, yes. She's wasn't fifty yet, so dying that young is a shock, but it's not that."

"She left you something?"

"That she did. She left me her daughter."

"Her daughter!" I shot up straight in my chair. A child? She left Mark a child? Like a gift?

"Apparently," Mark said. "She's also my daughter."

There was total silence while we both absorbed this news.

"You didn't know." It was a statement not a question because Mark never would have abandoned a daughter.

"No. She didn't tell me. We weren't together very long, maybe two months. I never heard from her after we split." He paused for a second. "A daughter?" He glanced back at the letter. There was wonder in his voice. "The solicitor is going to send the results of the girl's DNA. He suggests I have it matched to mine, so both I and 'my daughter' can be assured that we are related."

I swallowed. Took a deep breath and tried to think logically. "Will you do that?"

"Probably." He sounded bemused. "It would be good for both of us to be sure, but I expect it will turn out a match. Britanny would have known."

He looked at me then away. "I should tell you more." He was silent.

I waited. The hairs on my arms stood up. I cold feel a tingle along my back. *Keep quiet, Claire. He'll tell you what is important.*

"Britanny and I dated as I said for about two months. We decided it wouldn't work. I got this job opportunity here in Hampshire, and she didn't want to move. We said goodbye with fondness but not heartache. We didn't keep in touch. It seemed better that way." He shook his head. "Why didn't she tell me? I would have tried to be a father."

Part of me agreed with Mark. She should have told him. The other part of me wondered if Britanny didn't want to risk being trapped into a relationship with a man she had decided wasn't right for her. Mark would have wanted time with his daughter. Britanny would have had to share her. It would have been a difficult decision.

I ignored my own advice about keeping quiet and said, "Does the daughter know about you?"

He studied the letter. "Amber. Her name is Amber. She knows a little about me, apparently. Who I am. What I do for a living." He lowered the letter and stared at me. "A ten-year-old daughter! Me, a father?" He was quiet, then suddenly grinned, a huge, wide grin. "I'm a daddy! How do you feel about being a mum?"

I stared at him. "Oh my word!" *How did I feel?* "Gobsmacked,"

"That about sums it up. Here, read the letter."

We re-read the letter together and understood that one Amber Britanny Wilson was in need of her father. She had been living with her mother in Woking, Surrey, but after her mother's death, had gone to stay with her grandparents in Yorkshire. She couldn't live with them permanently. Both grandparents had heart conditions and were not able to care for her, although they would like to be involved in her life.

My mind hopped around like a flea. If she lived in Surrey, she'd probably have a home country accent not a Yorkshire one. That would be more like mine without Mark's Welsh lilt. Although I couldn't know that. What would she look like? What would she *be* like?

Mark read from the letter, telling me Britanny had instructed Mr. Churston to inform Mark Evans of the existence of his daughter and the request that he recognize her, provide a home for her, and love her. She had retained a private detective several months ago to inquire about his circumstances and realized he was married. She hoped his wife would accept Amber. She was sorry that they couldn't meet and talk this through. She had thought she would have more time but the cancer was relentless.

It must have been fast if she didn't have time to even ring Mark. Or perhaps she kept putting it off until the cancer caught her.

"When do we go and get her?" I asked. "Amber." I tested her name, trying to get familiar with it.

"You re just going to accept her? A daughter?"

I stared at him. "What else would we do?"

Mark surprised me by reaching over, pulling me out of my chair, and carrying me to the sofa. He cuddled me on his lap. "You are the most understanding, wonderful woman."

Gulliver barked, disturbed by the suddenness of Mark's movements, then trotted over to collapse on the rug.

"That's true," I said and kissed him. I didn't say I was one terrified woman. What did I know about being a mother?

"How do you feel about being a dad?"

He stared at me. "Excited? Happy? Worried? Panicked? All of that. I never thought of being a father. I thought my job would make me a right failure. It might still make me a failure."

I could hear the rising anxiety in his voice. I didn't know if I could help him. My own father was a total disaster who'd vacillated between sentimentality and rage, succumbing to drink at age forty to the great relief of all. I didn't know what good fathers did, although my stepfather had been a good man, and my sister's husband was attentive to his children. We had examples around us.

"Your parents. They are going to suddenly be grandparents."

Mark grinned. "My mum will love it."

Mark's mum and dad lived quite a distance away in north Wales, but they could visit. His only sibling, his sister, had died several years ago and not left any children. Amber would be their only grandchild.

I hugged him. "This is going to take some time to think through."

"It is that."

I tried to envision our lives with a ten-year-old girl in it. Those words in the letter were going to translate to a huge change. It was as though my quick acceptance of her and our transformed family life suddenly had become real. My heart started beating fast, I breathed quickly. "Just a minute. Mark. Just a minute." I tried to slow my breathing. I knew this rising heart rate and rapid breathing was panic. I'd experienced this only once, at the top of a Ferris wheel. My friend had calmed me then, and I hadn't jumped off, although I'd felt the urge to do that. I could control this. I could. I just had to concentrate. Mark held me and breathed with me.

"All right?" he asked when I finally relaxed.

"Yes, all right. It's just that I realized how this was going to affect us. We can't walk around the house naked. We can't swear in front of her. Someone will have to be home to look after her. Our life will be curtailed, narrowed, constrained." I barely controlled a wail of worry.

He stared at me. "No having my mates in for a beer after work. No hopping out to Jack's for a game of darts of an evening."

Imaging how it would affect Mark helped me calm down. "It's going to be a huge difference."

He reached for me again held me close "Yes, it will. It will be momentous."

"But we must do it," I said firmly.

"Indeed. We must." He murmured that into my hair.

We were going to need luck as we were without any parenting experience. A couple of booby birds with their blue feet and dozy approach to life had more parenting skills.

We decided that we would leave Amber where she was with her grandparents in Yorkshire for another two weeks while we registered her for the fall term in school here and got her room ready. We would need at least one initial visit with her. We had a lot to consider. We made lists.

I had some idea what ten-year-olds were like—my niece and nephew had both been ten at one point—but I had no idea what a ten-year-old girl who had just lost her mother would make of us. Surely, she'd be fearful of what kind of a father she was going to have and highly suspicious of a stepmother. There were so many questions: How do you help a child deal with the loss of her mother? How do you know what she needs? Who do we consult to help us? Would her grandparents help or be a hindrance? What legal steps do we need to make? How was Amber feeling about this?

The immediate problem was: Where would she sleep? At the moment, we only had a small pull-out sofa bed in my study for guests. That wouldn't do. I'd have to give up my study. I'd have to give up more than that: privacy, spontaneity, time, and money, although money wasn't a problem We would need a bigger house. I felt a pang of loss. I didn't want to give up my house. I *couldn't* give up my house. Maybe we could add on to it.

The whole idea of living with a ten-year-old was daunting, but I surprised myself when I realized I thought it would be fascinating to have a child with us. This would be a future neither Mark or I had imagined. Amber would not have anticipated it either.

"Blimy!" my sister Deidre said when I rang her and told her I was going to be a mum. "This will be an immersion experience."

I agreed. "Like jumping into a raging river. You and Michael had your kids as babies and grew into your parenting roles. Mark and I are going to just dive in."

"A baptism of immersion. Constant mistakes. Crying in the bathroom because that's the only place you'll have privacy. Taking long walks in the woods so your screams of frustration won't alarm the family."

"Deidre! Stop it. You're scaring me."

She laughed. "You're going to need a regular counselor. I know I do." Deidre gave advice as if I was paying for it. She was a barrister and people usually did pay her to solve their problems, so she almost automatically dispensed advice. I'd have to sift through it for what I wanted to do and what I didn't. After we disconnected, she texted me the number of an on-line counselor she recommended. That was useful. I had a feeling that counselor was going to be important to me.

The DNA results were a match. Mark was sure they would be, but it did remove any lingering doubt.

Every decision Mark and I made about Amber took a lot of discussion. We spent hours at our kitchen table, drinking tea and going over our choices.

"Mark, you grew up with normal, reasonable parents and a sibling in an almost picture-book family. I grew up with a loving mother, an alcoholic father and a sibling so much younger than me we shared very little except the experience of yells, hitting, drama, and hiding with our mother. Amber has grown up with a single mom. We have nothing in common." I could hear my voice rise.

"My family was stable for a long time until my sister skidded off into addiction. That tears you apart fast."

His sister had died some years ago. I expect I idealized his upbring because mine was so different. "The thing is, we can't rely on our own experience to understand Amber's."

I had to believe we would come to understand her. I could hope.

Mark took three days off work and went to Yorkshire to meet Amber, her grandparents, and their solicitor. We thought it best that Mark meet Amber alone, so she didn't feel overwhelmed, and I could attend to the renovations in the house.

I contacted the counselor, whose name was Maxine Morgan-Smith, 'Just call me Max". She gave me advice on how to interact with Amber for the first few weeks: keep a routine, listen to her, be reasonable. I could probably do that.

Mark stayed overnight at a hotel in York and called me when he was settled and had time to talk.

"We stared at each other when we first met," he said. "Britanny was blonde, but Amber looks like me with dark, curly hair and brown eyes. It's uncanny." His voice held that tinge of awe I'd heard before.

"And quite wonderful?"

"And quite wonderful," he agreed. "George and Freya, her grandparents, want Amber to come to us soon because they have some medical tests, and they would rather she got settled before they have to deal with all the traveling and waiting on doctors they expect. Also, they'd rather she had time with us before she had to start at a new school."

That was reasonable. "How are they with her? Caring?"

"I think so, in their Yorkshire, no-nonsense way. Amber seems to be comfortable with them. I guess she's spent quite a bit of holiday time with them in the past."

Mark's parents wouldn't have had that history with Amber. They might never become as close to her as her maternal grandparents.

Mark returned home and back to work. I put my energies into reorganizing the house.

Earlier in the month, I had contacted my handyman Peter Brown, my cleaner Rose Jones, and a carpenter called Desmond Parmar. Desmond, who was about thirty, slim, energetic, with brown skin, brown hair, and intelligent brown eyes told me he could do the design and oversee the renovations.

"I'm ADHD, you know, Mrs.," he said as he sat drinking tea at my kitchen table and occasionally patting Gulliver who sniffed around his knees. "I like moving all the time. Your project," he gestured to the rough plans he'd drawn, "is a bit of a lark for me. Fast, you know. I can get it done in a fortnight."

"Really?" I was astounded. Renovations in my experienced took forever.

"Yes, I can. I have a lot of trades I can get'" he paused, "mostly relatives, so I have some leverage, don't you know?"

I smiled greatly relieved.

Among his relatives he had a plumber, an electrician, and a carpenter. Desmond was a find. He did finish it in two weeks.

Mark arranged to travel back to Yorkshire and pick up Amber just as the renovations were completed.

I congratulated Desmond as I paid him.

"It was a doddle," he said. "My biggest problem was keeping Hardeep working. He's a lazy sod."

I recalled Hardeep. He was the electrician, about twenty-one, dark eyes, long dark eye lashes, full of good humor and quick smiles. "You did it."

"Ah, yes. I got his mum to nag him. She's my aunty. It's called the family-management-business model." He grinned.

"It worked."

Desmond and his crew had moved my desk from my former study to a corner of the living room where they'd created an office area. I set up my computer and printer there. It wasn't private, but it was, at least, a designated office space. I needed a desk, computer, and files to run my book tour business. Desmond's cousin Hardeep had replaced the wiring in Amber's bedroom to take the electronics I expected she would want, if not now, then in a few years. I had him rewire our bedroom as well. He'd done a good job and we now had a charging station and more plug points in each room.

One of Desmond's many cousins had plastered the wall of my former study and repainted the room in a pale green which I hoped would be restful. I had to take Gulliver out for many walks during the painting process as he was fascinated by the activity and smells in Amber's room and got in the way. I had visions of my white, black, and tan spaniel sporting patches of green.

There was no space for an additional bathroom which I expected we were going to need. For now, we would have to share.

I'd ordered a new bed which was delivered. Peter Brown struggled upstairs with the awkward package and spent an hour assembling it, grumbling all the time—but then he always grumbled no matter what he was doing for me. If he was planting bulbs I'd bought, they were the wrong color. If he was digging in my garden, it was in the wrong place. I was used to him.

I bought sheets, a duvet, and a fluffy rug to lay beside the bed, a cork board for the wall, hangers for her clothes, a laundry bag, and a smaller desk and chair. It looked inviting. I hoped she'd like it.

Mark drove to Yorkshire to collect Amber. That would give them time alone on the drive back to get to know one another. Two of us might be too much for her, so I opted to stay home.

Peter Brown came over on the day Amber was due home with a pot of tiny yellow roses, "For the wee lass." I had to blink to keep back the tears. I couldn't have imagined Peter Brown being that sensitive and kind.

Rose, after spending the previous day helping me clean the house from top to bottom, came over with brownies. "All kids like chocolate," she said. The village was prepared to welcome her.

I vacillated between excitement and dread. What if she hated us,? Me in particular? The villagers? The school? What if she was so upset she started throwing things? Or punching holes in the wall? Or screaming at me? I wasn't educated or experienced enough for this. I had no idea how to be a mum. I took a deep breath and faced the truth. I was going to be one. Amber had no place else to go.

CHAPTER TWO

At first, Amber was quiet, and prone to tears. She was polite but distant and rarely made eye contact with me. She was more at ease with Mark, talking to him and searching him out—that is, after she'd cuddled with Gulliver. He adored her and snuggled with her whenever she was still, sleeping in her bed and generally adopting her as a sibling. Mark and I missed Gulliver in our bed, but Amber's need was greater. After the first month, she stopped waking in the middle of the night and adjusted as well as anyone could after the loss of her mother. My counselor Max, who I contacted weekly, gave me advice.

"Establish a routine of wake and bed-time, snacks and meals, so she'll feel more secure, safer. Her world has turned upside down, you know."

"I know and I'm trying. But I don't know how she feels. She doesn't talk much."

"Don't expect miracles the first week, Claire. Are you generally a reliable person?"

I thought about it. "Yes, I am."

"Then you'll be fine."

I hoped so.

Mark and I did that as much as possible. We managed to live on top and around one another in this small house. I loved my nineteenth century flint and brick house and didn't fancy leaving, but if I stumbled over Amber's Wellingtons and Mark's briefcase one more time I might be reconciled to it. We were trying to live amicably together, but it was difficult. Luckily, the Stonnings who had the other half of this semi-detached were rarely at home, so we didn't have to try to control the noise; nor did we have to listen to their parties. Their attached house was a second home for them, and they had not been there for months. We were the last house in the village on The Street so had some space around us and some privacy.

"Why is our road called 'The Street'?" Amber had asked me about a month after she arrived. After the first month she'd finally begun to talk. Max told me to speak to Amber as if I expected a reply but not to complain when I didn't get one. The stone wall response had been maddening. It had made me feel as if I was invisible, but I followed Max's suggestions and eventually Amber recognized me as a fellow resident.

"It's called The Street because it's an old Roman Road. They called the roads that went directly through a village or town "The Street". You'll see that name everywhere."

"That's silly, really," she'd said. "Just because the Romans called it The Street doesn't mean we have to do that two thousand years later. We should call it…" She thought for a moment. "School Street" because the school's on it at the other end."

I didn't point out that the church and the library were also on it.

At the end of August, Amber had started at the local junior school in Year Six. Deidre had come for visit at that time and had given me so much advice my head spun.

"Year Six is multiplication tables and long division in math," she'd said. I was fine with that. I kept the accounts for my tour business.

"And fractions and ratios and geometry."

"Mark can help her," I abdicated.

"No reason why not," Deidre said. "Except he's often away with his murders."

While Mark was a Detective Inspector with the Hampshire Constabulary, he had an appointment on the Major Crimes

Investigations Team. He could be anywhere in England or Wales investigating crime. I couldn't be home all the time either.

"I have a tour booked in September," I fretted. "What are we going to do?"

We managed. Mark requested a week's holiday to stay home with Amber when I expected to be on a week's tour with four American guests. I would collect them from Heathrow on Sunday and tour with them until Thursday. At first, they would stay in Ashton-on-Tinch at The Badgers, a local BnB. I would be home to sleep at night but off with my group all day. Some of those days would be long. Then I would take them to Devon.

I hoped this schedule would work. It had worked on paper when I'd set out all the concerns and what to do about them. I liked planning. Deidre tells me that it's my way of controlling the future, but I see it as reasonable. I trusted that no murders would occur that needed Mark's expertise and that his chippy boss Superintendent Marjorie Addison would leave him in peace for the week.

Amber's Yorkshire grandparents had come to visit twice, staying for a few hours each time.

"You're doin' fine, lass," Freya Wilson told me when we were alone in the kitchen. "She's a good girl. Smart. Is she still quiet?"

"Not so much now. In fact, she chatters a lot."

Her grandmother smiled. "You're doing grand."

Freya's praise meant much to me. I was grateful for her visits. Mark's parents decided to wait until Amber was more used to living with us before visiting. They were excited about her, though, and sent her a welcome gift of books.

Gulliver was in heaven. There had never been so much food on the floor. It's not that Amber was deliberately messy, but she ate as she walked and managed to drop food all over the house. I didn't complain because I didn't have to clean it up, Gulliver, did that.

Food had been a problem for us with Amber. She was a vegetarian—a ten-year-old vegetarian—and Mark and I were not. I agreed with her that plant-based food was going to be more and more the choice of the British public, and I agreed her mother had made a good decision to eliminate as much dairy and meat as possible, but Mark and I weren't converts. The spicy smell of bacon still held an irresistible appeal.

"Pigs had to die for you to eat that, Claire," she admonished me.

I knew that.

"It's an inefficient protein source," she continued.

I knew that too. Where did a ten-year-old get that vocabulary? Likely from her mother. She'd been a good mother. Maybe I could learn to eat more veggies.

I pottered around the garden, tying up the chrysanthemums and picking a few late gooseberries and a Bransom apple, the only one on the tree. I took a few moments to admire the warm tones of the brick around the windows and the glitter of sunlight off the flint. Peter Brown, had planted purple and white asters in clumps around the front garden where they gave a soft ambiance like a Monet painting. He'd be horrified at the comparison.

"They're practical, give color, and can handle an early frost," he would say. Still, in spite of his curmudgeon attitude, he created beauty. Rose Jones created order inside the house. I stroked the door jamb as I passed it. I loved my house, and I did not want to leave it. We would make our cramped space work.

I had time to answer a few emails before Amber was due home from school. We'd scheduled a visit to the church to check out the youth programs. Gulliver who had been napping at my feet suddenly sat up, stared at the wall, then trotted to the front door. I closed the file and left the computer.

"Hi, Amber. How was school?" Amber was tall for her age, and strong as she bicycled or walked everywhere. She had her dad's curly dark hair but, she told me, her mother's pale skin. She was thin. I didn't know why, as she ate often.

"S'alright." She hung her rucksack on the pole near the door and shrugged out of her sweater. She dropped it on the floor. Gulliver pounced on it.

"Oops," she said, glancing at me. I waited. She play-wrestled on the floor with Gulliver who loved it and managed to get her sweater back while she rubbed his tummy. She hung the sweater beside her rucksack.

"Is there anything to eat?"

"I've been to the bakery. Help yourself." I moved after her to the kitchen and plugged in the kettle for tea. Amber found the tea cakes and fairy cakes and put three on her plate. I didn't comment as Max had said she would probably overeat for a few months to comfort herself and to just let her do it.

Now that Amber had decided to talk to me, she talked a lot.

"There's this girl in Year Six who is a real prick."

"Is there another word that isn't so vulgar that would describe her?" Deidre had coached me on how to get kids to change their vocabulary.

Amber thought for a moment then said, "No."

So much for tactful guidance. "Go on."

"She tries to take my bag and get my snacks out of it but I'm bigger, so I don't let her."

I brought two cups of tea in mugs to the table and sat opposite her. I pushed her tea toward her.

"She tells me I'm an orphan. 'Ya! Ya! You're an orphan. No one wants you.' I'm not an orphan." She stared at me.

"Of course, not. You have a dad and a step-mother and grandparents and a step-aunt and uncle and cousins and a dog." I touched each finger of my hand enumerating her relatives. "Definitely not an orphan."

"What a liar she is." She added sugar to her tea and blew on it.

"What's her name?" I asked.

"Priscila. Who calls their kid Priscila? A stupid name."

I liked that name but didn't say so. "How are you going to deal with her?"

Amber paused to finish the tea cakes and pull the wrapping off a fairy cake. "I'm going to ignore her most of the time, but if she tries to get my bag again, I'm going to smack her"

I didn't tell her not to use physical force. What did I know about bullying at school? The nastiness of sixth form in my school seemed mild compared to what happened in school theses days. My niece Kayla had been severely bullied at school last year, and I knew it could be serious and dangerous. At the moment, I thought Amber was handling it as well as she could. I hoped it wouldn't come to a physical fight.

"Why is she doing it do you know?"

"Bad temper. Total brain shrinkage. Bad diet. Stupid parents. Take your pick. I don't know, and I don't care."

"I see." She had a good point. She needed to protect herself more than she needed to psychoanalyze the bully. I changed the subject.

"We are due at a meeting with Mrs. Fotheringham-Whitley in fifteen minutes for a talk. Is that going to work for you?"

"About the youth groups?"

"Yes."

"Right." Amber chased the crumbs from the pastry around on the plate until there wasn't one left. "Is her name really Fotheringham-Whiteley?"

"It is."

She shook her head. "Stupid name."

I could see that 'stupid' was the word of the week.

"She doesn't lead the groups, though. She just organizes them. She's the vicar's wife."

"Is *his* name Fotheringham-Whitley?"

"Just Whitley."

She considered that for a moment. "Not quite a feminist then."

I didn't see how she worked that out, but I didn't pursue it. Some conversations with Amber were like mazes. I never knew where they were going. Sometimes she was blunt and direct with questions such as: When you're away, what happens to me?

I'd told her about my coming tour to Devon, how long I'd be away and what we'd planned for her care. She had just nodded. I didn't know how she'd felt about it.

At this moment, she was interested in her after-school plans.

"Stephanie goes to choir at the church. Maybe I could get into that?"

"We'll ask," I said. That might be a good fit for her. She would do well as I'd heard her sing. She had her dad's musical genes.

"Right." She took her empty cup to the dishwasher. "I'll just go to the garden with Gulliver for ten minutes. Call me."

She came when I called, and we walked to the St. Hilda's, Church of England, which was on our street about half-way between our house and the school. I had arranged to meet Joyce in the church proper as she didn't have an office. I wondered about that. She did so much work for the church, you'd think they'd give her office space—and a secretary.

I didn't go to church often, but I loved the peaceful atmosphere of this one. The wood was dark as befitted a Victorian edifice; the stained glass of the windows was brighter than the period usually allowed. Amber was distracted by a tabby kitten who was posing on a gravestone, stretching its limbs, revelling in the warm September sun. She stopped to admire and pet it which is why I reached the interior of the church before her. I stared, whirled, and blocked the doorway.

"What's the matter," Amber asked me, stopping on the top step.

"There's been an accident. I want you to go home and," I improvised quickly. "Take Gulliver for a short walk, feed him, then change into your riding clothes. I will be back as soon as I can."

"What happened?" She tried to peer around me.

I put both hands on her shoulders. "It's serious. I need you to do as I say." I controlled my voice.

She was still for a moment, then turned and headed back down the path.

When I was sure she was indeed leaving, I turned back to the church.

Draped across the bottom steps was a man. He was still, far too still. One hand was stretched out as if supplicating the deity. His face was turned to me. It was Jordan Cooper our riding instructor. I'd known at a glance he was dead. No rising of the chest, wide-open eyes, no small movements, no movement at all, just an awful stillness.

I fished my mobile from my pocket and called 999.

I moved closer to see if I could detect any sign of breathing while my mobile rang the emergency number. I knelt by the body. Jordan appeared surprised—not terrified or horrified—just surprised. It was difficult to suppress the urge to close those staring eyes. I put two fingers to is neck. No pulse.

"Emergency. Police. Fire, Ambulance or Coast Guard." The steady voice spoke in my ear.

"Police."

The call went through to the police dispatcher. "Name?"

"Claire Barclay."

"Location?"

"Ashton-on-Tinch."

"What's the trouble?"

"I am in St. Hilda's Church on The Street and have discovered the body of Jordan Cooper prostrate in front of the altar. Wide staring eyes. No pulse. He's dead."

"You need to call an ambulance."

"There is a bloodstain on his chest. No gun or knife that I can see."

"Are you alone? Are you safe?"

I hurriedly glanced around the church. "There is no one here but me. Oh, someone is coming in from a side door." I watched the door. The vicar came through.

"It's all right," I said to the police dispatcher. "It's the vicar, Nigel Whitley."

"Stay on the line," the dispatcher said. "I'm sending a car. Keep the vicar there."

I nodded as if she could see me.

"Vicar, stay back," I shot out the order as Nigel stooped over the body.

He glared at me, affronted. "What's this? In my church!" He sounded like Lady Macbeth.

"The police are on their way. They won't be best pleased if you contaminate the crime scene."

"I was just going to check on who it is." He stopped, turned to argue with me. "I need to close those eyes and say a prayer for him."

"I know who it is. Stand back. You can pray for him back here, and you are *not* going to contaminate the scene of a crime." Mark had ranted long and hard about idiots who wandered into a crime scene and created such a mess that the police could never determine the killer.

Reluctantly, Nigel started toward me. At that moment, Joyce walked in through the same door. It must be the shortest way from their house.

"Sorry I'm a little late, Claire. I got caught on the telephone by Mrs. Taylor and you know she can…" She stopped and stared.

"Jordan? Oh no! Jordan? Oh, my Lord! Jordan!" She ran toward the body.

"No, Joyce," her husband said as he grabbed her by the arm and jerked her to a stop "The police won't want you messing up their crime scene. What are you thinking?"

"Crime scene?" She turned to him a little bewildered.

"We are all going to sit here in a pew and wait for the police." My voice was firm. I had to keep everyone away from Jordan and get home to Amber as fast as I could. What would she be thinking? Not knowing what was going on was sometimes worse than knowing the details. What should I tell her. *Probably the truth, Claire. Then try to help her with her feelings about it.* I wasn't good at feelings. I dampened down my worries about Amber and concentrated on what was before me.

Nigel and Joyce followed me to the nearest pew and sat. Nigel was mercifully quiet, staring at Jordan's body. I stared at the stained-glass windows and counted the number of lead panes, forty-eight, and tried to identify the scent in the air. Furniture polish?. We were sitting like children waiting for our Sunday School teacher, obedient and quiet, except for Joyce's soft sobbing.

I heard the siren, then the crunch of gravel as the car stopped in the car park. The police had been quick.

CHAPTER THREE

The constable who arrived was Mira Walker. I hadn't met her, but there was only one black female officer in the local constabulary, so this must be Mira. She was tall, about five-foot-ten, and stocky, of course, because she was wearing all the paraphernalia the police carry with them: a flak vest with mace, taser, baton, cuffs and more. It was hard to know her physique under that load. She had an impressive background: a graduate in history and criminology from the University of Coventry. She was conscientious and ambitious, Mark had said. Behind her came a young, male constable bulked up with equipment in a similar manner, probably in his early twenties.

Cst. Walker strode up the aisle, glanced at us sitting quietly in the pew and headed toward Jordan's body.

"Bertie, check out this space, then the space behind the altar and then any adjoining spaces. Yell if you find anyone."

"Anyone?" her acolyte said.

She glanced at him. "Anyone you need help with." She pulled out her mobile as she moved closer. She spoke to the dispatcher.

"Definitely dead. Looks like a knife wound. Get me backup and Detective Constable Pemberthy if he is available, or a substitute if he isn't."

She listened, then said. "I only see witnesses here, but I haven't searched the premises yet."

There could be someone hiding close by. I had assumed the killer was long gone, but that wasn't necessarily true.

The last time we'd had a murder in Ashton-on-Tinch it was a visitor whom I hadn't known. Jordan Cooper was someone I had known and liked. Someone Amber had known and liked. This was added trauma on top of her mother's death and having to find a new family. How would she deal with this? What should I do for her? How could I explain it? I was not an accomplished mother. I was not good at feelings—mine or other people's. I remembered Max Hanson's advice: *Just listen to her, Claire. She will let you know what she needs.*

"Who discovered the body?" Cst. Walker moved to stand in front of the pew.

"I did," I said.

Cst. Walker took out her notebook and pen.

"Your name and address," she said to me.

I gave it.

A flicker of recognition passed over her face, although I was sure we had never met. She might have heard gossip about me down at the nick.

"Describe what you saw."

"My daughter and I had an appointment with Joyce here." It was the first time I'd called Amber my daughter. That had come out of my mouth easily. I started to continue but Joyce's weeping distracted me. I touched her shoulder, trying to giver her some comfort. Then, I took a breath and concentrated on my report,

"My daughter, Amber Wilson, and I arrived at 3:45 for a meeting with Mrs. Fotheringham-Whitley. Amber stopped to pet a cat outside. I continued up the steps and through the door. I saw the body of Jordan Cooper straight away. I sent my daughter home. She didn't see him."

"You know him?"

"He teaches…taught us riding, and he was a carpenter of sorts."

She wrote notes, nodded thanks at me when I stopped "Did you notice anything else?"

I thought back to when I'd first seen Jordan's body. I'd looked up then quickly scanned the nave. "The door where the vicar came in was a little open. Maybe someone came through that way or left that way. You might get fingerprints."

Cst. Walker agreed. "We might."

She'd probably get too many fingerprints. Many people used that door.

The young constable returned from his search and walked quickly up to Cst. Walker.

"Nothing, sir," he said.

That got through to Joyce. She stared at Cst. Walker, then at me. "Sir?" she whispered.

"A sign of respect." I whispered back.

She still appeared puzzled, but at least she'd stopped crying. Distraction was a useful way to keep feelings at bay. I didn't want to think about Jordan: his quick grin, his cheerful encouragement, his flirtatious and annoying habit of touching you when he was showing you something. I noticed he hadn't touch Amber. Too young to be interesting to him, thank God. I don't know what I'll do when Amber gets older to protect her from entitled males. In spite of his causal flirtations, Jordan had been a good instructor, making goals clear and showing you how to accomplish them. He was going to be missed. I wondered if he had a family somewhere: parents, siblings, children even. For all I knew he had a wife.

Joyce seemed calmer now. Jordan had worked on the church quite often. There was always something in need of repair in this medieval building. She and Nigel didn't have any children, maybe she saw Jordan as the child she might have wanted. I mentally worked out their ages. No That couldn't be. Jordan might even have been older than Joyce. Her meek, self-effacing manner made Joyce seem older than she was.

"Get some tape from the car and tape off all the doors to the church. This is now a crime scene." Cst. Walker was taking charge.

Bertie left. I caught a glimpse of his badge as he passed me, 'Witten, Bertie'. Probably Albert Witten. Obviously new. Obviously young.

Cst. Walker said to us, "We will talk to you more later."

"May I leave? I sent my daughter back to the house and need to get to her."

"Not yet."

I *had* to leave. Amber must be upset, not knowing what the "accident" was. She might ring Mark. I checked my mobile. She'd left me a message. "I'm calling Dad."

I responded with "That's good."

Cst Walker noticed. "Please don't spread the word about this. We don't want looky-looks here."

"I was going to ask Mark Evans to tend to his daughter."

"D.I. Evans?"

"Yes."

"Fine."

I texted Mark.

The answer came quickly. "On my way."

At that moment, two men and two women walked into the church. Three were in uniform but I recognized the one in civies, David Pemberthy. He'd been a constable, newly from Cornwall, when I first met him, but he'd been promoted to sergeant and was now a detective and not in uniform. He was tall with fair hair and brown eyes. I remembered him as a serious copper. He nodded at me.

"Hold on, lass. I'll be with you in a moment," he said to me. I stood and walked toward the door, but waited there. I wouldn't antagonize Cst. Walker by disregarding her instructions completely. I wasn't leaving, just getting ready to leave.

David spoke to Cst. Walker. "What do you have here?"

She glanced quickly at me then David. "I just arrived. I have the name of the deceased: Jordan Cooper."

David's eyebrows rose. "Indeed?"

"You know him?"

"I do. Most people here know him. He's a riding instructor. Won a lot of prizes when he was younger. Teaches riding and works as an odd-job man."

Then everyone except Joyce, Nigel, and me got busy. David was on his mobile calling for the forensic SOCO team. His supervisor, Superintendent Marjorie Addison wouldn't like that; her department would have to pay for it. The ambulance had followed the police and two medics hurried up the aisle, ducked under the tape and knelt over the body. The tall, thin woman held her stethoscope on Jordan's chest. The short, thin man checked Jordan's pupils with a flashlight. The tall woman pronounced Jordan dead.

"Out," Walker said curtly as she held up the blue and white tape. The two medics scurried back under the tape, reported to David, then left.

Cst. Walker took particulars from Joyce and Nigel.

Garman Bennet, our church treasurer, pushed through the connecting door, probably in response to a call from the vicar. I hadn't seen Nigel make that call. It was almost impossible for the police to control witnesses these days. We all had mobiles.

"Garman here hired Jordan to do some carpentry work," Nigel said. "He might know why Jordan was in the church." Nigel sounded as if he was directing the investigation. Pompous. There was no other word for him or rather there were a lot of words, but I tried to be relatively respectful. I have no idea why Joyce married him. She was probably too young and inexperienced to know how to judge him. I'd made mistakes myself when I was young, but thankfully, those days were behind me. Joyce was still living with her mistake.

Cst. Walker took Garman's particulars, then Garman joined Nigel and Joyce in the pew. He shot a few annoyed glances at Nigel. No doubt, he didn't see any reason why he should be involved. His eyes kept straying back to Jordan's body. It was hard to look at anything else.

I tried to distract myself with musings about Garman. He was retired or semi-retired now from his solicitor practice which, according to his wife Stella, a friend of mine, had been stultifyingly boring, as he worked mainly in banking, accountancy, and property law. He'd given up most of his business but was still the solicitor for a few clients, working from his study at home. He kept his muscular almost six-foot frame fit with regular cycling.

"He has cupboards full of supplements," Stella had told me. "He's so gullible. If the advert says it will take ten years off your life, he buys it."

He'd kept an interesting clientele, though, as they were rich and often from foreign countries. It was an echelon of society I'd rarely encountered. Stella said they were equally boring.

She enlivened her life with affairs. Jordan Cooper had been one of them. I remembered her telling me about that affair. She'd enjoyed it, she'd said, but ended it a few years ago.

The two men and two women donned their white protective suits and advanced toward Jordan. David finally gave us permission to go home.

"You have my mobile number," I said to David. "Call me when you need me to give my statement, and I'll meet you."

"Right you are," He smiled and waved me off.

I left the church and almost fell into Mark's arms. Warm, strong, solid.

"Are you all right? Amber said there'd been an accident?" He hugged me close.

He must have gone home before he came to find me. "Not an accident. Murder."

"Who?" He set me back a little and watched my face.

"Jordan Cooper."

He blinked. "Did you find him?"

"Yes. A...chest wound." I closed my eyes but I could still see Jordan. Why was I now shaky?

Mark pulled me closer. "Take it easy, *cariad*. Let's go home. I haven't been called in on this."

"We have to explain this death to Amber. She'll have seen the ambulance and the police cars. She'll be worried. I don't know how to tell her." I fretted.

"We'll do it together. No details. We'll just say he died, and it's suspicious."

"We were supposed to go to a lesson at five-thirty."

"She's got her riding togs on. Still go. Leah will have someone there to teach. We have to keep Amber's life as normal as we can."

I agreed, but I wasn't sure I could act normally.

"You can't tell Leah about Jordan yet, Claire. Mira would have fifty fits, David too, if someone told Leah before the police could get to her. She's Jordan's boss and important to the case. If you tell Amber, she might tell Leah."

I disagreed. "Amber has to know. She'll imagine worse things if we don't tell her. Besides, she's family. She's part of us now."

He was quiet for a moment. "Do you think a ten-year-old can keep a secret like this?"

I remembered my ten-year-old life when my father's drinking and rages were a family secret. "Oh, yes. I know they can."

"We won't tell anyone else."

"I'll caution Amber."

We headed home. Mark might be asked to investigate this, but since I found the body, they would probably keep him off the team—unless they were short-staffed.

CHAPTER FOUR

Amber had taken Gulliver for his walk and fed him. She was sitting on the floor, dressed in her jodhpurs and kit with her riding helmet on the chair nearby, playing with Gulliver. She had done exactly as I'd instructed.

I hugged her. "You are a gem."

She stared at me. "What was the accident? Who was hurt? Why didn't you let me help?"

I sat on floor beside her and petted Gulliver. "The accident was a bad one and the man was dead," I said. "There wasn't any help you or I could give."

She was still. "Dead?."

Mark lowered himself to the floor on the other side of Gulliver. "It was someone you knew, so Claire wanted to make sure you had only good memories of him."

She whispered. "Who was it?"

"Jordan Cooper."

She looked from Mark and then turned to me.

"My riding instructor?"

"Yes," I said.

"I didn't think he was that old but sometimes...." Her voice trailed off. She was likely remembering her mother had not been old. "Too bad. He was good. Are we going for a lesson?"

"Yes and I'd better get changed. Your dad will explain more," I said.

Did she understand that Jordan was dead? Was she pretending it hadn't happened? Or was she just pragmatic and concerned about how that would affect her? She was only ten.

By the time I returned to the kitchen, the station had called Mark in on the case. David Pemberthy had requested him and squashed any objections by saying that everyone in the village knew everyone else, so Mark might as well take the case. That meant his sergeant, Andy Forsyth, would be called in as well. Mark left immediately.

Amber and I climbed into my van and headed out to the riding stables. It was only fifteen minutes away. We would be on time.

"Who will teach us?" Amber said as she buckled her seatbelt..

I pictured Jordan lying at the foot of the altar. Not Jordan. "Maybe Mrs. Headly. Maybe Joyleen." Leah Hedly owned the stable; her daughter Joyleen taught there—when she wasn't competing.

Just then I got a text from Leah. Amber read it to me. "Jordan hasn't shown up. I will take your lesson."

I got Amber to text back "Thanks."

I drove toward the stables. "Are you going to be all right with this tragedy?" I asked her. "No nightmares or anything?"

"He's not my mother. He's like someone on the telly. I didn't see him dead, so I remember him standing in the center of the ring telling me what to do. I'm sorry he died. But people die."

Good point. I took another tangent. "I don't think Mrs. Headly knows about Jordan's death," I said. "We shouldn't tell her."

"Is she a suspect?" my sharp step-daughter asked.

"Your dad told you it was murder?"

"No, he didn't, but he got called out on a murder investigation, so it wasn't hard to guess."

She was much smarter at ten than I'd ever been.

I wasn't sure how to answer that question. Yes, of course Leah was a suspect. Everyone who knew Jordan was a suspect at this point, but I didn't want Amber to feel she was surrounded by murderers.

"Not particularly," I temporized. "It's just not our job. And we could compromise the investigation if we tell Leah about Jordan's death before the police do." I hesitated, trying to think of a simpler word than 'compromise'.

"Screw up, you mean?"

"Yes." She had a big vocabulary. I should remember that. "We could certainly mess up the investigation. Let's leave it to your dad and his team."

She was quiet for a moment. "I won't say anything, but that's hard."

Keeping a secret is hard at any age. You always want to tell at least one person.

"You'll be able to talk about it when the news gets out to the general public. Then you can tell your friends that you were close to the murder site."

She darted a quick glance at me. "I was, wasn't I?"

I shivered a little. "We were both a little too close. You don't expect it in a church. I don't suppose there has ever been a murder there."

"Maybe in Oliver Cromwell's time."

"Maybe."

The stables, called Headly Downs was situated in the rolling country a little north of Ashton-on-Tinch. The hills and meadows were a lush green, even after our dry summer. The hedgerows divided the fields into paddocks and provided a home for the Dunnock sparrows and yellowhammers I heard out here at the farm. I pulled up beside the stable block. We grabbed our helmets. I locked the car, tucked the keys into the small pocket in my jacket, and we presented ourselves to Leah Headly.

"That Jordan!" she complained. "I thought he was reliable, but he hasn't called. Amber I'm sending you out with Joyleen for a trail ride. Would that be all right?"

Leah looked harassed. Her long dark hair, usually in a neat chignon, escaped in straggling tendrils. She kept glancing at her outsized watch.

Amber smiled. Trail rides on the bridle paths that meandered through the hills nearby were her favorite activity. She glanced at the two girls around her age who were saddling their horses. She'd have company.

"You have Sadie today, Amber." Leah led out a grey pony.

"I like Sadie," Amber said and took the lead rope.

"I put your saddle and bridle by the door." Leah indicated the tack to Amber. Amber picked up a curry comb and a hoof pick and led her horse to the tack, tied her to a ring on the wall, and began the required grooming.

"Joyleen is taking the three of them over the bridle path toward Osborne along the river," Leah told me.

"Amber will like that." I reassured her.

"She's quite a neat little rider."

"Her mother gave her many experiences, including riding lessons."

"It shows."

I, on the other hand, had never had a lesson before coming to these stables with Amber and needed beginner's instruction.

Leah brought the big, chestnut mare Audrey out for me, and I began the brushing and hoof-picking that had become routine. I saddled Audrey and followed Leah who walked to a paddock.

Mark had been right about trying to normalize the day. It was relaxing to plod around the paddock at a walk as Leah stood in the center and corrected my posture, the way I held my hands, and in particular, the way I positioned my feet. As there was quite a lot to pay attention to, I stopped thinking about Jordan every minute.

"Well done,'" Leah said as I drew up to a stop in front of her. "That's it for today. Come to the office after you've groomed

Audrey and put her back in her stable box. I'll have tea. The trail ride will be another half-hour."

I found her in her office at the far end of the stables and thankfully accepted a strong cup of tea. She had smoothed her hair and looked as tidy as one of her horses.

Her mobile rang. She answered. "Police? Yes. Jordan Cooper works for me. What's he done?"

She listened. "I'll be here."

She disconnected and stared at me. "The police. They asked me about Jordan." She shook her head. "What's he gone and done?"

"Does he often get into trouble.?"

"Not the police kind of trouble. He's a menace to women as he seduces them left and right. The kind of trouble I can think of involves jealous husbands or boyfriends. Probably a fight. I wish he wouldn't get so involved with women. I need him here. He's an excellent instructor."

"He is," I agreed careful to keep my comments in the present tense.

"Has he come on to you?"

"I'm not interested in him, and he may be a bit afraid of Mark."

"Right. Your husband's a copper, isn't he?"

"That's right."

She sipped her tea. "I never had to warn him off Joyleen. He had sense enough to know that seducing her would cost him his job here and his living space. He has the apartment over the stables. He left her alone and, I admit it was difficult for him because Joyleen had a massive crush on him. He managed to dance around her while still letting her know he thought she was a good person. I'll give him credit; he never caused her any harm. I quite like him. I just wish he'd be more circumspect. I can't tell you how many women call here for him."

"A nuisance."

"Yes, and I don't have much patience with them."

I considered Stella's fling with him. She'd said he was great fun, easy to play with, and easy *not* to love. She hadn't been harmed. They'd parted friends. Still, I wondered if all those women and their boyfriends and husbands or fathers were going to be suspects of Jordan's murder.

Amber was full of her trail ride and chattered all the way home.

Mark had started supper.

"Pasta," he said from his position at the stove.

"Pasta's good," Amber approved, "but I'll do the veggies. My mum said we have to have vegetables," Amber said.

"Be my guest." Mark said.

"Change first," I directed. It was good Amber could talk about her mother, but it was like having a fourth person in the house. I didn't resent that. I might have, but I didn't. Amber needed the memory of her mother. I considered Britanny a friendly presence. She wasn't a ghost who whispered instructions over my shoulder, but more like an imaginary counselor. Amber's quotations from her mother could be some kind of guidance.

Amber collected Gulliver and headed up to her room.

Mark leaned over and kissed me. "How are you doing?"

"Better. The riding lesson was a good idea. I'd better get changed myself."

"Take your time. The sous-chef is on duty."

We smiled at each other.

"She's a dear," I said.

"Most of the time," he agreed. "I'm still on holiday next week, so let's talk over supper about your tour and my meal plans for the coming week." Mark was going to look after Amber while I was on tour.

"Good idea. How did you keep your time off while you're in charge of this murder inquiry?" It sounded as though he was going to be working and not working at the same time.

"I struck a deal with Pemberthy, and Andy will be here full-time. You can't cancel your tour, and I have to be home for Amber. They have a duty to accommodate me."

"Police union rules?"

"That's right. "

"You'll end up working and looking after Amber."

"People do it all the time."

"True."

I changed and came down in time to set the table. We talked about meals, which for some reason fascinated Amber and my Agatha Christie tour. We didn't talk about murder.

CHAPTER FIVE

The house settled for the night. I took Gulliver out for his last pee, cuddled with him, talked to him, and sent him up to Amber. I heard her door open and close. Mark and I retired to our room. I fervently hoped no one would call to roust him out for work.

No one did.

In the morning, he headed off for his last day before his holiday. He would probably work late, organizing his desk and delegating jobs so he could work from home because, despite theoretically being on holiday, Jordan's murder was going to keep him busy.

Amber collected her books, her gym clothes, her lunch ticket, and her water bottle. There must be some kind of peer competition over water bottles, as I had obeyed precise instructions on what kind to buy.

Stella arrived about eleven, bouncing in the door with the confidence of a frequent visitor. She was well-loved in my household simply because she was kind. We all appreciated that.

"Wine," Stella demanded as she shed her mohair cardigan and draped it over the newel post at the bottom of the stairs. There really wasn't room in the front closet; she might as well hang it there.

"Red?" I was sure she'd want red.

"Yes, Cab sauv if you have it."

I did have a bottle of Chilean cabernet sauvignon.

"I know it's early, but I've had a trying morning, and I need it." She followed me into the kitchen where I found the wine and the glasses. I poured the wine, found the serviettes, some nuts and a few biscuits, put everything on a tray, and headed for the living room. I set the tray on the sideboard and handed her a full glass.

She took a quick sip, set the glass on the little table by her chair and stared at me intently. "How are you faring?"

"I'm all right." I didn't know how much she knew about Jordan. I waited.

"The police have been to see me. A D.C. Pemberthy and the sergeant, Andy" She mimicked Andy. "'Jordan Cooper was murdered and what do you know about it?' Andy told me you found him."

"Yes, I did. In the church. At the altar."

"You poor thing." She reached out and hugged me. "How are you really?"

I amended my first statement. "I'm better than I was."

She stared at me for a second, assessing me, then sat back and raised her glass. "Well, you're used to finding bodies."

She made it sound like a hobby. I sipped my wine and ruminated on the bodies I'd known. I'd discovered some of them because of my close relationship with Mark. Murder was his business, after all. The others, I'd stumbled on by myself. On reflection, I don't think I searched for the dead; finding them had just been bad luck.

"It doesn't get easier. In fact, it gets harder. The first shock gets augmented by the next and so on. Accumulated trauma, or something. I don't know how the police and Mark stand it." I took another sip. My hand was steady. No shaking. The ride yesterday afternoon and the wine today were helping.

The police had investigated Stella. That wouldn't sit well with her. "I know you've met Andy at our house, but had you met David Pemberthy before now?" I asked her.

"No. He hadn't come my way. Is he single?"

I laughed. "I think so." Ashton-on-Tinch was a village where most people knew each other, but some segments of the social world here rarely met. Stella's husband worked with rich, international clients. Stella socialized with them and their partners. David Pemberthy certainly didn't. Stella managed to keep up relationships with less socially elevated people like Mark and me and a string of local lovers, but she hadn't come across David. She was an easy person to get to know. She was brilliant at languages and in demand as a translator. She worked in London and at home as a translator for a publisher, so David would be unlikely to cross her path unless they met at a pub or a sports event or he sang in the musical theater productions.

"David's a Cornishman with a sense of humor—but a serious officer." I heard the hint of warning in my tone. I shouldn't worry. Stella was irrepressible, but she had some standards. No married men. Andy was married to Bruce, so not an option on two counts—and no youngsters. David was too young for her and, perhaps, too principled.

"Stella, are you all right? You had an affair with Jordan, didn't you? Are you grieving him?"

"I'm sorry for him. Angry that someone killed him and, yes, I did have an affair with him. That's why the police came to question me. They were discreet and came when Garman was out. Nice of them."

"And?"

"And nothing. Jordan was fun, a fabulous lover, but just someone to play with. He wasn't serious and neither was I. And he'd passed his best-before date some time before we parted. That doesn't mean I'm not furious that someone decided he could no longer live. I am. Raging mad, actually."

I met her eyes and could see that she was upset and angry. She had made up her face with mascara, eye shadow, and a slight blush on her cheeks. Her long brunette hair was loosely held back with combs. Stella was, as always, gorgeous. The anger only showed in her eyes.

"Are you worried that the police might think you killed him?"

"For an affair that was over?"

"Can you prove it was over?"

She put her wine down on the table, deliberately as if she was afraid she'd spill it or perhaps throw it at me. "What's this," she snapped. "An interrogation?"

"Devil's Advocate," I said.

"Oh. well. All right then." She finished her wine. I got up and poured her another.

"I told them that Jordan had called it off about two or three years ago. I couldn't remember the date, but it may come back to me. He'd met someone else."

"That gives you a motive."

"I didn't kill him. I was relieved, as it's always easier if the man calls it off. I'd hoped he would."

"Did Andy and David believe you?"

"Not sure."

We sat in silence for a moment.

"Alibi?" I finally asked.

"Not too good. I was home, if you believe it. Garman was home working in his study. So we alibi each other, which I expect doesn't impress the constabulary. It's a big house and we were in separate rooms, so either of us could have slipped out and murdered Jordan. I didn't suggest that, but I'm sure they thought of it."

"Still, it's hard to _disprove_ that alibi."

I considered Garman and Jordan. "Garman hired Jordan to do work on the church so he knew him. Did he ever suspect that you and Jordan…?"

"No, he didn't." Stella laughed. "Jordan and I got quite a kick out of that. It was part of the fun. Garman is so stuffy. If he had known I was having it on with Jordan, he would have been angry. First, because I was having an affair of any kind, then furious because I was having it with a riding instructor."

"A bit of Lady Chatterley's lover?"

"Garman would think of it that way. I didn't; I liked Jordan. He was warm-hearted, you know. That's rare." She was crying.

"I'm so sorry, Stella. You are going to miss him."

She sniffed. "I am. We weren't lovers anymore, but we were friends."

We were quiet for a few moments. I thought about Stella going from one lover to the next. She was an independent woman in so many ways, but she needed those lovers.

She seemed to read my thoughts which sometimes happened with us. "I should leave Garman and find someone more loving."

"Stella, you are always going to leave Garman, but you never do. Why not?"

"Not sure. You're right; I'm always thinking of it."

I couldn't image life with Garman Bennett. It strained my imagination to try to think of him as joyous or spontaneous. Unlike Mark, who could burst into a song with all the vitality of a self-confident Welshman, Garman seemed a dry stick of a man.

"Stella?"

"Hmm?"

"Who was Jordan's new woman, not the one he left you for, but the one he was seeing now?"

"Again, not sure. But you know, as impossible as it may seem, I think it was Joyce."

I was stunned silent. Joyce? With her mousy hair, her diffident, scurrying gait, her good works, her devotions to the church, and her almost slavish care of Nigel.

I finally said, "Our Joyce?"

"That's my guess" She stood. "Got to go. Books to read. Translations to pick apart." She was at the door, collecting her cardigan from the newel post. I was left with the notion of Joyce Fotheringham-Whitney as Jordan's lover spinning round in my head.

My sister Deidre rang just then, and I had to concentrate.

"We'd like to come for the weekend. We'll stay at a BnB, of course."

"Who's 'we'?"

"Me, Michael, Josh, Kala, and the two dogs. Both kids had their sports games cancelled. Something about repairing the pitch, so we decided to come to visit. How are you with that? I know it's last minute."

"I'm wonderful with it." Both Deidre and her barrister husband worked full time and a spontaneous gathering like this was rare. Amber was getting to know them and would be pleased to see them. "Do come. We'd all like to see you, and we need a distraction."

There was silence for a moment. "You're not going to tell me there's been another murder, are you?"

"I am."

"Now, we're definitely coming."

"Want me to book the BnB?"

"I'll do it. We'll be there Saturday afternoon. Leave Sunday evening. Don't cook."

"There's no room here to cook for such a crowd. We could order from Jack's Pub or from the take-away on Princess Street."

"We'll have to keep the kids busy outside as well."

I thought of my garden. Not big enough for three kids and three dogs. The Green was across the street from our house; they could take their games there. Or, we could organize them.

"What about a trail ride?" I said.

"Good idea." Unlike me, Deidre had had riding lesson when she was young. My step-father had come into the family as I was moving out, but when Deidre was ten and in need of a father. She had a more middle-class upbringing than I'd had. So had her children. They would be comfortable on horses. If I had a docile horse, I could follow the others.

Deidre broke into my reflections. "Can you arrange it?"

"I'll do that." I disconnected the call and stirred myself to consider what groceries I had to buy before they arrived. Snacks for the kids. They ate a lot. Snacks for adults with wine and enough fruit to keep Amber happy. I'd better check there was plenty of dog food.

I'd enjoy Michael and the kids. I'd enjoy Deidre as well. She was both my loving sister, a ferocious prosecutor for the Crown—and, therefore, an expert in murder.

CHAPTER SIX

St. Hilda's church had a website. I clicked on it and registered Amber in choir. Even on this Saturday morning I could register her online.

"Wednesday nights seven to eight. Is that all right?" I asked her. Amber was relishing her breakfast which was avocado, poached egg, and whole wheat bread. A wise choice. I should adopt some of her eating habits.

"Does that mean I have to go to church on Sunday mornings?"

I'd checked that. "Yes, it does. Ten o'clock." I glanced at Mark who was making coffee for us at the stove.

"One of us will try to be at church every week," he said. "At best, both of us, but you know our jobs won't always allow for that."

Amber chased the last bit of avocado around her plate. "I know. Mummy had to work some Sundays too."

Britanny had been an estate agent in the city of Woking, Surrey, where they'd lived. She must have had to work many Sundays, but Amber's grandparents, Freya and George Wilson, would likely have attended church in York. Amber might have gone with them when she lived there.

"Your dad and I will go with you as often as we can."

"I can go with Stephanie sometimes. Who is the conductor?"

Amber had sung in a choir, so she was familiar with the discipline involved. The conductor was to be obeyed.

"Mrs. Fotheringham-Whitney. The website says she has a degree in music from Durham University. Her instrument is the flute, but she plays the organ and the piano as well."

Amber nodded as if she expected no less from her music teachers. "Stephanie says the conductor is ace."

I'd noticed that the music was excellent the few times I'd attended church services, but I hadn't realized Joyce was so well-educated.

Amber peered over my shoulder at the website.

"Not a good design," she said.

"The website?"

"Yes. Do you have a website for your business?"

"I do." I clicked out of the church site and onto my own site. I was slightly nervous that Amber would not approve.

"Oh, that's nice." She stood close to me and stared at my advertisements for tours.

"Can I click through?"

I sat back and passed her the mouse. She examined the various tours and clicked on some testimonials.

"You go some cool places, but they are all about mystery stories. Right?"

"That's right?"

"Why?"

I considered her question for a few moments. She shut down the site and waited.

"I love the magic of words, the way words can make us feel as well as the way words can invite us into an imaginary world. Add that to the confederacy of readers who read the same books and want to know more about where they are set and you get a fascinating experience with intelligent people." I qualified that. "Usually." Most of the people on my tours were lovely; a few had been annoying and one had been murderous. I didn't tell her that.

About ten o'clock, all was chaos. Deidre and Michael arrived with fifteen-year-old Josh and eleven-year-old Kala. Josh had surely grown another few inches and was now as tall as me. He was still in the gangly stage where his hands and feet seemed destined for a tall man but the rest of him hadn't caught on yet. He was skinny, probably all that football practice kept him that way; they run non-stop for forty-five minutes in that sport.

Kala was still a little girl, her freckles pronounced on her nose and cheeks, her dark hair curling around her face. She gave me a bright smile and an enthusiastic hug. Josh leaned down and gave me a stiff-armed, awkward hug. Both were loving. Their Labs jumped around Gulliver who hid behind my knees for a few minutes before recognizing Pike and Duff and tearing off with them to the kitchen. It was like trying to manage a circus.

I herded everyone to the kitchen and settled them with coffee which Mark distributed, juice for the kids, biscuits for everyone and dog treats for the canines.

At first everyone talked at once, then the kids took the dogs to the back garden and peace descended.

"Did you get us some horses for a trail ride?" Deidre asked me.

"I got three for the kids. The stables didn't have enough available for all."

"A trail ride for the kids is good enough. We can take the dogs for a walk."

"And we," Michael said, "will fix that back gate you've been complaining about."

I smiled at Michael. He was such a good match for Deidre: a little older, calm where she was excitable, deliberate where she was spontaneous. She was short with dark hair and dark eyes; he was tall and fair with blue eyes. Both were gems.

The kids changed into their riding togs. We loaded everyone with their water bottles. Why did they have to have water bottles? I suppose we had fads when I was their age, but I don't remember them. There was no money for anything but basic necessities when I was young so, while there may have been fads, I wouldn't have participated. I did put a water bottle into each of Deidre and my rucksacks, as well as other provisions for our ramble, then drove to the stables.

"Two hours," Leah Headly said. Again, she looked a little less tidy than usual. Her dark hair escaped from the tie which attempted to contain it; she had little make-up and Leah usually was in full paint. She passed Deidre the Square electronic device.

"Two hours is fine." Deidre used her credit card.

"Any more word from the police?" I asked Leah.

She turned to me her eyes wide. "It was murder. Someone stabbed him. I can't believe it. I'm that shaken. It's obscene."

"I'm sorry," I said.

"Who would do that? The police have been all over his apartment here. It's...it's...ugly. The whole thing is ugly."

"I am so sorry," I repeated.

She nodded and kept nodding. A tear escaped from the side of her eye. I reached over and hugged her. Deidre left us and waited outside the tack room door.

"It is ugly," I agreed with Leah, trying to comfort her. Cruel as well. Jordan's death was going to affect many.

"He wasn't the world's best man but he was a dear, really."

I patted her shoulder.

She straightened and stood back. "Thanks." She took a deep breath. "The kids will have a good time." She was all business now.

"I'm sure they will."

Deidre and I took the dogs for a ramble on the hillside. We left Ashton-on-Tinch and walked the easy path to the top of the hill. There was a bench at the top, but we weren't winded, and the dogs were still rambunctious, so we kept walking.

"Where are we going?" Deidre asked me.

I consulted the map on my mobile. "We can take the Woodland path. It's 3.61 miles and gives us a view of the South Downs."

"I can do 3.61. Do you have a map?"

I held up my mobile. "I'm looking at it. Besides, I know the path."

She gazed down at the village below us. "It's pretty with the river running through it. You picked a lovely spot to live."

I smiled. "I like it. And I like the walking paths around here. This one takes us away from the river and toward Chawton."

"Jane Austen's Chawton?"

"The very one, but we aren't going that far. This is almost four miles. Chawton's much further than that."

"I'm fine with a loop. Where are the dogs?"

She whistled and her two Labs bounded out from the underbrush. Pike was all black but Duff had some white on his chest. They'd picked up some mud from somewhere and looked happy. Gulliver had not wandered off with the big dogs but stayed within my sight. I called him over for a treat just to remind him that he needed to stay nearby.

It was a beautiful day for a walk. The path was wide, no scrambling over logs or struggling with gorse. We broke out of the woodlands into a meadow that stopped at the edge of an embankment. Below us were rolling hills with green meadows divided by the spreading beech, oak, and ash of the north part of the South Downs.

"Beautiful," Deidre said, sitting on the convenient bench with a thump.

"Tired?"

"My muscles aren't used to it. I'll have to get back to the gym."

We called the dogs and distributed treats and water. Each of us had a collapsible dog dish and a water bottle. I also had a thermos of coffee and some Bakewell tarts I'd bought from the bakery. I fished them from my rucksack, defending them from the dogs, passed one to Deidre, and scoffed down my own. I could manage Gulliver, but the two big dogs were another matter. Deidre held one hand out to ward off the sniffing dogs and ate her tart quickly. The dogs weren't interested in our coffee.

"So how did Jordan die?" Deidre asked. I knew she would ask.

"Stab wound to the chest."

"Pretty reliable method."

"If you say so."

"Some people do survive it, but not many. Who did it?"

"I've no idea."

"Well, who couldn't have done it?"

I contemplated that. "Not Stella. Jordan had been her lover, but they were done, and Stella doesn't make enemies of past lovers. It's not her style."

"Alibi?"

"Her husband, Garman."

"Hmm. Not the best alibi."

"She knows that. But there's no evidence against her."

"Evidence is what Mark is going to need, for sure."

I thought about evidence: the way memory is unreliable even in the most honest person, the way pieces of material, letters, wills, and even finger prints get lost, the way various police departments contaminate evidence so badly it's useless.

"What kind of evidence is important?"

Deidre reflected for a moment then said. "Actus reus, mens rea, causation, absence of excuse." She rattled off what she thought was an answer. She understood my blank face and explained. "You have to prove the actions or omissions that cause the death, prove the perpetrator's criminal intent, the voluntary nature of the act, and the absence of any justification or legal excuse for the perpetrator's actions."

Deidre did sound like a dictionary sometimes, a law dictionary, but she valued accuracy. She'd had to memorize reams of material to pass her qualifying exams and often had to quote that material in court, so she didn't forget it.

I translated that explanation into practical terms. "So, we have to find someone who intended to kill Jordan, who had no legal excuse to do so and was mentally capable."

"It sounds straightforward, but it's often hard to get evidence that, indeed, John X actually did the deed, and that he intended the victim to die."

"I suppose someone could claim they were defending themselves from Jordan."

"The defence is not the problem of the police. They just gather the evidence to establish the facts. The defence or lack of it is the barrister's problem when it gets to court."

The barrister for the defence would rely on the evidence the police had gathered, though. So evidence was of great importance.

"Hey! Pike!" Diedre stood and yelled at the dogs. "Get out of there!"

Pike obediently withdrew his head from a hole in the ground and trotted over for a treat. Deidre handed out the treat, a reward for obedience, then gave a treat to each of the other dogs so they wouldn't feel left out.

She sat back down and turned to me. "So, who else could *not* have done it? Besides Stella."

"I don't think Leah Headly, the owner of the stables, did it."

"Why not?"

"Because earlier she didn't seem to know why Jordan hadn't shown up for work."

"Can she act?"

I stared at Deidre for a moment. "She's not a professional actress, but she does act in the Christmas pantomime." I remembered her Alice Fitzwarren in *Dick Wittington*.

Deidre shrugged. "You can't rely on her reaction then. She might have been prepared to act shocked and surprised."

"She's just taken our kids on a trail ride." I shot up straight.

Deidre didn't move. "So she has, but we don't know if she is guilty. Just that we can't say she isn't."

I was uneasy.

"She's an unlikely murderer, don't you think?" Deidre said. "Leah needs Jordan for her business. Do you think Leah was one of Jordan's lovers?"

I shook my head. "I didn't see any indication of that. She seemed to have a boss and instructor relationship. Her daughter, Joyleen, though. She'd had a crush on Jordan when she was younger."

"That's pretty tenuous."

I shrugged. "Who else?"

"A recent lover, perhaps?" Deidre suggested.

"Joyce Fotheringham-Whitley. And she is going to be Amber's choir mistress!"

"She hasn't killed any choir members in the past, has she?"

I stared at Deidre, then laughed. "Do you think I'm getting slightly overprotective?"

"A little. You are convicting people without evidence. It's one thing to speculate; another to act as if your speculations are real."

I breathed deeply and viewed the vista spread before me, calming myself. I couldn't keep Amber away from everyone in the village because one of them might be a murderer, but one of them likely was a murderer. I'd have to be vigilant.

I considered who might have killed Jordan. "I'm curious about Joyce. She works hard for the church, and I found out that she has a university degree in music, so we are getting her expertise. I don't think she's paid."

"What makes you say that?"

"She doesn't act like a woman with an income of her own. You know, she has dowdy clothes, a long time between haircuts, and is free with her time but not her money."

"Maybe her husband collects her salary and doles out an allowance."

I was affronted. "In this day and age?"

"She'd have to agree, as she'd have to be paid directly with tax deductions and social service contributions."

"I could ask Garman Bennett. He's our church treasurer."

"Solicitor, isn't he?"

"Yes. Do you know him?"

"I've heard of him. He works in a different world from mine. Rich businessmen and women with trusts, wills, and banking."

"I'll ask Stella to get the information about how Joyce is paid from Garman. I don't think he'd tell me." Garman wouldn't do me a favor.

"It should be public information in the treasurer's report."

"I'll see if I can find that."

We gathered the dogs and headed onto the homeward bound section of the looped path. I picked the burrs and twigs from Gulliver's coat then let him loose to follow the Labs.

"What are you going to do about getting a new house?" Deidre asked.

"I will hate to leave my house," I said, "But we need more room."

"The Stonnings are hardly in their side any more. Why don't you buy their house and open the walls between to make one big house?"

I stopped and stared at her. One big house. I'd get to keep my lovely cottage. It would just be attached and open to the Stonning's side.

"Brilliant. That's brilliant."

I could see it: a large front parlour because I'd break down the wall between the houses, a bedroom for Amber and a study for me, even a separate study for Mark. I couldn't wait to get home and propose that to Mark and Amber. Plans for renovation buzzed in my head with such energy I could hardly keep a conversation going with Deidre.

We collected the kids from riding They were full of where they had gone, to the ridge, and what they had seen, other riders, sheep, "Lot of sheep," Josh said. "And an osprey and some goats."

The men were watching the end of the football match. Josh joined them while Deidre and I organized a pizza-delivery supper from Jack's pub. We fed the dogs outside in the garden, giving them space between each bowl which prevented arguments, and left them to enjoy themselves in the sandbox Peter Brown had constructed for Gulliver. All three dogs happily dug holes, spreading sand on the lawn.

"That's fine," I said to Deidre. "Peter tells me it's good for the lawn."

When the pizzas, seven of them, were on the table, soda for the kids and wine for the adults distributed, and everyone had satisfied at least the first pangs of hunger, I announced Deidre's plan for the house.

"How would you two," I pointed at Mark and Amber, "like to live in a house that was a combination of this house and the one next door."

Mark put his piece of pizza down. "*Gwych,*" he said which is 'fabulous' in Welsh. He smiled. "Oh, that would be good." He shot to his feet, grinned, picked up Amber and whirled her around the room, then placed her back on her chair.

Her eyes were wide and she stared at him, then matched his grin.

"What do you think, Amber?" I asked.

She turned to me and cocked her head. "Is it as big as this house?"

I pictured the Stonning's house. I'd been in it a few times. "It has a kitchen at the back, smaller than this one, but a separate dining groom, a front parlour, two bedrooms and a bathroom upstairs."

"You could have my room for a study and I could have new room in that part of the house." She was quick to understand the advantages of the combined houses.

"That would work. Brilliant, really." The three of us smiled at each other. We would live more easily with more room.

"First,' Deidre said, "you need to know if they will sell. Why don't you call them?"

"What? Now?"

"Why not?"

"It's Saturday night."

"Just try," Mark urged me. "Patrick's called you many a time when it was inconvenient."

Mark was right about that, but Patrick and Rita had been in quite a bit of trouble then.

Patrick's number was on my mobile list. I rang him.

"It's Claire," I said when Patrick answered.

"Is everything all right? I hope the plumbing didn't back up again. I had to get the plumber in last time, and he was a right idiot in his billing. And then Rita refused to clean it up, and I had to hire a cleaner. It isn't the plumbing, is it?"

I was about to deny any plumbing problems when he started again.

"Or the electricals. They're all right, aren't they. No fire or anything?"

I finally got a chance to speak. "Everything's fine, Patrick. But now that I have a child in the house I need more room. Would you consider selling your house to me?" I needed to get my request in before he started talking again.

There was silence. "I didn't do myself any favors by listing everything that goes wrong with it, did I?"

"I know all that, in any case, Patrick, because it's usually me that alerts you to the problems."

"That's true. So, you'd like to buy it."

"Would you consider it?"

"I have to talk to Rita but I'd say, yes, we would."

"Wonderful. Thank you." I could see the pleasure lighting up Mark's face and to some extent Amber's. Deidre was smiling and Michael gave me a thumbs up.

"You two talk about it." I continued, "and get back to me with a price and a time line."

"We liked living there, but it hasn't been the same since Nott died."

I remembered Oliver Nott with a shudder. He had been one of the authors from Patrick's publishing house and had been killed in Patrick's yard.

"Rita just doesn't like going to the house any more. She wants to buy something in Kent near the sea."

That sounded hopeful. If Rita was already thinking of getting rid of this house then they'd be likely to sell.

"Let me know soon, Patrick? All right?"

"Sure and thanks for calling."

He sounded grateful. Perhaps my call came at the right time.

I grinned at everyone.

"Yeah!" Amber cheered.

Mark's was enthusiastic. "We could open up the rooms on both floors so they'd join."

"One big house," Josh said.

"Where do you think the bearing walls are?" Michael asked. He rose and gathered Mark and the children to wander around the house knocking on walls to find ones that sounded hollow which we could take down and ones which sounded dull which we couldn't take down.

"I don't think they can tell with any accuracy," Dierdre said, "because all these old walls are thick."

"It makes them happy," I said.

We sat at the table and talked about how we could change the rooms. After about a half hour, I called the others back for ice cream, cake, and more wine. Everyone had an idea about how to improve the house.

"Can you afford it?" Amber asked. Everyone was quiet, waiting for an answer. Mark stared at me.

"We can afford it," I told Amber. I had money from my stepfather, a wealthy man.

"A good use of the money," Deidre said," an appreciating asset."

She had never been envious that I'd received most of Paul's legacy. She'd told me that she'd been ten and I'd been nineteen and supporting myself when Mum married him. She'd had all the advantages of his money growing up, so she wanted me to have it after he died. Mark had taken some time to come to terms with the fact that I had enough money to buy several houses, but he finally accepted it. It didn't come up in conversation much because it wasn't good form to talk about money.

After supper, I pulled out the games and the children chose Catlan, an elaborate game of greed and acquisition like Monopoly, that lasted for hours. Players aged ten can play with equal skill as an adult, so it was a fair game. We played on the kitchen table and everyone crowded into the room including the three dogs. No one took the game seriously, so we all enjoyed it. Mark won.

Mark, Michael, and I had another glass of wine, but Deidre joined the kids with soda. She was driving. About eleven they packed up the dogs and left for their BnB. Mark helped me clean up the kitchen, load the dishwasher, and tidy the front entry way.

Amber had gone to bed. I took Gulliver out for his last pee of the day and trundled him up the stairs to Amber's room. He bounced onto her bed.

"Oof," she said.

"Good night."

"Good night, Claire. That was fun. Josh and Kala are my cousins, right?"

They weren't legally her cousins because they were related to me and not Mark, but they were cousins in spirit if not in fact. *Keep it simple, Claire.* "That's right."

"It was fun. Cousins are fun. And our new house will be fab."

She was right. After negotiations, renovations, dust, hammering, delays, smells of paint, and unexpected problems, it was going to be fab.

CHAPTER SEVEN

It was quiet when we finally went to bed. At least, as quiet as a two-hundred-year-old house gets. A few creaks and rustles always accompanied the cooling night. I was used to those sounds and even found them soothing.

In the morning, Deidre and family arrived for breakfast about nine. We were ready. Mark had been busy frying ham and bacon. Amber had put out the plates and flatware along with serviettes and glasses. She had been in the kitchen earlier and sliced apples, drizzling them with lemon juice to keep them from browning, added segmented oranges, and sliced pineapples to create a pretty fruit plate. That was on the table as well.

The kitchen in my house comprised of what was two rooms on the Stonning side. I had renovated when I'd bought the house to make it commodious. I wouldn't need to change it when we combined the houses. I'd be gutted if I didn't get the Stonning's house, and stymied as well. What would we do?

"Do we have blueberry syrup?" Amber asked.

"In the pantry." The syrup, along with the coffee, was imported from Seattle.

Amber returned with the blueberry syrup, the maple syrup, and some brown sugar. I mixed the pancake batter, one of my few culinary competencies, set the oven to warm and began pan-baking pancakes. These had been a staple for me when I'd lived in Seattle. Amber and Mark loved them.

I had a stack of about twenty keeping warm in the oven when Deidre, Michael, and family arrived. We put the dogs in the back garden where they headed for the sandbox.

Everyone settled at the table and Mark transferred the pancakes from the plate in the oven to a platter and circled the table, forking them onto plates. Josh took four. I expected he would be two inches taller the next time I saw him.

We had a coffee and talked over breakfast, but the family left soon after.

"I still have some work to do on a file," Deidre said. "And Michael has to meet a client later in the day."

"I have a tiny bit left on my homework," Kala said.

"I thought you said you'd done it all."

"Almost all," Kala said.

They left in a flurry of activity.

The house was strangely quiet. We looked at one another.

"Do you have plans?" I asked Amber.

"I'm going to Stephanie's house after lunch. She's at church. She sings in the choir, remember?"

I remembered. I guess we'd be going to church next Sunday. It was a big sacrifice of my Sunday. *Now that is pitiful. Get a grip, Claire. You aren't sending her to church without you. Accept the responsibility.* I was ashamed of myself. I would turn my attitude around—because I had to.

"Want to go to Jack's for supper?" I asked them both.

That would be a treat. Besides, a pub meal would suit me as I had a tour starting tomorrow and didn't want to cook. Pancakes I could manage. Anything else took effort. If we went out for a meal tonight, we might all enjoy it, and I could give Amber some attention. I had calculated without factoring in Amber's inclinations. She had other ideas.

"I might stay at Stephanie's. Her mom does a meat and potatoes and two veg supper every Sunday. There's lots of vegetables."

Plans were now going to be made as a family from now on. I adjusted quickly.

"Right you are, then," I said.

She packed snacks in a rucksack: leftover pancakes with cheese rolled for easy finger food, along with some of the leftover fruit. She added some for Stephanie, and rode off on her bike.

Mark and I had lunch by grazing through the fridge, munching through enough food to satisfy us, then retired to the front parlour. I knew Mark wanted to watch a sports match on the telly—I think it was rugby—and had just taken a sip of coffee and settled himself to watch the first half when the doorbell rang, or not rang so much as clamored. It's a harsh, rattling sound. I keep thinking I should change it but never do. It makes me think I have a grumpy gnome living in my front door who demands "Get this door!" Involuntarily, I smile. I may never change it.

Mark hit the 'Record" button but kept watching the game. I answered the door.

David Pemberthy stood there with Cst. Mira Walker behind him. Neither was in uniform. Mira Walker turned out to have a sensation figure when it wasn't hidden by the flak jacket and accoutrements. She wore a blue tank top, with a light, oversized shirt in a paler blue over it, jeans, and trainers—casual, but stylish.

"Is this an official visit?" I knew that, as I was a witness, they would want to talk to me.

"It is. Addison gave us overtime. Mira's been assigned to our team." David sounded apologetic. Didn't he want Mira Walker on his team? What was that about?

"Andy's just home from his holidays and isn't coming to this meeting."

I held the door wide. "Dear Marjorie must be worried about this one. She rarely grants overtime. Come into the living room."

Mark stood at the living room door. "How goes it, mate?" He shook David's hand. "Hello, Mira. I heard you'd been assigned to us. Getting experience before your boards?"

She smiled. "Yes, sir." So Superintendent Marjorie Addison had assigned Mira to Mark's team because Mira was trying for her detective boards. Good for Marjorie for mentoring a female applicant.

Mark accepted the 'sir'. This was not a social occasion.

"Coffee," I asked. I didn't want this meeting to be too formal. If it was too formal, I wouldn't be included.

"Sure," David said. "Some of that great coffee you have."

"Coming up. What about you, Mira?" I asked.

"Thank you. Flat white if you have it."

"Easily done," I said and fetched a tray with the coffee, cream, and some store-bought biscuits.

When we were all served, David began. "First of all, Andy's back from his holidays. Hale, hearty and ready to work—just not today. He said he'd check in with you tomorrow, but he knew you had guests, and he had to settle his own house, the bairns, you know."

Andy Forsyth, Mark's sergeant, had two rambunctious boys who were probably tired and fractious from traveling and so a handful for him and Bruce to settle down.

"I have your proper statement here, Claire, for your signature." David placed it on the low table in front of me. I reached for it. They were quiet until I'd read and signed it. David signed as a witness.

He took a gulp of coffee. "You're in charge of this twisty case," he said to Mark, "and I know you have to stay with Amber this week, so how are we going to manage the communications? What's the plan?"

Mark leaned forward. "I've thought about it. Andy will direct the co-ordination of all the interviews and the co-relation of the material and meet with me every day. I'll be at the station between just before 8:30 until 3:30. It's only the late afternoon and evenings that you will have to come here. I can have my calls transferred from the station after 3:30, if any come in for me."

"We can make that work." David said. "The only problem will be any late afternoon, any evening interviews, or, God forbid, over night emergencies."

Mark contemplated David for a second. "You'll have to pick up for me on that."

He stared at Mark, then nodded. We were all silent, wondering how that would work. Mark was used to being in charge at all times: reacting to new information and pursuing lines of inquiry without any concern over his hours, as long as he didn't bill them as overtime. While David might be happy to take on the added responsibility, Mark might chaff at giving it up. The logistics might be difficult as well. I imagined our living room with two or three detectives trying to corelate information and discuss the case while I worked on my computer and Amber did her homework.

"Occasionally, Amber could go to Rose's house for a few hours," I said. "Or her friend, Stephanie's."

"I'm not sure about that," Mark said. "She needs to know one of us is here for her." Mark had read the material on childhood trauma, and he wanted to augment Amber's sense of safety. It was a complicated choice: too much protection created a fearful child, not enough did the same.

"All right," David said. "We'll tease it out. Maybe use Bertie a bit more."

I remembered the young constable who had accompanied Mira at the church. He appeared far too young to be part of a detective team.

"So now," David said, with enthusiasm. "We have several suspects."

Mira glanced at me then turned to Mark. "Excuse me, sir." Her words were differential but her voice was firm. "I think we should not include a civilian in our discussions."

David and Mark turned, stared at her, then stared at me.

She persevered. "I'm sure Ms. Baclay is discreet, but it's unorthodox and not recommended to give civilians information about an on-going investigation."

The silence stretched. I saw a flicker of annoyance pass over Mark's face.

"An excellent rule to have," he said, "but not in this case. I can vouch for Claire's discretion." Mark spoke quietly, his casual words were underlined by his sharp glance.

Mira shifted in her chair but only mumbled a "Yes, sir." I gave her credit for courage. She didn't think I should be there, and she was making that clear even if her superior officers objected. However, they were her superior officers, so she should accept their decision. She didn't.

"With all respect, sir, she doesn't have any experience with murder."

This time the silence stretched longer. Mark coughed. He was trying not to laugh. That would humiliate Mira.

I said quickly. "Unfortunately, I do have a fair amount of experience with murder. That is what these two are thinking right at this moment." I thought of Mrs. Paulson, Oliver Nott, Phillip, and that poor university student I'd found. "You can rest assured I won't be gossiping about the investigation, but I can find out information that doesn't come your way. For instance, you will need to investigate Joyce Fotheringham-Whitley." I glanced at Mark and David.

"We didn't have her down as a suspect," David said. "Where does she come in?"

"I'm not sure, but I expect she was Jordan's latest lover."

Mira's eyes widened and she blinked. "Mrs. Whitley, the vicar's wife?"

"That's right." It was easier to persuade Mira to cooperate by giving her information than by arguing. I remembered being young when I was sure there was only one right way to do things.

"Well, well. Who would have thought it?" Mira's voice held a note of awe. "Do you have any evidence?"

"No, that's your job." I smiled. "I just pick up the information. You'll have to make something of it."

"I see." I think she did.

"David, you took the vicar's statement. What did he have to say?" Mark checked the papers David had handed him on his arrival. "It says here he knew Jordan."

"Aye, he prattled a bit. Jordan did some carpentry work for the church. According to the vicar, anything as old as medieval church needs constant repair. He said Jordan did good work, when he came. He charged a great deal 'although everything is more these days'. That's a direct quote from the parson." David studied his copy of the statement. "Other than the cost, he had no problem with his work. Jordan taught at the equestrian centre as well as did odd jobs around the town. Well-liked. Has had many girl friends, although Whitney had begun to suspect he had a new girlfriend recently but never met her." I have always been impressed with the way David could slip from his relaxed Cornish speech to the clipped, official police reporting vernacular. It was as though he'd learned a second language.

"What made him think that?" Mira asked.

"Jordan insisted on leaving at a certain time to meet someone. Vicar Whitney assumed it was a woman because he needed time to go home to shower and change."

"Reasonable, but not necessarily true," Mira said. "He might have been meeting a business associate, a prospective new employer, his booky."

"The vicar didn't know."

"Where was the vicar when we suspect the murder occurred," Mark asked.

"He was having lunch in his house which is adjacent. He went to the church just after lunch. He was in the right place at the right time."

"But then, he's always there," Mark said." The church is his place of business, so it's not necessarily suspicious that he was there."

"He never suspected that girlfriend might be his wife?" I was still fascinated at the notion of Joyce and Jordan as lovers. She had been shocked and horrified when she saw his body, but she was a kind woman. She might have reacted that way seeing anyone lying dead in the church.

"We need to find the lover if it wasn't Mrs. Fotheringham-Whitney. You're on that, Mira?" Mark said.

"Yes, sir."

"Check out possibilities with Andy."

David glanced at me and raised his eyebrows as Mira, head down, wrote in her notebook.

I interpreted that to mean I should also chase that lead. I'd do my best to ferret out the information. I wouldn't have much time as my tour started tomorrow.

They had Stella's statement and Garman's.

"I see you have Leah Headly's statement. Anything there?" Mark asked.

"She has an alibi. She was in the barns getting horses ready for the afternoon lesson for the pertinent time."

"Which is?" Mark asked.

"1400 to 1600. "There were several other witnesses to this: a groom, a woman who takes a class from the daughter, Joyleen, and a feed salesman."

"Was Joyleen there all the time?" I asked.

David sounded unsure. "I took her mother's word for it that she was around the whole afternoon, but I didn't check that. Should I have?"

"Perhaps. On the outside chance that she was upset by Jordan's rejection of her. Mind you, I think that was years ago. She had a crush on him when she was about twelve and Jordan wisely avoided her. That's a weak motive." Once I stated it, I felt foolish. That definitely was a weak motive.

"We'll check out her alibi to make sure she was in the barns and farmyard all afternoon and that Jordan hadn't decided she was now old enough to pursue."

"What a job," I said. "If you interview everyone Jordan has had an affair with, it could take weeks. If you interview every girl who had a crush on him, it might take months."

"Good point," Mark said. "We could get into rabbit holes following the girlfriends."

At about four, I abandoned them as they were creating a plan of inquiry. I retired to my side of the room to do some of my own paperwork. I was going to enjoy having a dedicated study when we renovated. I was definitely counting on buying the Stonnings' house. For now, I concentrated on blocking out the other voices in the room and opened my computer. They lowered their voices. I started checking all the reservations I'd made for tomorrow's tour group to make sure no one had lost my reservations, ignored them, or had gone out of business. All was as I'd booked. I tidied my work space and stood.

"We're off now," David said. "Thanks for the hospitality."

"Anytime."

David and Mira gathered their papers and left. Mark clicked the telly on and immersed himself in the taped rugby game.

I had more to do to get ready for tomorrow. I loaded my seven-person Mercedez van with some of the equipment I'd need for the Agatha Christie tour. I had a first aid kit with aspirin for stroke victims, band aids, gauze, tape, a sling for the accident prone, a sling for those with an injured a hand or arm, a cane for those who might injure a foot or ankle, and Prenoxade, naloxone, for drug poisoning, I added calamine lotions for any itches and some headache tablets. With luck no tourists would meander too close to a cliff edge, or suddenly stumble into traffic I locked the van and returned to the house.

Amber sent me a text. *Staying for supper at Steph's.*

I responded with *Okay. We'll be at Jack's Pub until about 6:30. We were planning on eating early.*

Amber texted back. *Will b home @ seven.*

Good, I sent back. Stephanie's family was large and noisy. She was the youngest of four children and everyone seemed to bring friends to Stephanie's house for Sunday dinner. Amber would be welcome and only one of probably about five extra guests. Beth, Stephanie's mother, told me she had given up on a career in teaching after her third child was born and committed to being a full-time mother and manager of the house.

"There's no time for anything else," she'd said. It was hard and constant work, but she seemed to enjoy it.

Mark, Gulliver, and I and met Amber at seven at our front door. We had all eaten well. Gulliver was happily full of floor scrapes. It never seemed to hurt him. Mark unlocked the door, and we piled into the house.

CHAPTER EIGHT

I dressed for my trip to Heathrow and my meeting with my tourists: tan linen trousers, pale cream tank top, tan, and lavender subtle patterned shirt—and my handmade Italian Girotti multicolored platform slip-ons. They were comfortable and gorgeous. Mark was up and eating breakfast with Amber, discussing singing. At least, Amber was talking; Mark was eating and nodding. Neither he nor I chatted at breakfast. I managed a 'Good morning' and left them to their one-sided conversation while I collected a cup of coffee and some toast.

I headed out for Heathrow about half eight. There was a steady line of traffic on this Monday, but I made good time. Gulliver was sleeping, safe in his crate at the back of the van. With only four women on this tour, his crate could ride in the far back seat; he wouldn't be regulated to cargo space. He'd stay there quietly while I went to collect my guests.

The four women were arriving on the same flight, as they were friends who lived and worked in the Seattle area. The organizer, the one I'd corresponded with, was Dr. Philberta Blake. She was a professor at the University of Washington. Her friends, all university teachers, had an interest in the life and works of Agatha Christie. *Did they teach mystery writers in university classes these days?* I wondered. I'd ask them.

I'd never attended university. My wonderful step-father had come into my life when I had already left school and was working. I'd liked my independence and hadn't taken advantage of his generosity the way Deidre had. She'd grown up with the expectations she would go on to advanced studies; I hadn't. I didn't resent it. Paul had left me so much money I didn't miss the difference in living style our income-generating abilities would have created. I loved my tour-guiding work, and Deidre loved her barrister work. We were lucky. Still, I was intimidated by the thought of four intelligent university women expecting me to educate them about Agatha Christie.

Dr. Philberta Blake was just as her passport picture showed her: thin with short brown hair. She was about my age and walked with big strides. She wore expensive casual clothes in blues and browns. On such a tall woman, the clothes looked fabulous. She wore Fluvog shoes in a soft plum color. They were wonderful shoes. Perhaps we had something in common.

She approached me. "Claire Barclay?"

"Yes. Dr Blake?"

"Berta. I recognized you from your website photo. Thank you for being here to meet us."

"It's a pleasure." I glanced behind her.

Three women were patiently waiting. Berta Blake stepped back. "My friends: Kim, Tessa, and Mallory."

Kimberly Sutton was much shorter than the others, about five-foot-one and dressed in kaikai coloured, loose cotton trousers and top. Over those she wore a light blue cardigan. She smiled at me.

A tall, slim woman, with long grey hair in a simple plait stepped forward. "I'm Tessa." She wore jeans, a purple shirt with what looked like a patch-work vest. She was definitely colourful. "Pleased to meet you. We are so looking forward to this.' She shook my hand with more energy than I'd expected from an older woman who had just flown about ten hours. But then, they'd flown with KLM and in the premium economy class. That would have been comfortable, even relaxing.

"And I'm Mallory." A much younger woman leaned toward me and offered her hand.

She was beautiful: smooth brown skin, huge brown eyes, tall with substantial weight behind her, and long straight hair that gleamed in the sunlight. I guessed she was Indigenous but I had no idea from which Nation. I'd read that Mallory was a grad student at Seattle University who was looking for information on war poets for her graduate thesis. The others were going to help with her research.

This tour was going to test my own research abilities. If I fell short, I was going to feel foolish, and they would be disappointed. I don't usually lack confidence in my knowledge, but this group would have research abilities beyond mine, and I might be wrong about some stories or facts. *So, you'll be wrong. They will, no doubt, correct you and feel kindly about it. Don't fuss.* I'd pay attention to their comfort. That would be a good start.

They each had a checked bag they had piled on individual carts, so I led the parade to my van. It was a reasonable amount of luggage. They were going to be in England for another fortnight after finishing my tour.

"We've come all this way," Berta said, "and all of us made care-taking arrangements, so we might as well stay for a holiday."

I opened the back of the van and reached for a suitcase.

"Woof." Gulliver greet them.

The four women stared at the back of the van.

"Gulliver," I indicated the back. "He's in a crate. Gulliver is a Cavalier King Charles spaniel and my best friend. Does anyone have any concerns about Gulliver traveling with us?"

"Not me," Mallory said. "I like dogs."

"I'm good," Tessa said.

"As long as he doesn't yap," Berta said.

"I'm okay with him." Kim added her approval.

"He won't come with us every day because I don't like leaving him in the crate for long, and some days that would be necessary."

Berta huffed. "I like your priorities." She sounded sarcastic.

I was startled. "Did you mean I put my dog before my guests?"

"Do you?"

I paused for a moment. "Sorry, but I expect I do."

"Of course she does, Berta." Tessa came to my defence. "Anyone with the least caring nature for animals would do that. You can complain or do something about it if you aren't comfortable, but a dog can't."

I didn't agree with her. Gulliver made it clear when he was unhappy. He had a variety of woofs and yips when he wanted me to pay attention to him, but I wasn't getting into the argument between Tessa and Berta.

"I can leave him with a sitter some of the time."

"Not necessary," Berta said curtly.

I took note of Berta's objections, though, and would leave Gulliver when we went to Devon. They climbed into the van.

"As you can see there is plenty of room, so you can sit wherever you like."

"We'll get a good view of everything from these high seats."

"You can see over the hedgerows," I agreed.

They settled into their seats, and I drove them via the M3, the quickest route to the Badgerhouse, their BnB in Ashton-on-Tinch. Carol Badger was on hand to welcome them.

She had six rooms to let so my four each had their own room as requested.

"I'm too old and full of routines and bedtime rituals to share a room," Beta announced.

For a moment I wondered if she practiced an exotic religion then realized she probably meant she had a bedtime routine such as a cup of tea or cocoa, a read for precisely thirty minutes, then absolute silence. She wasn't as old as some of my fussy tourists who were in their late seventies and insisted on heating pads and herbal tea or black-out curtains and a bottle of scotch.

The Badgerhouse was Victorian with the gingerbread enhancements of trellis work. It was small compared to some edifices to Victorian wealth with only eight bedrooms, but it was charming. The right side of the ground floor had two long sash windows. The floor above had identical windows directly above, but the top floor had only one window set in a mansard roof. A wide staircase made a gracious entrance to the carved, wooden front door. The house was painted a forest green with rust brown on the windows frames and the lacey decorative wood at the eaves. I loved this house. It was, in its way, symmetrical but had enough additions, bump-outs at the side and elaborate decoration to satisfy the heart of any romantic tourist.

I left Gulliver in his crate and led my group into the house. Carol Badger was in her thirties, energetic and fit as she scurried up and down the stairs of this guest hotel many times in a day. She was short, about five-one, had a fair complexion and wore her nut-brown hair in short curls around her head. She told me she cut it herself to save time and money but, since it was so curly, her bad hair cut was hidden in the curls.

"Welcome, all. Let's get you settled."

Carol efficiently sorted out which person went to which room, paying attention to who had trouble on the stairs and who didn't like morning light. I stepped back and left her to it.

Before they disappeared into their rooms I offered them a choice of activity. "I am happy to conduct a walk around this village and get some lunch. I live here and know it well. If you'd rather rest after your flight, we can walk another time. After lunch, you might like a rest for a few hours, then we will head out for supper."

I assumed Mallory, the youngest of the lot, would like a walk but it turned out they all preferred a walk, lunch, then the rest.

"Meet me in the foyer here in thirty minutes then. Can you do that?"

"For sure," Tessa said. "That's enough time."

I watched them leave, wondering what it was going to like to guide a group who already knew one another. Usually, my guests either didn't know one another or knew only one or two others.

I drove home and parked on the street outside my home. I let Gulliver into the garden, walked back to the van and checked each seat to see if the woman had left anything behind. Tessa had left a purple, velvet, drawstring bag. I'd only seen pictures of those. In Edwardian times they were called dance bags. They were popular also in the early twentieth century. By the feel of this one, there were glasses in there. I took it with me.

Inside the house, I gathered the mail off the floor and set it on the table, and answered a few emails. I called Gulliver in from the garden and left him with a new chew toy. Then I walked back to Badgerhouse, leaving Gulliver at home, as he was not welcome in every shop in the village, and the women might want to explore some of them.

The women were in the foyer, changed from their travel clothes, and ready to walk. That augured well for the tour as waiting for a late guest always strained the mood of a group. I passed the velvet bag to Tessa who thanked me and stashed it in her rucksack.

"We'll walk along the river here to the alleyway between the houses then up to Princess Street, cross it, skirt the cricket pitch, then up to The Street." This wasn't a big village but there was a book shop, a dress shop, a tea room, and the post office on The Street. "The church here is medieval and has an ancient cemetery"

"How old is the church?" Mallory asked me.

"About seven hundred years, the oldest building in the village. My house is nineteenth century so not as old."

"Shit! Seven hundred years!" Kim said. "There's nothing that old in Seattle. Of course, Indigenous people lived there for thousands of years, but they built with wood, so their villages didn't last, and the white settlers, who didn't arrive until 1851, built mostly with wood as well. Nothing lasts *this* long where I live. It gets ya'." Hers wasn't an unusual reaction. North American tourists usually took some time to readjust their notion of 'old'.

We walked past Thomas and Mary Greenwood's house. They were teachers but also gardeners and the late roses tumbled over the wall in crimson profusion with the heady spice scent I always associated with this corner of the village.

Kim stopped to smell the low-hanging beauties. Her clothes in drab kaki almost blended into the stone wall while her chestnut-colored hair caught the light in bright auburn sparks. Her face, pale with a reflected blush from the roses, was beautiful. I clicked a few pictures. I would send them to her if they turned out well.

Once we were on The Street, they stopped at the book shop.

"I'm always looking for early editions of Agatha's work," Berta said. "Recent editions take out some of her prejudices. As offensive as she sometimes is, her prejudices reflect the times and give me a more honest look at the world at that time. Some objectionable opinions were considered normal."

"Such as?" I asked.

"She considered adoption a motivation for matricide. Now really, that doesn't make sense."

"She isn't particularly accepting of Indigenous people as *Ten Little Indians* tells us," Mallory added.

"They have changed that title to *And Then There Were None.*"

"Sure. What? Eighty years after she wrote it."

"Agreed. It's disgusting, but my point is, that it wasn't disgusting to readers of her day, and we should pay attention to that fact. Words reflect attitudes."

"So we accept she was prejudiced and blind to the danger of those prejudices and set it aside as she's long dead and we can't educate her?"

"We can educate the readers," Berta insisted. "But readers should know how objectionable some of the accepted attitude of the past were."

I stayed out of that argument.

They dispersed within the book store, looking for books that were special to them. A half hour in the book shop was enough before we moved onto The Street and headed east. The knoll on which the church sat rose on the other side of The Street. I knew they'd want to visit it, but I hoped to give the constabulary enough time to finish their work and remove the crime tape. There was no need for this group to know about Jordan's murder. The hill was high enough that we couldn't see the steps of the church from directly below it. The women wandered into the dress shop next and tried to get Kim to buy a colorful shirt. Mallory picked out one that would look good with the kaki.

"Not on your life," she said. "I don't care how I look and neither does Felicity." Felicity Thomas was listed as her next of kin to be informed if anything happened to her on this trip. I assumed she was Kim's partner. It sounded as though they had similar taste in clothes.

"Are you ready for lunch?" I asked.

"Sure." Tess pushed her grey hair back and shook her shoulders as if trying to loosen them. Her voluminous draperies shook and settled around her in an interesting array of blues, turquoise and rust.

I herded the four women into the Blue Heron Café. I'd reserved the room at the back which had comfortable chairs and light oak tables. The woman settled down distributing their packages around them and picked up the menus.

"Ordinary fare here," I said, "but a good variety, and they make most of it here, so it is fresh and usually very good. We're having a more elaborate meal about eight tonight."

Three pairs of glasses appeared. Everyone stared at Mallory who had picked up her menu and started to read it without glasses. The three older women went back to their menus. I'd worn glasses for distance since I was ten. I didn't need help for close reading yet. In fact, I could read without glasses and just needed them for seeing distances. Somehow, taking my glasses off to read in this company smacked of competition. I left them on.

"There are the usual burgers, sandwiches, omelettes, as well as Cornish pasties or a more substantial meal of beef Bolognese, chili, or lasagna." This was one of the meals I was paying for along with tonight's.

The waitress took orders. It was Vi Taylor, Rose Jones' younger sister. Vi, short for Violet. Rose and Violet. What was her mother thinking? Luckily, there were only two girls in the family. I wonder what Mrs. Taylor would have named another girl. Daffodil?

"Nice to see you, Vi," I said.

"You too, Claire. How's little Amber making out?"

"So far so good. It's a big adjustment."

"The kids at school like her—so Rose's girl says."

I smiled. That was good to hear. They weren't all bullies then.

The women made their choices. I had the Cornish pasty, as I can't resist them. We were down to the coffee stage, tea for Mallory, when I asked about their particular interest in Agatha Christie.

Berta leaned forward, her coffee cup in one hand. "I'm the one with the particular interest in Agatha. I am a full professor at University of Washington in the English Department with affiliation with the Creative Writing Department where I mainly teach grad students and do my own research. It is precisely the position I've always wanted. I got my PhD studying twentieth-century novelists. I did my thesis on Doris Lessing, a totally acceptable author to academics. Now, Christie is a twentieth-century novelist as well, but there was no way I could study her seriously until I got my PhD, then tenure. With the tenure I have now, I can study whatever I please. I have accumulated time for a short sabbatical which I've taken to investigate Agatha."

Did she see herself as an academic rebel? "That's impressive," I said. "I hope I can provide enough material for you."

"I don't expect you to be a scholar. I gave you a list of the places I wanted to visit. Getting me there will suffice."

I was relieved, but also a little annoyed. Not a scholar? I was doing a bit of research myself on Agatha Christie's missing eleven days, but I was reluctant to tell Berta that. I didn't want her to belittle my efforts. Besides, I hadn't had much time to work on it lately.

She continued as if she was the chair of a meeting. "Mallory is studying... You can tell her what you're studying, Mallory."

Mallory put down her tea cup to speak. "I'm studying War Poets. Tessa is my supervisor as she's ace on poetry." She smiled at Tessa and continued. "I don't understand male violence, and I have studied it. So now I'm looking at war as the manifestation of male violence. Did poetry act as a balance or a safe haven for soldiers? I hope to find poems, epitaphs on gravestones, or anything that will help me understand how soldiers who were poets and soldiers could reconcile such a dichotomy."

I felt as if waves of politics, social attitudes, and the big concepts of humanity were rushing at me. I was not knowledgeable in those fields. Politeness urged me to inquire about the interests of Tessa and Kim, but I was a little afraid that they, too, would be outside my ability to accommodate.

Malory nodded at Kim.

Kim explained her studies. "I am a tenured professor at Northwest University's English Department. My field is queer writers of the twentieth and twenty-first-centuries. I am trying to broaden or narrow, depending on how you look at it, into non-defined gender writers."

I had no idea what she was talking about. Luckily, Tessa spoke before I said something inane.

"I'm a full professor at Seatle University. My specialty of study is nineteenth-century poets, particularly women poets when I can find them, but I'm willing to help Mallory with her thesis and get into the war poets and violence. It will be interesting to see how the poets of history developed into the twentieth-century war poets. I can see an article on that."

I could almost understand that research.

They were beginning to yawn and look tired, even Mallory, so I started toward their BnB.

"The church is medieval, isn't it?" Mallory said as we left the café.

"Yes, it is."

"Can we just walk up to it. I won't take the time to explore it now but I'd like to see it and the graveyard."

I hoped the crime tape had disappeared.

"Just a quick walk up and then back down to the Badgerhouse," Berta said. "I'm flagging."

"All right."

I took them across The Street and up the short driveway to the church. The crime tape was still there.

"Do you have a film crew working here?" Berta asked. The women had stopped and stared up the steps to the heavy wooden doors now festoons with blue and white police tape.

I was tempted to lie, but living in a village kept a person honest, as someone would always spill the truth or, at least, their version of the truth.

"No," I said. "We had a tragic accident here yesterday. And the police are looking into it."

"What happened?" Tess asked.

These were academics. They would always ask questions.

"A local man was murdered."

They looked at one another. There was silence then Berta said, "I suppose I naively thought that just occurred in Christie novels."

"I could be in LA," Kim said,

"Or Seattle," Tess agreed.

"It is rare here," I defended my village. "I'll find out when the tapes are coming down and let you know."

"How do you find out?" Berta asked.

"My husband is the detective in charge."

They all stared at me now. "Interesting," Berta said, "but I can't cope with anything more. I need my bed."

I walked them to the Badgerhouse and stopped outside the front door. "Have a rest or a walk if you like. The river walk is beautiful, and it is right at your doorstep. I will be back at seven to drive you to Basingstoke where I have reserved a table at a lovely restaurant in a period Georgian house."

They all smiled at me. I hoped they would have a rest, concentrate on their studies, and leave the idea of Jordan's murder alone. His death was not entertainment for tourists. I've had tourists interested in helping solve a murder before, but this time I would resent it. Perhaps because I knew Jordan and, for all his faults, he didn't deserve to be murdered or to be treated as a puzzle to be solved by them. I wanted nothing to get in Mark's way as he investigated, particularly not my tourists.

CHAPTER NINE

I was home before Amber's school was out. I hugged Gulliver and let him out in the back garden. Then I texted Mark. *I'm home. You can stay at work after 3:30 if you like.*

Thanks, he replied.

How is it going?

As usual. Too many suspects. Not enough evidence.

Good luck.

Amber banged the front door shut. Gulliver barked and danced around her. I called from the kitchen. "I'm home, Amber. How did it go?"

"Okay." She responded from the hall. I expected she'd flung her uniform sweater to the floor as usual. She came into the kitchen, with her shirt pulled out of her blue tartan skirt and her tie askew. I remembered treating my uniform just that way many years ago.

"Tea?" I lifted my cup.

"Sure."

I poured her a milky tea and pushed the sugar bowl her way. She settled onto her chair and ladled in two spoonfuls of sugar. I drank it that way as a child.

"Any more trouble with the bully?"

"That's all over."

That was so last week. I had to learn to keep up. Gulliver came into the room fighting with Amber's sweater.

"Uh, oh." She said and retrieved the sweater. She was kind to Gulliver and slipped him a piece of biscuit to distract him. The sweater went on the back of the chair. and would make it up to her room eventually. She drank her tea then headed up to her room to change out of her uniform, taking Gulliver but not the sweater. I took a vegetable lasagna from the freezer and set it to thaw on the counter. Amber didn't come back to the kitchen until just before five. She took an avid interest in food preparation.

"Lasagna's going into the oven now. It should be forty minutes." I sat back down with another up of tea.

"I'll make a salad later."

"I'll have a taste, but I'm eating out tonight."

"Oh, right. You have those ladies from America. What are they like?" She'd poured herself another cup of tea, wrapped her hands around the mug, and leaned forward. Her dark curly hair bounced as she moved.

"Busy. Chatty. Super smart. All university professors."

"Are they annoying?"

"You mean do they make a point of showing how smart they are?"

"Like that," she agreed.

"No. Not that I've noticed. They're just smart and curious about everything." I thought about it. "Intimidating at times when I realize they know more than I do about some things, but they don't do that deliberately."

"It's hard, sometimes, to be smart. People want you to act like you aren't. You know. Just be quiet and don't ask questions."

My mobile rang just then, but I registered her comment in my memory. Was that a problem for her?

"Patrick Stonning," I read aloud from the display on my mobile.

"The guy next door?" Amber sounded eager.

I smiled. "Here's hoping. Hello Patrick."

"Hello, Claire. I have to tell you, your call about buying the house couldn't have come at a better time. We were dithering. You know how sometimes you dither back and forth on a problem and never do anything because change could be worse than the present situation?"

I let Patrick's words wash over me. Eventually, he'd come to the point. Amber raised her eyebrows. I shrugged to indicate I didn't have the answer yet.

"So we set aside some time, and we really got down to the pros and cons and, actually, it was simple really. Rita will not live in the house because Oliver died there. That's all there is to it. So there's no point on holding the house for any longer. You can buy it."

I grinned and did a thumbs up to Amber.

She left her chair and danced around the room, setting Gulliver off in a merry chase of jumping and barking. I made a shooing motion with my hands, and Amber danced into the hall and the living room; Gulliver chased her.

"If it's okay with you, we'll get the house evaluated by an estate agent and pay him for doing that. If you could share that cost, then we won't need the agent after."

"I agree," I said quickly.

"Then whatever cost he comes up with is what we will agree to sell it at and what you agree to pay."

"That sounds fair, Patrick. And because we are both paying the agent, we are assured he or she isn't slanting the price either way."

"That's what I thought."

I wanted to sing and shout. My own study again. Room for Deidre and family to stay. A den for Mark to watch those rugby games. My brain was buzzing. I focused on Patrick.

"What closing date are you thinking of?"

"We think we could arrange to be out in a month. Is that too soon for you?"

"No. A month would be fine." I could get my solicitor, Mr. Greenwood, to cash in some securities and get the money into my bank account and then over to Patrick in a fortnight. I'd have to set everything in motion soon.

Patrick continued to speak. "I'll book an evaluator this week. We can have the price set by the end of the week then go from there."

I knew Patrick ran a successful publishing business, Stella sometimes did translations for it, but tonight he was demonstrating his ability to make deals. I expect he dealt with contracts every day.

"Patrick, that's wonderful. Thank you."

"It works for us as well. Rita's grateful to you. She thinks I would have held onto it forever if I didn't find a good buyer. I don't think that's true, but it's what she thinks. I am glad it will be you. We're both going to be interested in what you do with it. Make it into one house, I expect. That'll be a big job."

I let Patrick rattle on as he is wont to do in any conversation and drifted into a haze of speculations about "one big house".

"Well," I heard the goodbye preliminary in Patrick's tone. "I'll text over the evaluation to you when I get it and the invoice for your half of the cost. Should be a week."

"Many thanks, Patrick. Give my love to Rita."

"Will do." He disconnected.

"Amber," I called.

She dashed in. "We got it?"

"Yes! We got it! At least, we've agreed to the sale. It hasn't gone through yet."

"We're going to get it!" she amended. Amber is a precise thinker.

While the lasagna bubbled away in the oven, I fetched a long sheet of paper and two pencils.

"First," Amber said, "What's their house like. How many rooms? Is it like this one?"

"Not quite." I'd been in the house several times. "It has the same front parlor. Where I...we have a big kitchen, they have a small room they use as a study." I must use 'we'—we're a family now.

"So, we could connect all the rooms and have a giant living room."

"That's one plan," I said. "I'll sketch the house as it is, both floors, then we can start moving walls."

She grinned. "I'm going to move walls so I get a big bedroom."

I laughed. This was going to be a big project but a wonderful change. I'd need to talk to Desmond Parmar, my efficient builder, after the sale went through.

Amber suggested I go over the house plan in ink. Then we could put our ideas over it in pencil. That way we could always see what we started with. I almost forgot the lasagna but pulled it from the oven with only a few scorch marks on the edges.

I served Amber and a smaller portion for myself. We shoved the plans aside and used the end of the table, ate quickly and were still at the plans when Mark arrived.

I left Amber to explain our exciting news and dashed upstairs to change for the elegant evening out.

I heard Mark say, "That's grand, *bach*."

"I want a desk and wifi in my room."

I thought about that as I changed. Young people tended to isolate themselves in their rooms. Perhaps it would be better to make a study on the ground floor that she and Mark could share. Perhaps I'd offer her a two-piece *en suite* in her bedroom and an extra bed so a friend could sleep over. That way there wouldn't be room for a study in her room.

I threw on my deep purple, silky trousers, a turquoise shiny tank top and a long multicolored light sweater in shades of purple, lavender and turquoise. I added my Tory Burch Georgia pumps and silver dangling earrings of North American Indigenous design. I grabbed my clutch handbag.

I stood in the hall and transferred my mobile, purse, keys, and tissues from my rucksack to my handbag, and listened to Mark and Amber's conversation. Amber had served Mark some lasagna and was sitting at the table with him.

"See that's where I want my room."

"Have you thought about the fact you can have either a front view of the garden, the street and the green beyond or a back view of the garden and hills beyond."

Amber was silent. I waited to see what she would decide.

"There's pros and cons, aren't there?" she said.

"Yes," Mark said. "There are pros and cons. Let's look at them."

I let myself out the front door before tears welled up and spilled down my cheeks. I was surprised at my reaction. It was spontaneous. They were so earnest and sweet. So bonded. I was lucky to have both of them in my life.

The ladies were waiting when I walked into the foyer at Badgerhouse where they decorated the space with glitter and color.

"What an elegant group," I enthused.

Berta wore a muti colored dress of azure blue, black, and silver with long sleeves made of some frothy material like chiffon that emphasized her tall, elegant figure. I realized how practical it was as it would scrunch up into a small ball in her suitcase. Over it, she wore a long black vest. Her shoes were Girotti's. I'd seen them online. Gorgeous. Metallic, peacock blue with gold buckles, block mid-heel. I'd love to own them. I saw her glance at my Tory Burch's. We smiled at each other.

Tessa wore a dress as well. It was reminiscent of a nineteen-century Jane Austen dress with its deep mahogany color, high waist, and small drape almost to the floor. I wasn't sure if those were trainers underneath that dress.

Mallory wore black trousers, a black shirt, and a long tunic vest with Indigenous patterns in red, white, and black applicated down each side of the front. Her earrings, like mine, were silver, engraved, and dangly.

"You vest tells a story. Am I right?" I asked her.

"It does." She smiled. I supposed the story was personal as she didn't expound.

They gathered their bags and sweaters while I took in Kimberly. I had yet to see Kim in anything the least bit elegant, but she had made an effort for this evening. She wore trousers, of course, but they were black, her shirt was a bright yellow, made of a shiny material. Her sweater was lightweight and a muddy beige color. But it was her shoes that attracted attention. They were bright gold and sparkling, as if they'd been sprayed with glitter.

"Great shoes," I said to her.

She grinned. "My partner, Felicity, gave them to me. She said I had to be glamorous occasionally."

"Is *she* glamorous?" I asked.

Kim thought about it. "I'd say, 'No'"

L'Ortolan was in Shinfield, south of Redding and about forty minutes from Ashton-on-Tinch. It stood in its own large landscaped grounds off Church Lane and opposite St. Mary's Church. The restaurant was in a handsome red brick Georgian building with a diamond pattern on the upper story and white stone cladding at the corners and on the edges of the chimney. I had reserved, so we were escorted into the conservatory where the tables were dressed in white linen over purple table skirts. The chairs were upholstered in purple velveteen. It was a bit rich for my taste. Still, it was kept from being garish by the muted gray carpet. The surroundings did justify our sartorial splendour and fabulous shoes.

"Beautiful," Kim said as she gazed out the windows at the greenery, darkening now with shadows in the September evening.

"Very nice," Berta agreed. She took a menu from the waitress who had glanced at me and, at my nod, came to me last.

"On your bill?" she murmured.

"Yes." This was one of the meals included on the tour.

The menu was elaborate and should satisfy everyone's need for a Michelin three rosette experience. It was going to take some time to browse amid the Cornish Cod with Scallop Mousse, Grapefruit Beurre Blanc, Girolles and Yorkshire Salt-Aged Lamb, Lamb Faggot, Savory Puree, and Wye Valley Asparagus.

"Girolles are Chanterelle mushrooms," I said. "And Lamb Faggot is a few usually rounded pieces of meat. I think you might call them roundels."

"Cornish Monkfish," Berta read. "Anjou Pigeon. Pigeon, really?"

"It's farmed squab," I assured her. "It tastes like chicken."

They took their time over ordering starters and the entrée. Dessert was going to be another studious affair.

Kim ordered the eight-course tasting menu which would be delicious. Mallory ordered the Orkney Scallops with Trout Roe, Decana Pear and Fennel. Berta chose the pigeon, Tessa the lamb, and I ordered the monkfish. We all ordered minestrone for starters with homemade bread. A thick book with a leather cover contained the wine list.

"Why don't you order the wine?" Berta said. "Consult with George here," She waved at the hovering sommelier whose name tag indeed said "George". He smiled.

He was young to be a sommelier, but he held the book and was ready to advise. I wasn't buying a bottle for each person so confined my choices to the front page where I could order by the glass. I sorted out the Pino noir to accompany the minestrone, the Pinot Grigio for the fish, a hearty red for the lamb, and a Bordeaux for the pigeon.

"You can refill their glasses as they wish," I said.

The presentation of the plates was a work of art. Mobiles flashed as my guests sent pictures of artistically arranged food to their friends and relatives—always a good sign.

Berta and I limited ourselves to one glass of wine but the others managed two and Tessa managed three. She was mellow and happy when we selected our desserts.

Tessa passed on the sweet liquor with her peach melba, but the others had a small taste.

They dozed on the drive home. I helped them into Badgerhouse and drove the few blocks to my home, satisfied my tourists were content.

Mark had left the front light on for me. The mellow yellow glow was welcoming. I let myself in and took off my shoes. The house was quiet; I didn't want to wake anyone. Gulliver had heard me, though, and padded down the stairs to lick my face and accept pats and endearments. We parted at the top of the stairs, as he returned to Amber's room. I opened the door to our room. Mark was asleep. I checked the time. Midnight.

Ah, well. It had been a wonderful dinner. So far the tour was going well. I undressed, and slipped into bed beside Mark.

He roused. "All right?"

"Mmm." I said. "Fine. You?"

He took a deep breath and rolled toward me. "Fine now." He reached for me.

In the morning, I got only a quick report from Mark on the murder investigation.

"More interviews today. Andy's working on the case book. Lots to consider. Call me tonight."

"I will."

"Anything you need, Amber?" I asked.

"I'm good," she said and waved a piece of toast at me.

I would be away to Devon with my tourists for two days. I hoped Mark would let me know what he discovered. I have never found a cure for my curiosity.

CHAPTER TEN

The morning was sunny and warm with that deceptive brightness of late summer which can turn to fall in an hour. We'd started at nine o'clock as, even on the fast roads, it was two hours and forty minutes to Torquay. I took the M3 for a short way then turned onto the A303, heading west.

The women gazed out the windows at the green and rolling lands of Hampshire. They were enthusiastic about the coming two days.

"Agatha Christie's home," Berta enthused. "I am going to research every minute."

"And shop and drink and eat," Tessa reminded her.

"That too."

We were heading to Devon, to the town of Torquay where Agatha Christie had lived for many years. Berta waved her Agatha Christie Festival brochure to get my attention.

"Yes?" I asked, one eye on the road.

"Do we have tickets to festival?"

"I have them and will hand them out when we get there. You have tickets to two days entrance to the festival as well as dinner tonight at Greenway house." Greenway House had been Agatha Christie's home.

"Really. Greenway House? However did you manage that?"

"You gave me lots of time to plan, and I knew someone." An old friend of mine from my working days at *English for Executives* snapped up some cancellations for me.

I drove for an hour through the patchwork of green and yellow fields with hedgerows marking them into patches. Farm land surrounded us all the way to Martock where I took an exit off the highway to The Old Dairy Café. It was a good restaurant to stop for coffee as it was light and airy and had interesting vegetarian choices as well as light snacks.

"How do you keep people from buying up the farm land and putting up tracts of houses," Kim asked me. "Your population is about sixty-eight million. Where is everybody?"

"Yes," Mallory said. "My people wandered all over the natural land until settlers arrived and pre-empted and fenced it. How did you keep people from doing that?"

The land defined our history. "To start with tribes controlled the land and defended it from other tribes as it was done in many other places." I explained to Mallory. "Then we had the Christians with their rules and their hierarchy who established monasteries. The monks controlled much of the land and farmed it, so they kept people from building on their farms. We also had the feudal system where the lord was given huge tracts of land for his own use."

"No matter who was already living on it?' Mallory asked.

"No matter who was living on it." I agreed. "Everyone was subject to the king. Some got land rewards from the king or the queen, and the rest didn't. Those feudal lords protected their land for centuries as producing farms. They often used them for grazing sheep and that wasn't compatible with human settlement, so that's likely how the lands came to be house-free. Now, we have many government rules about where you can put a house. We do need agricultural land to feed ourselves."

"It's beautiful," Tessa said.

"For another hour or so it is," I agreed. "Then you are going to see acres of housing tracts as people crowd close to the sea. The land-protection rules sometimes give way to housing needs."

I rejoined the 303, headed west then south of Exeter to the A380. There were houses all around us here as people clustered around the city then spread south toward the sea. There were trees and open green fields alongside the road as we approached Torquay, but no farmland. I drove up to the Grand Hotel in Torquay, pulled over at the loading zone, and stopped.

"This is where we will stay for two nights."

The hotel was an impressive, a white, Victorian edifice in a vaguely French style with turrets, claiming the sea front on Corbyn Beach with unimpeded views of the English Channel. The green lawn sloped down to the road before the sea and the whole impression was one of elegance.

"The Grand Hotel," Berta breathed almost reverently. "Where Agatha Christie spent her honeymoon."

"With which husband?" Kim asked.

"The first," Berta said. "Archie Christie."

"After I unload your luggage, could you could wait in the lobby until I park the van at the station across the road? I will be right back to arrange your rooms. The lobby is something to behold."

"Oh, wow," Mallory said, taking in the wonder of the hotel. "Art Deco extravagance. I bet it was just like this during the war."

"Yes, madam." A smiling young porter dressed in dark trousers—no jeans here—and white polo shirt reached for the cases as I pulled them from the back of the van.

My guests were still on the sidewalk gazing at the tall white rendered sides of the Grand.

"It looks like a wedding cake," Tessa said. "Let's go in and check it out."

They moved off. The porter, a young Asian man, gave me a grin. "It takes some like that," he said. "American?"

"From Seattle."

"Seem like a nice bunch," he said, as he piled the cases onto his cart.

"They are lovely." I smiled at him.

"Makes it easier, doesn't it?"

I agreed. In the hospitality business, good manners went a long way. I moved the van to a car park near the station, bought a two-day parking pass for twenty pounds and walked back to the hotel to join the ladies in the lobby.

They were staring at the marble pillars, marble floors with a central circular pattern which reflected the circular light above, an arched ceiling with cove detail, and in the halls, an expanse of parquet floor.

"They have an Agatha Christie suite," Berta said enthusiastically.

"I know. I'm sorry I couldn't manage to get it for you. It's booked years in advance."

"I suppose so. Lovely to be here, though."

I settled the women in four separate rooms with sea views and myself in a single at the back of the hotel, and arranged to meet them for lunch in a half hour at the Pier Point Bar and Restaurant on Rathmore Road just below the hotel. It was informal there, not expensive, and had delicious fish and chips as I'd found when I'd spent a day in Torquay last month checking out restaurants and looking for interesting excursions. I gathered the tickets I would need to hand out: the Agatha Christie Festival brochures in case they'd lost the one I'd sent and a map of the town. I had circled in red on the brochures the events which they had tickets for and ones that might interest them. The town was full of people. The bar would be lively, but we were early, so perhaps we'd get a table.

We were lucky and got a table near the window with the ocean view. The buzz of conversation was steady but not yet loud. This lunch was not a meal I paid for, so they studied the menu, ordered, then turned to me, expecting to be entertained.

"You know Agatha Christie honeymooned here in 1914." They nodded. "And you probably know she lived near here for some of her life."

"She was born here," Berta informed us.

"And she had that beautiful mansion near here, didn't she?" Kim said. "I included her in my 'Writers of the Twentieth Century' class."

"That's right," Berta said. "Greenaway House. That's close by, I think?" She turned to me.

"It's her holiday home on the River Dart, and it's about a half hour from here. We are having dinner there tonight."

"Greenaway House belonged to Agatha Christie?" Tessa was incredulous.

"It did."

"Greenaway House," Berta breathed with reverence. "That dinner will make my trip."

"What so important about Greenway House?" Mallory asked.

That's all the encouragement Berta needed. "She usually went there to relax after she finished writing a book. As well, she set at least three novels in that area: *Five Little Pigs*, *Dead Man's Folly*, and *Ordeal by Innocence*."

"It's a National Trust Property now," I said.

"So they will have artifacts, memorabilia, and articles I could study?" Berta asked.

"You'll get more at the museum on Babbacombe Road here in Torquay. I can drive you there. Text me when you want to go."

"Wonderful. Thanks." Berta looked as though I had just handed her the winning National Lottery ticket.

I didn't have a solid sense of these women, their tastes, ideas, or needs, except Berta. She was a scholar who was sufficiently established and secure in her university position that she could pursue any research project she liked. The life and work of Agatha Christie was her driving goal at this point. I expected that she was such a strong personality that the others just came because Berta wanted them with her.

"Tell me, Kim. What is your interest in Agatha Christie?"

"Not much more than other women novelists of the twentieth century. I'm on this trip to support Berta, although I am enjoying it a ton."

"Do you teach at the same university as Berta?"

"No I teach at Northwest U. It's in Seattle though, so we see each other at events."

"And your goals?"

"I'm trying to decide if I should move from studying woman novelist to trans writers."

"Hard to get research on trans in the twentieth century critical articles," Tessa said.

"There's that limitation," Kim agreed,

"And you, Tessa?"

"I teach at Seattle University mostly women poets of the nineteenth century. I'm here to help Mallory with her lit review for her War poets thesis. We're going on a war poets' tour after this one. But, like Kim, I'm enjoying this. The Grand Hotel. Dinner at Greenway House. What's not to like?"

"And I," Mallory said, before I could ask, "am trying to get enough research to stuff my thesis and get that PHD. Tessa is my supervisor."

"I got her the grant to come on this trip."

Malloy grinned. "That's what finally convinced my husband that this degree is financially worthwhile."

The three other women smiled at her. I had heard that it was difficult to get support when you were working in upper-level academia. Mallory was getting substantial encouragement. I hoped it lasted, at least for the duration of this tour.

"And I," Berta said, "am going to write a series of mystery novels. I've made a start."

Here was another tourist who was sure she could write a mystery. Several of my previous tourists, avid readers of mysteries set in Britain, had plans to write their own mysteries. Berta just might do it.

"What do you think is essential in a mystery," I asked.

"A good solid motive."

"Which is?"

"Any of a combination of greed, anger, love, or fear."

"Fear?" I thought about that.

"A murderer may kill in order to make his or her own life safe."

I expect there were more motives than those, but I didn't dispute them with Berta.

The waiter served our lunch and, afterward, I handed out tickets to the International Agatha Christie Festival.

"You can walk through the park and take in all the displays and events that are going on there before you get to the festival proper. If anyone gets tired and wants to come back to the hotel, just text me. I'll pick you up. We have a late sitting at Greenway House, so you are free to enjoy the festival until we leave the Grand at half seven,"

They looked at me.

"Seven-thirty," I amended.

They paid their bills and bustled off.

I sat for a time with my coffee, thinking about the lives of those four women. They were each busy, independent, active, and full of purpose and energy. All that drive and ambition, accomplishments and curiosity made me long for one practical, pleasant, unambitious, good-natured tourist. I'd have to be on my best tour guide behavior not to let them know I found them a bit too energetic. I loved Agatha Christie, and I wanted to do some research myself. My local mystery club in Ashton-on-Tinch counted on me to write up articles to accompany the books we were preserving that had special significance. I was working on Christie's missing eleven days with a librarian in Wallingford. We had amassed a significant number of articles, and we're in the process of writing a literature review. It took time. Like many scholars, probably Berta as well, we were interested in why Agatha left Archie. Well, not why she left him, that was understandable, but why she disappeared in such a public way and was discovered eleven days later at The Old Swan Hotel in Harrogate. I'd been to that hotel; I wouldn't have chosen it.

The café was starting to fill. I thanked the waiter then went back to my room, did some accounting on my computer, and made sure all was in order for the next few days. At four, I called Mark.

"Is Amber home?"

"Yes, she came directly from school, complaining that she should have a riding lesson at least three times a week if she'd going to get any good."

"Did you point out the cost?"

"I did, and she said it was important to keep young people busy and learning. I sent her to do her homework on the kitchen table."

I laughed. "She's only ten. Anything is possible. She'll become a good rider; she already is a good rider."

"She's a smart, our girl."

"She is at that."

We were quiet for a moment, appreciating Amber. I observed other children her age, particularly when I saw her with her school mates. They were not as clever as Amber, nor did they have Amber's bright spirit and cheeky attitude. It occurred to me that other parents might have the same view of their child.

"How is the investigation going?" I asked.

"At the fact-gathering stage still. No one has come forth to confess. And we have staffing problems as usual. We can't use Bertie Witten. For one thing, the super won't let us, and for another he's too inexperienced."

Mark was always looking for more staff. "What have you learned?"

Mark had tried to hold back information when we were first dating, but he doesn't do that any more. I learn it one way or another, and he says I help him think.

"I interviewed Joyce and Nigel separately. Andy took Stella. Nothing telling there, although Joyce did admit to having had an affair with Jordan which she says was over. Nigel hadn't been aware of it, and she hadn't told him. Stella's affair was long over Andy says, and, well, you know Stella. She's an unlikely murderer. She just doesn't care enough."

I considered Stella's attitude to men. Mark was right.

"David and Mira interviewed Garman because he was working on the church books, and a man named Anthony Michel because he came to practise the organ in the morning. So, we know Jason was alive at eleven when Michael left or, at least, Jason wasn't lying dead in the church."

"You already knew that because Leah said he was working until two."

"It's a check on her statement."

Of course, he had to check statements. "What next?"

"Andy, David, and Mira have yet to interview the staff at the Blue Heron Café and inquire if anyone saw Jordan arrive—or anyone else arrive. Because it's directly across the street, someone might have seen the killer approach the church."

"It's up on the knoll, and you know people don't often look up."

"True. Still, we need a list of customers who were at the café after two and before four when you found the body to see if they remember seeing anyone. Also the staff at the DIY store beside the café. And their customers."

"That's going to take a week."

"It might. But it has to be done, and I still have to interview Joyleen Headly."

"Better take a female officer with you. She's prone to crushes, and you don't want that."

He protested. "I'm old enough to be her father."

"So was Jordan."

"Hmm. I'd better take Mira."

Mira was closer to Joyleen's age. She might be helpful.

Mark had more to say. "We found the knife in the bushes besides the church. The pathologist is swabbing the knife *and* around the area on Jordan's clothes where the knife entered. The thinking is: the murderer might have had sweaty hands and no gloves so left DNA on the knife. Most criminals or even first-time killers know enough to wipe the knife. They might not think about Jordan's clothes, though. Also, the pathologist thinks he or she might have put a sweaty hand down on Jordan's chest to get the knife out. That's a long shot but worth trying. I'll take DNA from some suspects. The department won't pay for more than six DNA tests. Too expensive. When it matches, it's grand evidence, but it takes as long as three weeks to get results. In the meantime, we have to get as much evidence as we can in case there is no DNA captured."

"You have a lot to do. It's hard for you to only be at work part time right now."

"Ture, but Andy's *achubwr bywy*d."

I interrupted. "What's that?"

"A life-saver. He's reliable and, because Bruce is at home, he can work long hours. Having to be home by three-thirty is restricting me. This isn't going to work in the long run."

I definitely didn't want to give up my work. "We'll talk about it when I'm home."

"Enjoy your tour."

I rang off. He had distracted me from the murder. What were we going to do? We couldn't leave Amber alone after school. Perhaps Rose would take her after school until one of us got home. How did other parents manage?

My ladies enjoyed both the dinner at Greenway House and the tour the staff took us on after dinner. Back at the Grand Hotel they departed to their bedrooms, and I made my way to mine. It was midnight, and I was tired.

A sumptuous bath with musky salts relaxed me, and I tumbled into bed prepared to drift away immediately. Hazy thoughts floated in and out of consciousness. Something Berta said resonated for Mark's investigation. Something about motive. Right. Greed, anger, love, and fear. The motive was likely buried in a passion from a lover or an ex-lover. What if it wasn't? What if it was greed? Or fear? What could Jordan have done to cause such a reaction in his killer?

CHAPTER ELEVEN

The women were up by eight and in the dining room for breakfast: Responsible, disciplined, orderly. They had their festival brochures beside them on the table. The older three put their reading glasses on and off as they alternatively read and talked. They'd studied their brochures and were full of the choices they'd made and the expectations they had for their experience. I paid close attention; it was my job to make sure they were happy.

We spent the day at the festival. The panel discussion on comedy and mystery had the audience laughing at the improv one-liners. I scouted through the trade displays of new mysteries, noting the ones I wanted to buy. My ladies had wandered off to satisfy their own interests, but I got a text from Berta just after lunch, asking me to drive her to the Torquay Museum. I wanted to do some research on Agatha Christie myself for my mystery book club at Ashton-on-Tinch, so I was happy to accompany her. The Agatha Christie Gallery in the Torquay Museum has some artifacts from her life such a clothes and some notes she wrote, mixing the real Agatha with her fiction, and including memorabilia from the telly shows of her books. I was trying to get a sense of the real life of Agatha, but it was hard because she didn't gush with opinions or emotions in interviews the way celebrities do today, so we knew more about her writing than her real life. We heard a lecture on the plot lines of three of her books. Berta took notes. I was looking for material relating to the missing eleven days when she must have had an emotional crisis to run to Harrogate, but I didn't find anything new. I'd have to go back to the museum in Wallingford, a market town where Christie spent her later years.

By late afternoon, the ladies were tired and ready to return to Aston-on-Tinch.

I drove them along the coast until just past Dawish then north on the Exeter Road and through the farmlands to join the familiar A303. Aware that I was on duty as a tour guide, I deviated south to Salisbury and pulled onto Ox Row Street Market Square, stopping in front of Ox Row Inn.

I swept my hand to encompass the surroundings. "The cathedral and the beautiful town are all yours for an hour-and-a-half. I will meet you inside the restaurant after I find parking." I blocked the traffic on the street until they had exited. By then, I had four cars patiently waiting behind me. I honked my thanks and drove almost a block before I could park near the library. That was lucky. Parking is a pain in Salisbury, especially with a van.

The Ox Row Inn served a quick and sustaining meal in comfortable British Pub style décor: wood paneling, wood floors, and wood chairs that didn't match. That seemed such a brilliant idea. If one chair broke, you didn't have to try to find a match.

"Can we have an hour to check out the cathedral?" Mallory asked. "Since we're here."

"Yes, of course."

They all left but Tessa who said. "I've seen the cathedral, and I can use time to rest my feet." We ordered another cup of coffee. Tessa eased her feet out of her sandals and sighed.

"New shoes."

"Yes, bad idea. I'll get my Birkenstocks out to wear for the rest of this trip."

Birkenstocks would fit in well with her loose trousers, long vest, and vaguely hippie-style shirt. She'd tied her long, grey hair with a leather thong. The overall look was relaxed if slightly theatrical.

"I've lived in Seattle," I said to Tessa, "but I don't know anything about your university."

"It's right in the heart of Seattle on the hill where a number of hospitals are."

I recognized the area. "We used to call that 'Pill Hill'."

"That's the place. I work there, but I live out by U of W."

"Near the lake," I said. I knew that area better. "Do you have a family?"

"I have one daughter who lives in New York and is a journalist. It's a precarious living, but she landed a job with an on-line magazine and she manages. I'm quite proud of her, actually."

"And you have friends." She hadn't mentioned a partner, so I assumed she didn't have one.

"Yes, good friends. Relationships are important, especially as you grow older. I am recently divorced. I shouldn't have stayed with my ex as long as I did." She shrugged. "Habit, maybe. He left me for the typical younger woman for fun and games, but he was so incredibly boring I should have left him much earlier. At least our divorce was civil. I have to admit a feeling of euphoria when he told me he was leaving. He sent me an email."

"An email? To say he wanted to leave?"

She smiled, not at all upset. "His message said: I think it's time we separated. I want a divorce."

"I answered. 'Certainly. I will arrange it.' Then I yelled 'Yes!' at the computer."

She smiled as she reported on her marriage breakup. It sounded as if it had been past time for a divorce.

"He responded politely. 'Thank you.' That's how much passion was left in our marriage. We didn't argue or even discuss it. Sad, isn't it?"

It was sad that after years of marriage they had little to say to each other. "Do you regret it?"

"Not in a millions years," she said and grinned.

We were back on the road shortly and home at Badgerhouse by nine. I promised to pick them up in the morning at half eight.

Both Mark and Amber were still up when I arrived home. Gulliver was ecstatic. I fussed over him then kissed Mark. I hugged Amber who gave me a slight hug in response.

"What are those ladies like now?" she asked.

"Talkative, intelligent, curious, and energetic as we expected. I'm tired."

She grinned. "The old ladies are wearing you out. Shame, shame. You need more exercise."

"Probably." That made me feel even more tired.

Amber called Gulliver, and they headed up to her room.

Mark poured me a cup of tea while I unloaded my computer onto my desk in the parlour, and put my suitcase near the stairs. I sat down heavily on the chair and reached for the tea.

"Thank you."

"Demanding, are they?"

"Not really. Not in the way of being petty or wanting special treatment. But they pay a lot of money for this tour, and I'm aware that they expect a lot for it. It's fair, but it's a strain. They're interesting women: curious, reflective, polite. So far, no one has gotten lost, or sick or annoyed anyone."

"A good tour, then."

"So far. How did you get on today?"

"I interviewed Leah and Joyleen. I'm interested in Joyleen. She seemed secretive. I took a swab for DNA because she was twitchy. I'm supposed to have better reasons than that to request an analysis, but I'll include her sample in the mail out."

"Did you take Leah's?"

"I didn't like her for a suspect. She was straightforward. She seemed clear."

"Clear about what?"

"About Jordan." Mark hit a key on his computer which brightened to show a page of text. It must be his notes.

"She said he was excellent as a riding instructor, had a professional background which attracted customers, was unreliable around women but agreed not to bring them to the stables. She said 'We suited each other. I'm going to miss him.'"

Mark was reading directly now.

"Did he try to pursue your daughter?" I said

"No She had a crush on him when she was a teen, but he avoided her and made it clear to her that there was nothing doing. It would have cost him his job, and he liked it here."

"So you don't think there was anything going on there."

"No. He wanted to stay here. All those adoring women clients. And I made sure he had time off if he needed to judge a show somewhere. It as good for my business if he was seen on the circuit.'

Mark swivelled around in his chair.

"Now what?" I asked.

"We're looking for a current girl friend."

"Thwarted love as a motive?"

"It seems logical. Joyce looked good at first."

"She's so unlikely. I can't believe she had an affair with Jordan. She's so worthy, and meek."

"She did. And she has a lover on-going at the moment."

"No! Who knew? She looks so…I…don't know…uninterested in sex."

"She's interested. She admits Jordan made overtures about a month ago, wanting to rekindle the affair, but she's hooked up with an old boyfriend and wasn't interested. Jordan had been her lover, but he was in her past—recent past."

I pondered that rationale for a moment. "What if the vicar thought she was attracted to Jordan, or if he'd just realized she had been involved with him? Would the Vicar be a suspect?"

"*Ei*, of course. As you know. At this stage, everyone's a suspect."

Mark thought the motive for the murder lay in Jordan's affairs. I thought about Berta's list of motives that included greed. "Was there any financial aspect to this?"

"Not that I can see. I think Jordan's long line of lovers is our best bet."

I mulled it over in my mind as I had a quick bath. Mark was no doubt right. With Jordan's predilection for affairs, husbands, fathers, and rejected lovers might be standing in line to elicit some justice.

In the morning, the ladies were ready at half eight for an hour's drive to Wallingford where Agatha had her permanent home with her second husband Max Mallowan. The museum there had an extensive collection of books and artifacts about Agatha's life and works. It also had Carla Hancock, a knowledgeable curator. She was short, slim, with bright blue eyes and the unflappable air of calm that I associated with most librarians.

We spent the morning with Carla. She and I had done some research on Agatha's missing eleven days. We were working at a slow pace, as I didn't get to the museum often, and Carla had other work to do. I wasn't prepared to tell Berta about our research, as Carla was doing most of the work, and I suspected Berta would not be able to resist taking that research and using it. If Carla wanted to share it, then I wouldn't object, but I wouldn't gift it to Berta. In any case, there was enough other material to keep Berta happy. Academics were like magpies in my estimation. They picked up whatever they could. If you didn't want them to acquire yours, then you had to hide it.

This museum tried to give the visitor some idea of Agatha's personal life at nearby Winterbrook, her home with Max Mallowan for forty-two years and where she wrote most of her books. Because Winterbrook was now a private residence and didn't allow visitors, artifacts from Agatha's life were housed in the museum.

"Look, Berta. Here's a letter she wrote complaining about being sick," Tessa pointed to a glass cabinet where several letters were encased.

"We have a collection of letters written by her," Carla said. "Would you like to look at them?"

"Lead me to them," Berta said.

Carla soon had Berta at a small table with a pile of manuscripts, books, and papers beside her. The others were happy to wander around the museum, so I took a few minutes with Carla.

"Any results from your inquiries in America for information?" Carla had approached a historical association in Maryland for letters from a correspondent of Agatha's.

"Nothing yet," she said.

We ran down tentative leads looking for hints of why Agatha had run away and left a trail that appeared as if she had killed herself. We could guess why she did it, but we didn't know. She had never talked about it and neither had her daughter. We'd <u>like</u> to know. We were even <u>determined</u> to know.

The four of us left Berta for a couple of hours and wandered around Wallingford. Malloy wanted her picture taken outside, sitting on a bench with the statue of Agatha Christie which was also sitting on the bench. That inspired the others to have their picture taken, Kim looked as though she was talking to the statue.

We walked along the Thames and into the old town proper with its narrow streets and crowded shops where first floors leaned above the ground floor giving it a medieval feel.

"Wallingford is where they film Midsomer Murders,'" I told them.

"I saw one of those. Is this Causton?" Tessa asked, naming the town in the film.

"It is."

While the women were gazing at shop windows I checked my messages and found a text from Stella.

Meet me this afternoon. I MUST talk to you."

It sounded ominous, but Stella did dramatize.

Back in town this afternoon. Meet you at The Blue Heron at 2:30.

It could be important, or it could be just Stella fussing.

We went back to the museum to collect Berta and to go for lunch in The Old Post Office housed in a stately, brick Georgian-style building. It had a relaxed atmosphere with wooden floors, wooden table tops, and wood paneled walls. The food had been good the last time I ate here; I hoped the same chef was on today. It's a bit of a gamble because occasionally what I expected didn't happen. Today the food was delicious, although I think Berta could have been eating sawdust she was so enthusiastic about what she'd read.

"Do you know how long Agatha was in Egypt? I think she must have married Max because he went to Egypt to work. She loved it there."

Berta held forth all through the meal giving us the highlights of what she'd learned at the museum. The women asked her intelligent questions and kept her eagerness for her subject high.

I drove them past Agatha's house in what used to be Closey but is now part of Wallingford. Winterbrook, her house, is a beautiful Georgian-style house on the banks of the Thames.

"It was the setting for Littlegreen House in *Dumb Witness*," Berta said.

"She did all right," Kim observed. "That's one huge house."

"She did make a lot of money," I agreed. "But not as much as one might suppose for someone who sells more than anyone else and all over the world."

"Why not?" Kim asked.

"Because," Berta said definitely, "she didn't have a good contract, and she ran into problems with her taxes."

They dozed on the way back to Ashton-on-Tinch and were wide awake and ready for entertainment when we arrived at Badgerhouse. Consulting Berta before hand, I'd planned a golf game.

"It was Archie, her first husband who was an avid golfer," Berta said.

"Yes that's true," I agreed. "But Agatha used golf many times in her books. I have a list of books where Agatha mentions the game as well as a golf brochure of the Ashton River Golf."

Breta's eyes brightened. "I don't have that list of books."

Thank goodness I'd found something to add to her knowledge.

"I have arranged a golfing afternoon at private links close by."

"What's the dress code," Tessa asked.

"It's not enforced for guests," I reassured her. Some golf courses were scrupulously insisted on collared shirts and golf shoes, but this one was happy to take the money for guest players without dress restrictions. I'm not sure if that is a normal rule here or if the manager of the Tinch River Golf Club, Ron Silverton, made an exception for my group. He is a retired sergeant from Mark's constabulary who had become bored with retirement.

The women changed and piled back into the van for the short drive to the golf course. I stayed while Ron set them up with clubs, provided them with a cart and set them off on the first tee.

I paid. I hoped they enjoyed it because it was costly.

Stella was waiting when I arrived at The Blue Heron. Her lush figure showed to advantage in the pale tan trousers, cream shirt, and primrose yellow sweater. Her long brunette hair held copper tones that glinted in the sunlight. Her eyes appeared dark and large as she was never without eye shadow and the mascara that enhanced them. She'd taken a table outside in the courtyard and was the only person there. She had two coffees and two slices of Victoria Sponge waiting.

"Thanks," I said.

"How's it going with Amber?" I knew she hadn't asked to meet me to talk about Amber, but I was willing to let her have a few minutes to gather her thoughts.

"Not bad. We're all learning."

"I should be a better honorary aunt. Why don't I join you riding this week?" Stella was an accomplished rider.

"Do that. We'd both enjoy it."

We were quiet. "So what's up?" I finally asked.

"The plods were over this morning."

I raised an eyebrow at her over my first sip of coffee.

"Well, alright. It was Andy Forsyth, Detective Sergeant Andy Forsyth."

"And?" What else did she want to tell me?

"I'd rather have had Mark."

"Not likely. You're my friend. Conflict of interest."

"Oh. Right."

"What did he want to know?"

"He wanted to know about my time as Jordan's lover. It was years ago, but I remembered and told him about it." She grinned. "I made his ears burn."

Stella couldn't resist teasing or flirting. "It's a murder investigation, Stella."

"I know. I know."

Did she kill Jordan? Why would she? "Did Garman know about your affair with Jordan?" That might have been a motive for Garman, but if the affair was years ago he surely wouldn't have been in a rage now? If he ever <u>was</u> in a rage.

"At the time, he knew I had a lover. He didn't know who. Garman accepts I need someone to love, and he's not it."

"How does he feel about it?"

"He doesn't feel. You know that."

She was convinced that Garman was devoid of emotions and only operated through reason. She might be right. He was methodical and always reasonable. She was missing so much being married to him. Still, I'd come to understand that Stella needed Garman's solid respectability to live as flamboyantly and impulsively as she did. Without him and dependent on herself, she would have to be more circumspect, probably be more dependent of the publishers who employed her. She'd have to be her children's sole support. Although she was their emotional support, Garman was their financial support, as both girls were beginning their careers and needed their rent and groceries paid for while they went to school and climbed whatever ladders a financial whiz kid and an artist climbed.

We were quiet for a moment. I was thinking how odd Stella and Garman's relationship was.

"It's time I divorced him," Stella said.

"Really?" She'd talked about it before, but perhaps this time she meant it.

"I had to stay until the kids were on their way to a stable future. I've stayed long enough."

"Will you be all right financially?"

"I will be fine for a few months because I have my own bank account, and I will be fine after our lawyers divvy up everything, although I truly don't know how much money Garman has or how he's invested it. He won't talk about it. I know he gets monthly income from different sources—his pension and other investments because he has certain days he pays certain household bills and those are connected to income coming in. I've tried getting into his bank account, but I can't crack his password. I'll have to think about it. He might have a list of passwords somewhere. It would be just like him. I'll have to find it."

"But if you don't get much from the divorce settlement, you'll still be all right?"

"I will."

She was fidgeting with her cup, her serviette, and her hair. It might be the interview with Andy that had set her anxiety meter high, or it might be something else.

"What made you decide on divorce now?"

She stared squarely at me. "Face it, Claire. Garman is incredibly boring."

That was true enough.

"It hit me, when the police were at the house that if I was in serious trouble, Garman would never stand by me."

"No?"

"Not in this lifetime. He'd pick up his stocks and bonds and disappear. I wouldn't impress his rich clients, his rich friends, or add to his image of himself. So he'd dump me. I'd better dump him first."

"Do get on with it!" I said impulsively. I was fed up with her complaining about Garman for years and never doing anything about it. I'd been in an abusive relationship myself during my twenties, and I remember the excuses I had for staying with Adam. I remember also what a relief it was when I was finally alone.

"Just do it, Stella!"

She blinked and sat back. "I suppose I shall."

I don't think that is what she planned to tell me, but whatever it had been, she'd changed her mind.

CHAPTER TWELVE

I left Stella and drove home to catch a few minutes with Mark and Amber. Mark was making supper—pasta again but they both seemed to like it—and Amber was chopping vegetables.

"School, all right?" I asked Amber

She sent a quick glance to her dad. They seem to have been discussing something. I didn't have time to delve into it, even if they'd welcomed me to the conversation.

"I'll catch up with everything later. I have to dash."

"Where are you off to?" Mark asked.

"Basingstoke to a 60s musical concert. It starts at half seven."

"You'd better get moving."

I flew upstairs, changed into a pair of dress trousers, a deep blue shirt, multicolored vest, and my Fluvog, chunky-heeled, blue and turquoise shoes.

The women were waiting for me at the golf club door. "A good game?" I asked.

"I can't hit the ball straight," Mallory complained.

"It was your first time," Kim told her. "You can't expect to hit it straight yet. You can certainly hit it far."

"Far into the trees," Mallory grumbled.

"We did have a good game," Berta answered my question.

They buckled themselves into the seats. Tessa asked. "What's on for tonight?"

Theses women had energy.

"We are going to a 60s Beattle concert in Basingstoke."

"Jeans, long shirt, big glasses," Berta said.

"Big hair," Kim said and laughed.

"Before my teen years, but I like the music," Tessa said.

They all agreed they liked the music.

I drove them to the Badger's BnB and waited for them while they showered and changed, then drove them to Basingstoke.

I liked the music as well, which was a bonus as I sat through it with them, then drove them to dinner at The Holly Blue, just out of Basingstoke on the way home, where there was a good menu, a relaxed ambience and superb views, although it was almost dark when we arrived.

I deposited my tired guests at The Badgerhouse and was home by half eleven.

Amber was asleep, but Gulliver came out to greet me, lick my hand then return to Amber's bed.

Mark was in the kitchen.

"Tired?" he asked.

"Yes. I could use a cuppa."

Mark made the tea and sat at the table with me.

"How's it going with Amber?" I asked curious about the conversation I'd missed earlier.

"Good, I think. Half the time she chatters away about telly shows and fads. This time it was about how she feels like a misfit at the school, and if it wasn't for Stephanie she'd stay home."

"She's new at the school. Maybe it will get better." I could hear my counselor Max in my head. *And maybe you should pay attention here. If she feels like a misfit, that's how she feels. Don't trivialize it.*

"I don't know what to say to her," Mark said.

"What <u>did</u> you say?"

"Not much. She seems to like me listening, not talking."

"Most people do."

"True." He stared at me for a moment.

"What?" I sipped my tea. Jasmine. Heavenly.

"I wish I hadn't missed all those years of her growing up. What was she like at three? At six? She's a good rider. I wasn't there to put her on her first pony It's frustrating. Sometimes, I'd like to have her mother here and give her a piece of my mind."

I took my own advice and just listened.

His anger at Britanny was justified. How dare she decide he was not to be Amber's father? When I thought about it, part of me applauded her courage in deciding to raise her daughter herself. It wouldn't have been an easy decision either way.

My mind wandered a little. Britanny had only gone to her parents when she was ill. Before that, she'd made a life for herself and Amber on her own. Her parents had been loving and supportive, but there was no getting around the fact that they were old. I wondered if we should try to create a ground-level bedroom for George and Freya, so they wouldn't have to use the stairs when they visited. Then we'd need a downstairs loo as well.

"Sorry," he said. "You've heard all this before."

"It's all right. I'm just relaxed," I lied.

He didn't believe me. "Let's get to bed. We haven't had nearly enough time there, lately."

"I'd fancy that," I said, miraculously energized.

I was at The Badgerhouse by eight the next morning. My guests were leaving today so had to take time to pack their bags. While they finished their breakfast and brought their luggage to the foyer, I paid Carol Badger for their accommodation.

"Nice women this time," she said. The last group from my tour who had stayed with her included one fussy traveler.

"They are," I agreed. This was a short tour. Today was our last day, so I hadn't had much chance to get to know them well. I suppose the fact that they already knew one another before they arrived meant they came with a core cohesive feeling and made for less of the awkward social fencing that a group of strangers displayed. I felt a little cheated as if I was outside their experience, and they didn't need me to create a group feeling. I would have known them better if I'd had them for a fortnight. Mark and I needed to talk about our work and our child-minding duties.

My tourists and I were off to Oxford for the day, then I was driving into London to leave them at a hotel near Tower Bridge. They were going to explore London for few days, then join a tour on War Poets of the Second World War. I'd left Gulliver behind again. It was going to be a long day, and he would be better alone until noon when Mark came home and let him into the garden for a break. He'd dog-nap in the afternoon, and hang out with Amber when she got home just after half three. That was another adjustment. Gulliver was sometimes better off without me.

"Tell me about this St. Hilda's College Crime Fiction event," Berta said before she'd even sat down in the van.

"As soon as we are underway," I promised her.

Once we were headed north to Oxford I activated the mic.

"The Crime Fiction Event is held every year," I said, "usually in August, but they had some conflict with the venue so are, luckily for us, holding it later this year."

"What's the plan?" Berta asked.

"We should be there before ten," I said. "I have your tickets for today and for the dinner this evening. There are several sessions during the day. One is with Richard Osman,"

"The Thursday Murder Club Mysteries?" Kim queried.

"That's the man." I said.

"Is he English?" Berta asked.

"He is. He works in television as well as in print. There will be other literary luminaries there, but you war historians may be interested in the writers of the Second World War which is one of the session for the early afternoon. Then, the P.D. James dinner will produce another popular writer and no doubt good food."

"It's sounds fine," Mallory said. "I don't know how much I'll pick up at the mystery session, but I've always wanted to go to Oxford. My mom isn't going to believe it. She's an English major. Teaches English at our high school. She texted me last night and said I had to climb some tower."

"The Carfax Tower," I said. "It's seventy-four feet tall." There weren't any Canadians in this group, so I didn't have to translate that to meters. "You do get a beautiful view of Oxford."

"I'll do that and send Mom a picture."

Kim might accompany her but not Tessa. All those steep steps would likely make her feet ache.

"The Colleges in Oxford are not in one place but scattered all over the city. St. Hilda's College is just across the River Cherwell, so you will need to text me when you want to go across to the center of town, or you can hop a bus. I will be around so feel free to call me and I'll take you wherever you'd like to go. St. Hilda's was founded in 1893 as a woman's college but it's inclusive now."

I glanced back. They were reading their material and nodding, so I continued.

"I've given you a goodie bag with a map of Oxford in it. There are cafés marked where you can get lunch, and I've circled the location of several bookstores: Blackwells of course, Waterstones, and Gulp are near the center of Oxford. I also included a sweet and a bottle of water."

We drove through the green and gold farmlands spread out on either side of the road, arriving in Oxford via Botley Road, crossing the Thames at the edge of the city. St. Hilda's was on the south-east side of the city on the other side of the River Cherwell. I pointed out Carfax Tower as we passed it on the High Street and Magdalen College just before St, Hilda's. "It is spelt Magdalen but pronounced 'maudlin'. And no, I don't know why. The bridge is pronounced 'maudlin' as well."

"The word that seems peculiar to me," Mallory said, "is derby pronounced darby."

"And clerk pronounced clark," Kim said.

"English," Berta said, "is inexplicable."

I met a linguist once who explained the spelling of many words that seemed odd to me lay in the origins. English has many origins: Anglo Saxon, Viking, Celtic, Roman, and more.

I stopped outside the college and pointed out the banners that indicated where they were to join the festival. They picked up some of the excitement from the surrounding crowd and, grasping the tickets I'd handed them, left the van.

"The copper beech at the back of the main building is beautiful," I called to them, "and the library in impressive. There will likely be a marquee set up along the river, so it should be a wonderful venue. I'll park the van and be around here today, so do call me if you'd like to be driven any where."

I had my own tickets to some sessions. I wanted listen to Richard Osman expound on mystery writing, so I hoped they wouldn't ask for the van when I was enjoying the events. It was my job to look after them, though, so I would jump to and accommodate them.

I didn't see them all morning. There were so many attendees that they disappeared into the throng. It was about two when Mallory called for a ride to the center of Oxford and Carfax Tower. When I picked her up, Kim was with her. I dropped them off and asked them to call me when they were ready to return. I reminded them that the dinner was at six.

"We might walk back," Kim said. "Where's the Bodleian Library. We might go find that."

I showed where the University Church of St. Mary the Virgin was on the map. "Just go north from there about two blocks."

Mallory clicked onto her mobile. She entered Bodleian Library Oxford, UK, and came up with the directions.

"We'll be fine."

I left them, found a place to park the van, and set off through the streets. I wandered over to Blackwells and started on the top floor, managing to limit my book buying to eight books, including one on sustainable farming that I knew my niece Kala would like. I studied the window of the Shoe Embassy but didn't buy any of the tempting shoes on offer. I stopped at the Quod café for tea.

I was surprised to find Berta in the Quod. She was on her mobile again, so I hesitated to disturb her, but she saw me and gestured to the chair across from her.

She disconnected her call and put her mobile in her bag. "Join me. I've ordered high tea."

"High tea here? Lovely." I arranged my parcels around me, caught the eye of the server and asked for another order of high tea.

"You've had enough of the conference?" I asked. I'd thought Berta would be immersed in it.

"I just wanted a half an hour away. I'm going right back. It's excellent."

Berta seemed to be on her mobile often during the day. I hadn't asked what was so important that she couldn't leave it behind when she was on holiday. It was none of my business, but I was curious. I kept a firm grip on my curiosity, but she answered my unspoken question.

She patted her handbag. "I check up on my husband," she said.

Visions of an unfaithful spouse, an incompetent cook, or an overly generous party-giver flashed through my mind.

"My husband has dementia," she said. That was one problem that I <u>hadn't</u> envisioned "It's early dementia. so not too bad yet. I have a housekeeper living in while I'm away. He still calls me to find out where his glasses are, or what he is supposed to be doing at the moment. With the time change that's a bit of a challenge."

We were interrupted by the arrival of tea, teapots, cream and sugar, and a three-tiered cake serving stand filled with sandwiches, scones, cream, jam, and fairy cakes. It was impressive. When the server left, I turned my eyes from it and back to Berta.

"I'm sorry" I said. "It must be heartbreaking to see him change."

She was silent for a moment and sipped her tea. "It is. The deteriorating aspect of it is frightening, and I know it's going to get worse. I've done the research as much as a non-medical person like me can. It is not a prognosis anyone wants to deal with."

She helped herself to a watercress sandwich. She seemed matter-of-fact, accustomed to the situation I supposed. I reached for a sandwich. I wondered where they got watercress at this season.

"We're doing all right. I have help, so I can go to work and take time away from him. I do miss his old self. We used to go together on these jaunts."

"I'm sorry," I repeated. I didn't know what else I could say.

She smiled. "John was such good company. He was an amazing researcher and professor, studying the effects of climate change. He was ahead of his time and important in his field. I think he missed work more than anything else when he had to stop. There are so many losses a dementia patient has to deal with."

I imagined them: inability to remember people's names, the way to the grocery store, the way home from the store, what day it was, and worst of all, who your loved ones were.

"I'm going to make sure he gets everything I can possibly provide for him. He'll stay home with me as long as possible."

She sounded fierce and capable. For a moment, I wondered if this intense sense of purpose to protect and defend her husband would ever be a motive for murder. She might want to murder his doctor, the health care administrators, even the neighbors. I was convinced there were as many motives as there were people. Not just passion as Mark and his crew seemed to think.

We sipped our tea and worked our way through the sandwiches, the tiny pink fairy cakes, the fruit scones with clotted cream and raspberry jam while Berta talked.

I got a glimpse of her life as a university professor, her children, two—both married with children, her appreciation of the lush green world of the Pacific Northwest of America, and her amazing curiosity about almost everything.

She picked up the bill when we finished tea. "You've saved me a counselling session," she said. "You're an excellent listener."

"It's been a privilege," I said and left her to return to the conference.

Kim and Mallory didn't call me. I stayed in town until about half five then moved the van to St. Hilda's. I waited by the door to the banquet room and texted everyone my location. They arrived by six, and we trooped into the banquet hall for dinner and the famous author speaker. This year it was Elly Griffiths. I'd heard her before. She was a witty and engaging speaker.

"What does she write?" Mallory asked me.

"The Ruth Galloway series, among others. She's excellent."

"It's been a good week," Mallory said. "I'm glad we came on this tour. "

"When does your next one start?" I remembered they were going on a War Poets tours.

"Three days from now. We're going to see a bit of London: The British Museum, the National Arts Gallery, Trafalgar Square, and a couple of plays before we join it."

"What a trip!" I applauded their plans.

"Yeah. It's been great, and it's going to be great." She smiled. "These women pulled me in with them, you know? I'd not even thought of going."

"When you are a revered academic, you can do the same for another student."

"For sure," she said.

We left Oxford about half eight, and I drove in relatively light traffic to London. I took the M40, then the A40 to London and to the Tower Hotel right beside the bridge. This was where their next Tour started. They had booked there for the three days they planned to explore London. The hotel was central, so, easy for them to get around. They were tired, but seemed happy and, bless them, tipped well. I unloaded their luggage and bade them all a fond goodbye.

The roads were fairly clear, no major hold-ups out of London, and I was home just before midnight.

Gulliver was the only one awake.

CHAPTER THIRTEEN

In the morning, Mark headed out to work. He wore a casual sport's shirt with a jacket over it. His curly dark hair, fell on his forehead. I smoothed it back and gave him a quick kiss. That was all I was willing to do when Amber was watching.

"I hope I can get one more day out of Andy. He's coordinating all the material into a composite file. I know the super is pulling him off the case because there is a suspected homicide near Portsmouth, and she thinks I have too many officers."

"She'll pull him off, then complain you aren't getting results fast enough."

"She will, indeed." He dropped a quick kiss on my hair.

Amber waved a goodbye from her position in front of a bowl of fruit and muesli. Mark patted Gulliver and closed the door behind him. I finished my coffee while Amber got ready for school. When she was at the door with her rucksack, I joined her with Gulliver.

"Would you like Gulliver and me to walk with you? We're heading out as well." I wasn't sure if ten-year-olds walked with their parents or if that made them feel like a baby.

"All right. Sure."

It was a fine late September morning with sunshine lighting the oak trees in the church yard. There was a hint of crispness in the air, but it would be warm this afternoon.

Gulliver did a play bow in front of Mary Greenwood's big Golden Retriever, but it ignored him and trotted across the street.

"That's like me," Amber said.

"How so?"

"I want to play but the other girls won't let me."

I was shocked. "All the other girls?"

"Well, not Stephanie. She'll hang out with me, but most of the girls have this like club, you know? It's a fantasy club and they let me join sometimes, but they never let me be Marya when they play Dragomir Academy."

"Do the other girls take turns on that role?" It was the first I'd heard they were playing fantasy games at school.

"Almost everyone."

We stopped at the edge of the playground. Gulliver sat, panting a little, his eyes bright watching the girls who were swooping around like birds.

Four girls about Amber's age stood in front of us.

"Can we pet him?" one asked.

"Yes, he likes people," I said.

"He is so pretty." Soon the four girls were kneeling on the ground, crowding around Gulliver.

Amber shot me a quick glance. Obviously, Gulliver gave her social cachet.

The bell screamed a high buzz. The girls reluctantly rose.

"Amber," I said. "Can you walk Gulliver after school?"

She blinked, then said. "I can."

"You get to walk him?" one girl said as she walked beside Amber on the way to the entrance.

"Yeah, and feed him. He sleeps with me."

"You are sooo lucky," another said. "My mum won't let us have any pets." Their voices faded out as the school swallowed everyone except me and a tall, elegant slim woman, with remarkable blue eyes. She approached me.

"I'm Isobel Cameron."

"I remember you, Mrs. Cameron." The headmistress. I'd met her when I registered Amber in the school.

"I haven't seen you walking Amber to school before." I felt an implied criticism as a new parent. Did most mothers accompany their ten-year-olds to school in this village, I wondered?

"I don't usually walk to school with her. I should have done it before—and brought Gulliver."

She smiled. "Yes. Amber's status just rose." Mrs. Cameron bent down and patted Gulliver. "Beautiful dog."

"Thank you." I was quiet for a moment and then said, "Mrs. Cameron, what's Dragomir Academy?"

She laughed. "It's an imaginary school for troubled girls in a book by Anne Ursu. The ten-year-olds are currently fascinated with it."

I knew it must be something like that. "The girls haven't let her join in that game, at least they haven't given her any important parts. Amber is feeling left out. I'm worried she isn't fitting in here."

I remembered when my niece Kala had serious bullying problems. I didn't think that was going on here, but I didn't want to miss it and only pay attention when Amber was desperate.

Mrs. Cameron continued to pet Gulliver. "That's a common problem for ten-year-olds, even those who have socialized with their peer group for years. Amber, of course, has the additional difficulties of being a newcomer and, of course, losing her mother." She straightened and faced me.

"Does that mean she might never fit in?" I was worried more now.

"Oh, no. Rotating leadership is one of the practices of this age group. She will likely have her turn."

"Really? Girls take turns being a leader? Is this Dragomir Academy play normal?"

"Absolutely. That kind of play comes with social rituals which help to teach group dynamics."

Groups dynamics? Rotating leadership? I felt inadequate as a step-mother. "I didn't know any of this."

She was reassuring. "It's my job to know it. Yours is to support her, love her, and give her a safe haven."

Could I do that? I could try. "But I want to understand what her life is like."

"She'll let you know what you need to know—if she trusts you."

I wanted more information. This parenting was intimidating. Mrs. Cameron had turned and started toward the school.

I raised my voice. "I understand my job is to be an emotional support. I still would like to have more information about ten-year-olds."

Mrs. Cameron hesitated, then turned back to me. "I don't have much time this morning, but here is a quick analysis: Amber came us at a time of flux in her life where she didn't have a past solid relationship with the group here. This makes her unsure of her status, and, of course, makes her anxious."

"I see."

"Amber has qualities that indicate she will manage this very well. She is kind which goes a long way with others; she is clever and does well in class which in this school is accepted if not admired. She has one good friend."

"Stephanie".

"Nice girl. Encourage that." She started to walk away.

"Thank you," I called after her.

She waved.

I dropped Gulliver off at home and picked up the book I'd bought in Oxford for Kala, slipped it into a mailer, addressed it, and hopped into the van. I was headed for the grocery shop where I planned to buy more than I could carry. I parked at the grocery store and walked back to the post office.

Nigel Whitley was just leaving and held the door for me. I stepped in but stopped him.

"How is Joyce doing?"

He politely stepped away from the door and joined me inside. "She's not doing well. She should set an example and be more stoic. Death is part of our journey. We must learn to accept it."

I stared at him. Was he really so insensitive? How did he get to be a vicar? My silence must have disconcerted him because he shifted on his feet, then said. "Well, frankly, she worries me."

"She's not taking Jordan's death easily."

"No and she didn't even know him well." I wondered if he was saying that in order to discount any rumours about Joyce's affair with Jodan, or if he truly believed it. I'd best assume he didn't know about it.

"You didn't know Jordan well, did you?"

"I knew him but not well. He did work around the church, and I liked what he did, but I can't say we ever had any common meeting ground. He wasn't a scholar, not educated except in equestrian skills, so we wouldn't have had much to talk about."

I wasn't educated either in the sense that I didn't have a university background, but I felt quite capable of talking to Nigel. It may have occurred to Nigel that I didn't have his Cambridge background.

"I mean he didn't read. If a person reads, they're educated. He didn't read."

That was a condemnation indeed. How did he know Jordan didn't read?

"Do you think I should visit Joyce?" If she had been Jordan's lover, then she was in mourning which would be made worse by Nigel's dismissal of it.

"Yes, do that. Kind of you."

"Were you at the church that morning?" He was a suspect.

"When Jordan died?"

"Yes."

"I was there. You saw me. I told the Detective Constable Penberthy that." He frowned.

"And you didn't hear anything?"

"No, of course not. I would have come out to see who was disturbing the sanctity of the church if I had heard anything."

He would have unless he was disturbing it himself.

He frowned, his bushy eyebrows a grey line, like an ancient caterpillar across his forehead, his scant, sandy hair losing the competition with the eyebrows,

"Jordan wasn't supposed to be working in the sanctuary. He was supposed to be repairing a door in the hall. He must have been meeting someone."

That was reasonable. It might even have been his wife Jordan was meeting.

"Possibly," I agreed.

He nodded briskly at me and left.

I took the book I was mailing to Kala to Helen Taylor who was the postmistress. My cleaner, Rose, gets her love of 'news' directly from her mother. Helen is a short, plump woman who seems at home in her body with its extra pounds. I've always admired the way she ignored current fashions and wore what she liked. Today it was an old-fashioned housedress which she probably made herself. I'd only seen that shirtwaist style in movies.

"This is going to that niece of yours, Gulliford, right?"

"That's right."

She bustled about, weighing the package, measuring it with the measuring tape she kept strung around her neck like a seamstress. "I heard the reverend."

The room was small. She couldn't help but hear.

"That man is a bit..." she paused as she searched for the word," hypocritical. That's the word. Hypocritical."

What did she know? "In what way?"

"He goes on about how he's so concerned about his wife."

"I think he *is* concerned.'

She snorted. "Not so much, I don't think. If he was, he wouldn't be swanning off to London to meet up with another woman."

I was shocked. It was the first I'd heard of this. "He has a...a...a." Now *I* was searching for the word, "a liaison in London."

"So I hear," she said with some satisfaction as she entered information into her computer. "There you are, love. Two pounds."

I handed over the two pounds

"Yes, my Rose's husband. You know her Frank."

I agreed I did.

"Well, Frank was up to London for the car show. That man is besotted with anything on wheels. He went up with a bunch of his friends and they saw the good reverend with this woman looking at cars."

That didn't seem like enough evidence to convict the man of adultery. "She might have been his sister, and he was helping her look for a car."

"Not according to Frank. She was no sister he said."

I left feeling some sympathy for Nigel. I suppose some members of a congregation always looked for transgressions in their minister. Perhaps they wanted him to be more on their level and Nigel with his hubris might invite that kind of speculation. It didn't mean he actually had a mistress. I'd tell Mark, though.

I stopped at the butcher's, Sam's Place, to buy the meat Mark and I enjoyed. I noticed some veggie burgers.

"I'll have a couple of those, maybe six. I can freeze them, can't I?"

"Certainly can. This is for your little girl?"

"Yes," I beamed at him. She was my little girl.

I stashed my meat in the van and proceeded to the long list of groceries I'd need. I would do a proper grocery shopping which should last us a fortnight. The cost always surprised me. I left the groceries in the van and stopped at the cash point beside Sam's Place and deposited most of my tip money. Those university profs had been generous, even Mallory who, as a grad student, probably didn't have much.

Once I was home, I unloaded the groceries, stacked the freezer with future meals and called Gulliver in from the back garden.

"A long walk is what we need, Gulliver, my man."

He was stimulated by the word 'walk' and by my upbeat tone. Before I reached for the leash, his tail was wagging, as he danced to the door.

Out in the sunshine and on the path to the river, I moved quickly. Gulliver would have liked to tarry at the riverside, investigating the ever-elusive ducks, but I hurried him on past the vet clinic and up the path toward the ridge. We climbed steadily for about ten minutes and came to the lookout point where we could see miles into the farmland and distance hills. I sat on the bench and unsnapped the leash. Gulliver would now come on recall, so I didn't worry he'd wander away. He bounded toward a gorse bush. I heard a rustle, then a quail shot into the sky in a flurry of wings. I hadn't seen a quail fly before; they tend to scurry along the ground. Gulliver barked and twirled in an awkward chase.

"Give it up, Gulliver. You'd need wings."

I let my mind drift. Mrs. Cameron seemed to think Amber would work out her social problems and that she was in no danger at school. Maybe I needed to let her do that and just be there to listen. I definitely didn't have the knowledge of ten-year-olds that Mrs. Cameron did. I should take her advice.

I wondered how Mark was getting along with the investigation of Jordan's murder. It was a dreadful thing to take someone's life. It wasn't just their life, it was their future contributions, interactions, loves, and opportunities that they took away. Jordan's death affected others: Joyce for one, and adjacent to her, Nigel. He was worried. I suspected even Stella was looking back on her relationship with Jordan and comparing it to the one she had or didn't have with Garman.

I shook off introspection and headed up the trail. Two hours later Gulliver and I returned home. I filled Gulliver's water dish. You'd think he'd been a day on a desert. He lapped up all the water and demanded more.

"Yes, your highness," I said and obliged.

I made myself a sandwich, sat outside under the rowan tree, and had my tea, sandwich, and an apple. It was peaceful here. I loved my home. I glanced at my mobile. I should check with Patrick.

He answered on the second ring.

"I was going to call you. We need to get an architect evaluator into the house, so we can get a good idea of what needs repair and what is fine."

I started to agree, but he kept speaking.

"The drains are always the point of contention, so let's get him or her to check those out and the electrical. Sometimes the electrical can hold surprises like that old knob and tube. That's dangerous. I don't think there is any there, but we'll get the architect to check. And then there's the plumbing. Well, you know we had that redone when we had the flood under the stairs."

I remembered that incident. "That would be fine, Patrick," I managed to interject. "When can we do that and would you like to arrange it?"

"I've already got someone on tap. Sean Battersfield. Do you know them?"

"No."

"Good company. Rita's parents used them when they sold their flat."

Rita's parents had several flats in different parts of the country. They no doubt picked a good architect, although perhaps expensive.

"That will be fine, Patrick," I repeated. "When is the inspection?"

"Soon. I'll let you know."

"Excellent."

He disconnected.

I felt like singing. Even dancing. This was going to be wonderful. I hoped we'd have our new house in a month.

My next call was to my solicitor, Arthur Greenwood. I had to sell some stock to pay for the purchase.

"A bigger house is a good investment, Claire," he intoned. "Prices are rising quickly in Hampshire, and you will be in a good position to sell the house in twenty or thirty years should you wish to."

Twenty or thirty years seemed impossibly far away.

"In the meantime, "he continued. "You could borrow against your house should you ever need funds in an emergency, although your other investments should cover most contingencies."

I was impatient with his flat, deliberate tone. I knew that information, but I reminded myself I was a civil person and good manners cost nothing, as my mother was wont to say.

"Thank you, Arthur. Let me know when the sales of stock are completed and the money in my account."

"Oh, they should be there tomorrow," he said.

"Wonderful." I disconnected.

Arthur was the last person to celebrate anything, but I could celebrate on my own. I clicked on some old music and danced around the kitchen to *Mama Mia*.

It was my night to make supper, so I started a chicken stew. Amber will eat chicken—just not red meat. I chopped vegetables for a salad and put out some chocolate brownies I'd bought for afters.

The stew was cooking slowly on top of the stove when Mark arrived unexpectedly early with Andy Forsyth.

"Coffee?" I offered.

"A quick one, Claire," Andy said. "Just coffee, no treats. I need to get home to Bruce and the boys."

"You're still on the case then, Andy? I thought the super took you off."

"She did. I'm gone as of tomorrow. Today we need to exchange as much info as possible."

"I'll get the coffee," Mark said and proceeded to do so. I sat at the table with my tea.

"Andy's been interviewing Rose." Mark said as he returned to the table.

"Rose Jones?"

Andy answered me. "Yes, your house cleaner."

"What for?"

"She was at the cemetery at the relevant time looking after the grave of her granddad".

I remembered Rose saying he had died last year. "Did she see anything?"

"She says no," Andy said

"If there was anything to see Rose would have noticed," I said. "She is as curious as a puppy."

"She may have seen something but not registered it as anything important." Mark said. He picked up some papers and glanced through them, then turned to me. "We wanted to ask you if you have heard anything we could follow as a lead. We're coming up blank here."

"It's early days yet," I reassured him. Then, I thought about Helen Taylor's tale of Nigel. "I have gossip," I said.

"Gossip would be a start," Mark said, responding to the bubbling coffee maker and brought two cups of coffee to the table, then the milk and sugar. "Spill that gossip,' he said."

I told them about Nigel.

"What do you think?" Andy asked Mark.

Mark gestured to the notebook Andy carried "You're keeping the composite record. Add that."

Andy opened the notebook, activated it, called up a file and began typing.

"Tell Mira to chase that story. She can interview Frank Jones," Mark said. "It will give her some detective work to do and get her out of our way for a while."

Obviously, Mark was not happy with Mira.

"Is she a problem?"

"Just a little straightlaced. Rule-bound. Narrowly logical." Mark said. "Which is why we're hiding out at home." He turned to Andy. "I don't think there's anything in that gossip. Parishioners always gossip about the vicar. And even if there is some truth in it, the reverend might not be motivated to kill to protect that secret. If Jordan had tried to blackmail him, he would have told him to spread the gossip. He could just deny it. Parsons are gossiped about all the time."

"I suppose so," Andy said.

"What have we got then?" Mark asked.

Andy read from his screen. "The reverend, his wife, your friend, Stella." He glanced at me then continued, "The stable owner, her daughter, the organist? "He looked at Mark.

"Might as well include him."

"Right you are then. The church treasurer, husband to Stella, some unknown lover of the reverend if we can believe the post mistress, and your housecleaner who was at the cemetery and maybe a new lover of Jordan's, maybe a creditor of Jordan's, or women we haven't met yet."

Mark was quiet for a moment. "Right then. David interviewed Stella, Joyce, Nigel, and Garman. You'll need to re-interview Nigel and Garman. Also interview Rose Jones again and look for Jordan's new love. Put Mira on that. She can sift through addresses from anything we have from his apartment."

Andy typed those instructions into the notebook.

Mark continued. "We need to interview Joyce again. I'll do that as well as Garman, Leah, and Joyleen. I'll liaise with Mira. She can hunt down any new love or desperate creditors."

"Right, guv." He shut down his notebook and rose. "I won't have time to do three interviews. Which one do you want."

Mark grunted. "I'll take Garman."

"All right. I'll leave the reports on the main file. Call me if you need any clarification. Thanks for the coffee. I'm off."

"I'll be right behind you," Mark said.

I went to the door with them and spoke to Andy. "Give my love to Bruce and the boys."

"I will. It's a good thing Bruce works from home, or we'd never manage all the work and running about the kids need. How are you two managing with Amber?"

I answered. "She's a dear, but it's a challenge to manage our time. We're working on it."

He smiled, waved and both were gone.

I mused about our time management skills as I returned to the kitchen. We *were* managing, just.

CHAPTER FOURTEEN

I loaded the dishes into the machine and let Gulliver out into the garden. When Gulliver heard Amber open the front door, he barked to join her. She had come home immediately after school had been dismissed.

"Riding at four," I said to her. I'd decided to try to keep her schedule as normal as possible.

"I know. Hi, Gulliver." She dropped to the floor and rubbed Gulliver's belly. He loved that.

"Better..." I started.

"I know, change." She headed up the stairs with Gulliver trotting behind her.

I'd changed to my tan jodhpurs, white shirt, brown boots, and black hard hat. Amber soon appeared wearing the same. It was almost a uniform. Stella was wearing identical clothes when she pulled up in her Land Rover Defender, one of the perks of being married to Gorman. We piled in.

"Do you think we'll get to go on a trail ride, Stella?" Amber asked.

"I'm counting on it," Stella said. "We'll leave Claire to her plodding lesson."

"She's getting better really fast." Amber said quickly.

I glanced at Stella.

"She is," Stella agreed, registering Amber's resistance to criticism of me. "She'll be on the bridle paths with us very soon."

Mollified, Amber was quiet.

Stella raised her eyebrows at me. Acceptance by a stepdaughter is not a given and so it's something treasured. I wouldn't count on it to be consistent yet, but I felt a warm glow.

Leah sent Stella and Amber off on an hour's ride to the ridge. It was a beautiful day for trail riding, and I hoped to be a good enough rider soon to join them.

"Still on your own, Leah," I said when we were finished the lesson, and I was grooming Audrey.

"I put in a call into the editor of the Riding Instructor Association's newsletter. He usually knows who is looking for more work."

"Is a replacement for Jordan hard to find?"

There were about ten horses boarded here besides Leah's five. She'd need someone to help manage the stables. Sam White mucked out the stalls and did the heavy lifting. He was an institution around the village as he managed, in spite of his mental handicaps, to work hard under direction and was much valued in the community. Still, there would be plenty of instruction and stable management that Jordan must have done.

"I'll never get an instructor as good as Jordan—he was a star—but I might find someone, at least, competent. I heard about a stable girl working at a racing barn who's fed up with the bosses. That can be a hard place to work with forcing the horses to win when it might be hard on them and all the scheming the head boy does."

"Do they really hurt the horses?"

"Some of them do."

"I hope you find a replacement soon. You'll run yourself down."

"Joyleen's stepping up real well. She sees she's vital to me, so she's working harder. That's big help."

Audrey gave me a gentle nudge with her nose. I took that direction from her and fed her the carrot I had in my pocket. I'd finished cleaning Audrey's feet and brushing her coat and was putting the tools in the equipment box when I stopped for a moment and studied them. The hoof pick I was using wouldn't have been anything like the knife that stabbed Jordan, but there were knives in the box and one of those could have been the weapon. I was going to ask Leah the name of the long wicked-looking knife in an open compartment but stopped. I shouldn't let her know I, and by association Mark, was interested in her knives. I'd tell Mark.

I deposited my equipment and turned back to Audrey, untying her lead rope and giving a slight tug. She, no doubt, envisioning hay and oats, followed me. Leah opened the stable door, and I led Audry in. I slipped off her halter, checked she had water and hay, and left her there. Leah closed the door as I stepped out of the stable.

"You must certainly miss Jordan," I said.

"It's such a shame," Leah said. "His life was horses. I got that. I keep imagining that he's in the tack room, coming in from the paddock, forking hay down from the loft. It's like having a ghost around, but a friendly ghost. I do miss him. The horses do as well."

I took a whiff of air, smelling the musky spice of horses, the grassy smell of the hay, and the underlying aroma of manure, although it wasn't as strong here as other barns I'd been in. Jordan must have felt at home here.

"You sound as if you knew him well."

Her face stilled, and she blinked. "Once I did, a very long time ago."

I wondered how close they had been.

"Jordan wasn't one you could count on, you know. He was ambitious, and he was right to be ambitious. I got that. I really did. Look what he did. Made the Olympic team. Was a star in the world competition. No, he had to go."

What did she mean: he had to go? He had to leave her and go pursue his Olympic dreams, or he had to die?

We stopped at the rails of the paddock, looking at the grazing horses and out over the rolling Hampshire countryside. I'd assume she meant he had to leave her.

"You had an affair," I said softly.

"It was long ago."

"Did it bother you to see him with other women?" I probed a little.

"A little, but I didn't want him if he was seeing other women, so I couldn't complain. He was respectful. I'd say he was affectionate but not sexy with me. I was good with it."

"And your daughter? "

"What about Joyleen?" She spoke sharply.

"Did he leave her alone?"

Her face which had looked tense, relaxed. "Oh yes. Her crush on him was at least ten years ago. He handled it then; they got along fine now. He treated her like a niece She just accepted that as her due. You know girls; they don't think through relationships."

I didn't know if she was talking about Joyleen or her former self.

"Your Amber now." She suddenly became professional. "She's got a good seat, steady hands, and she's calm on a horse. She could go far. Do you want her to come more often?"

I didn't know if Amber was that good or Leah was upselling me. I was careful. "We'll have to talk about it. She needs to settle in here make friends, join in with other kids in activities. We aren't sure yet what is best."

"Take your time, but she would be worth the teaching."

I smiled at her. "That's nice to know."

I sat on the wooden chairs near the barn, waiting for Amber and Stella and checking through my emails on my mobile. Berta had sent me a picture of the four of them at Buckingham Palace. They must be hitting the tourist spots of London. I smiled at the camaraderie they shared.

Amber and Stella returned and talked horses all the way home.

"I'm looking for a good hack," Stella said. "No more jumping."

"I'd like a jumper," Amber said.

"Just rent horses until you grow because you get so attached to your horse, you can't stand to replace her when you're too big to ride her."

"Oh." Amber considered that. "How old do I have to be to get my own horse?"

"Depends on how fast you grow? Maybe twelve? Fourteen?"

"That's a long time to wait."

"There are other things for you to do. What about the theatre? There's a theatre group in town. They're going to put on *Pirates of Penzance* this year. Lots of singing."

She began the policeman's chorus. "When a felon's not engaged in his employment, or maturing his felonious little plans, His capacity for innocent enjoyment is just as great as any other man's."

She sang full-throated and filled the car with music. Amber and I joined in "A policeman's lot is not a happy one." Amber joined Stella's soprano, and I sang alto. The harmony rang around our heads.

Stella broke off. "You should try it, Amber. It's great fun."

I shot her a grateful look. That is what Mark and I wanted for Amber. Several activities with others, so she could make friends. A theatre group had people of all ages in it, including kids her age.

"Will you sing in it?" Amber asked Stella.

"Of course. I'll be Mabel."

Of course, she'd get the lead. Stella had tried many things and done them well. Operetta was one. We were lucky to have her beautiful voice in the village.

She glanced at Amber. "You should persuade Claire to sing in the chorus this year. She's always been too busy."

Amber might rather I stayed away from her activities.

"We could get Dad to join too. He can really sing." I ignored the slur on my musical ability, but she didn't seem to object to including me. It was wonderful idea. We'd all enjoy it. It would take a lot of time, though.

"You ask him," I said.

When we walked in the door, we smelled bay leaves, rosemary, and savoury chicken. Gulliver acted as if we'd been gone for days, spinning in circles and making snuffy, woofing entreaties. Amber sat on the floor and rubbed his belly. I checked the chicken, turned the stove off and headed up the stairs to change.

I was slowly expanding my repertoire of recipes and could make chicken stew, vegetarian lasagna, and various salads. Other meals came from frozen packets. Mark had a fried chicken and chips recipe that was delicious but made a mess of the stove. His pasta with tomato sauce was good as well.

Mark was home by six, and we ate together.

Amber chatted about her school day. There was no talk of bullying or her feelings. She talked about her science lesson and her math. Mark didn't talk about murder but about the new uniforms the constabulary was considering adopting. I brought up the possibility of singing in the musical theatre group.

"Come on, Dad. It will be fun."

Amber set out to persuade him, but it wasn't hard. He couldn't resist her.

"I will. Sign me up, but I may have to miss some rehearsals."

Amber had math homework, so I cleared the table and left them to it. When she needed it, I took on tutoring her English assignments; Mark took the math. After Amber and Gulliver headed up to bed about half eight, Mark and I finally had a chance to exchange information. We took our tea to the front parlour.

"Did you get the lab results on Jordan?" I asked. "It was a stabbing?"

"It was. Long knife. Possibly a common one."

"Knives are everywhere," I said. I told him about the knives in the equipment box at the stable.

"They're in every barn and in every kitchen," Mark agreed. "There are knives in the cupboard off the sanctuary of the church. It's where the women work on the flower arrangements."

"So, someone could have grabbed one from there and used it without having to bring it with them. A crime of sudden rage, not necessarily premeditated."

"That's right, but the knife was a long one and thick so not a kitchen knife. Could be a gardening knife."

"Or one used in a stable."

"Or in the homes of people with horses. Stella had horses so she might have one in her boot room."

I stared at him. "She might, but so might any number of people in this village. Anyone who visited a stable could have taken a knife."

"True. It doesn't help much unless we can find the knife." He leaned forward. "I had a word with Joyce."

"How is she?"

"Still shaky, but she could talk to me coherently. She told me about the flower arranger's cupboard. It has shears, secateurs, loppers, and several knives. She could describe them all. It's never locked."

"She's used that cupboard for years."

"Very likely. She knew it well."

I sipped my tea and thought for a moment. "Rose was putting flowers on her grandpa's grave. I bet she used that room."

"On that day?"

"Possibly, but she doesn't have any motive."

"Andy talked to her. I'll check his notes and reinterview her myself if he didn't ask her about going into the church. He would have, I'm sure. She might have noticed if any knives were missing. I'll need to know what time she was in the cupboard."

I sipped more tea. Yorkshire tea, robust without being overwhelming.

"When I think about motive, I think of women," I said.

"Hard not to, with Jordan," Mark agreed.

"There are other women in his life who weren't lovers. What about Joyleen? It's possible that Joyleen is his daughter."

"What? Leah's daughter is Jordan's daughter?"

"She might be. I don't know what difference that would make. Perhaps it would make it <u>less</u> likely that either Leah or Joyleen would kill him." Why would a former lover or a daughter kill? Did he leave a will?"

"Andy found a strong box in his apartment. He said he'd bring it in before he went home tonight, and we'd open it in the morning. If Jordan left a will, there might be a copy in the strong box."

"Are you thinking of money as a motive?"

"We don't know how much he had." Mark considered his remark and amended it. "The trouble is there is no set amount that constitutes enough money as a motive."

"He didn't live as if he had much." I hadn't seen any expensive cars, watches, or clothes on Jordan, but he might have been spending money on something else I couldn't see—like gambling.

"We'll find out. I should make a note." He moved to his desk computer which wasn't far, typed in some words then returned to his chair and his tea. "I will be glad when my desk isn't in our living room."

"Oh good news. Patrick has found an evaluator, and she's coming this week."

"Progress, then. Amber's been looking on-line at bedroom plans. She has grand ideas."

"I'll have to try to restrain her. I'll be glad to get her present room back for my study. I miss it."

He glanced around our parlour. "I'd like to have a study for myself on the ground floor, perhaps in what was the Stoning's front parlour because we could keep the separate entrance to that room, or maybe their old dining room. What do you think?"

"Why do you need a separate entrance?" That was curious.

"I'm thinking of creating an office open to the public. I may have to leave the constabulary."

I stared at him. My heart raced. What was he thinking? This was the first I'd heard of it. I was half-expecting him to ask for a reassignment within the constabulary, not leave the police force entirely. We both had to readjust our lives and consider how we could accommodate Amber. Leaving the constabulary would be a huge change for Mark.

"And set up a business?"

"I'm not sure what's possible for me, but it's obvious I'll have to do something. Having Andy come to the house to report isn't ideal. And my hours aren't conducive to parenting. I can't go hieing off to Yorkshire or Norfolk the way I could before Amber. You have to go with your guests, and it isn't always going to work that I can stay with Amber when you're traveling. I don't want her to feel that she's being shuttled off to a sitter. I don't want her to feel she's an inconvenience."

"I don't think that has occurred to her."

"Not yet. But how is she going to feel if, for instance, if I'm away twenty days out of a month on a big case up north? I am going to have to face this and soon."

I was quiet, thinking of all the ways in which Amber had impacted our lives and would impact our future.

"It's a big sacrifice." He might regret it or resent Amber for it.

"I don't look at it like that. It's an opportunity for me to be something different—a dad."

"That's true." He was a complex and generous man and more flexible that I had expected. I loved him, and I admired him. I reminded myself how lucky I was to have met him.

We took our empty cups to the kitchen and headed up to bed.

I hung up my clothes. Mark did as well. He's neat and tidy. No clothes on the floor for him. Even his shoes are matched and in orderly line in his closet.

I climbed into bed beside him. "I quite fancy being a stepmother. I could take shorter trips for a few years. Perhaps more specialized like the Agatha Christie tour or a Jacqueline Winspear tour." That would be my sacrifice. I loved the longer trips. "That might help until she was much older. Have you thought about taking time off, a suspension of sorts, just holding your rank and your option to come back?"

"If I did that, the union wouldn't let me work elsewhere, and I need to work."

He propped himself on the pillows against the headboard. "I have to think of something I can do nearby or online."

"Let's see." I wiggled back and up beside him. "You have many transferable skills: critical thinker, solver of puzzles, someone who pays attention to detail and has incise interviewing techniques—you can be obsessed with details. You're able to understand your autocratic superintendent. You're a passable cook, fabulous baritone, and a duffer at gardening."

By now, Mark was laughing and reached over to tumble me onto my back.

"And you are one cheeky wench."

CHAPTER FIFTEEN

The next morning I was determined to finish my office work, calculate my VAT, and organize my other taxes. They weigh on my mind if I don't do them immediately after a tour. I had just finished entering all the numbers on my spread sheet when my mobile rang.

"Ms. Barclay?"

"Yes."

"This is Isobel Cameron."

The headmistress. My heart beat fast, and I breathed deeply. "Is Amber all right?"

"She's fine."

I hadn't been ready for that sudden fear. I took another deep breath to calm my pounding heart. "Yes, Ms. Cameron. What can I do for you?"

"I wonder if you were aware that Amber has a piece in the art show this morning."

"No," I said, slowly, thinking: *Why didn't she tell us?*

"I did send a note home."

"It didn't make it home."

"Hmm. Perhaps you could give me your email, and I will add it to the parents' list."

I gave it to her. "What time does the show start?"

"Ten-thirty."

"We'll be there and thank you."

Why wouldn't Amber tell us? She had deliberately withheld that note.

I called Mark. "We have an art show where Amber is exhibiting at ten-thirty at the school."

"Whew. Not much notice."

"Amber didn't want us to know."

"Should we show up if she didn't want us to?"

"Too bad," I said. "She should have discussed it, not just neglected to tell us."

"Agreed. See you there."

I knew Mark had wanted to study the comprehensive file on Jordan's murder. He'd have to make the time for that later.

Just as I was leaving Stella called.

"Pippa is coming today and staying for the weekend because she has to give a talk in art history to a grammar school in Alton. How would you like to join us?"

"At the lecture?" Stella's daughter was studying art at the uni and enthusiastic about it.

"Yes, and afterward for lunch."

"That sounds fine, but I'll take my own car because I have to attend a function at Amber's school first. What time is the lecture and where?"

"Spitalfields Road just off Church Street at noon."

"I can just do it. I'll meet you at the school."

That seemed to be my day sorted. I wouldn't get to my taxes until this evening, if then.

Mark and I joined other parents in walking around the inside of the gymnasium, looking as the pictures on display. Amber's was easy to spot as it was a fairly large and charming picture of Gulliver in the back garden, I saw Amber standing in the back row of the choir on the stage, but she didn't meet my eye. We took our seats and listened to Mrs. Cameron explain that a similar presentation would take place at the end of term, so we could see the development of talent. We listened to a short, lively piece sung by the choir in four-part harmony. Amber filed off the stage with the rest of singers. She did not look pleased.

"Now, as the note to parents informed you, the children are free for the afternoon while the teachers plan the up-coming programs."

Mark stared at me. I rapidly went over my plans.

"I can take Amber with me," I said. "Can you go home and let Gulliver out for a pee?"

He agreed. "That will work."

I hoped it would work.

I texted Stella that I was bringing Amber and got a *Fine with me* response.

I waited for Amber at the classroom door. She glanced at me but said nothing.

"We are going to Alton," I said, "as I made plans with Stella."

"Okay."

"Her daughter Pippa is giving a lecture to the fifth and sixth form students. We are gong to attend and then go for lunch." I was miffed that Amber hadn't told us about the art show. I realized I was curt.

Once we got underway to Alton, I decided to put the problem to her. "I'm hurt that you didn't tell your dad and me about the art exhibition. Did you have a good reason?" I tried to keep annoyance out of my tone.

She was quiet, then said softly, "I wanted to give you the picture as a surprise. I didn't know how to tell my form mistress that I didn't want to exhibit it. I wanted to surprise you."

I saw a layby, pulled over and shut off the motor.

"It is a fine picture. Thank you."

The tears dripped down her face. "It wasn't a surprise."

I unhooked my seat belt, then hers, and gathered her to me. I rocked her. "It was a lovely surprise. I was gobsmacked. You caught Gulliver's spirit, that kind of mischievous, lively look in his eye."

"Yes. That's what I was aiming for. I got it?"

"Nailed it." I said. She snuggled in until her head was under my chin and her arms around me. "I love Gulliver."

"Me too." We stayed like that for a few minutes.

"All right now?" I asked her?

"S'alright," she sniffed and scooted back to her seat.

I started the car and pulled out into the traffic. "We'll get a frame for it. Where do you think we should hang it?"

"Well." She considered that for a moment. "We could hang it on the landing at the top of the stairs, then we'd see it every time we went up and down. But maybe we should wait and put it in the new house?"

"There's a thought. There will be more wall space once we have the new house."

She seemed to be happy enough at the moment. I felt my shoulders relax. That could have gone so wrong. I had not been attuned to her feelings. I had only been aware I was annoyed. Parenting was like navigating a narrow bridge over a pond full of crocodiles. It was hard to keep balanced.

Amber was quiet for a moment, then asked, "Which one of Stella's girls is going to talk today."

"Pippa."

"Is she the one that talks all the time?"

"She is." Amber was right. Pippa talked even more than Stella.

The school was a handsome, red brick building with a large parking lot. We met Stella at the door of the gymnasium. I noticed Amber had removed her tie, unbuttoned the top button of her shirt, and rolled up her sleeves. She looked less formal now and was probably more comfortable. I remembered doing that with my unform whenever possible.

"Pippa's gone on ahead. We need to grab a seat. Hello, pet." Stella addressed the last comment to Amber.

"Hello, Stella. What's Pippa going to talk about?"

"Some woman painter in the Baroque period."

Stella talked as she herded us into the gymnasium and the waiting seats. The room was filled with about sixty boys and girls of around fifteen years old.

Pippa was on stage with three adults who were likely teachers of the art program. Pippa was about my height, slim with dark hair. and as beautiful as her mother. She began with slides showing eighteen women artists of the seventeenth century, then swung into a lively talk about the life of Mary Beale (1633-1699). She was an English Baroque artist who managed, even in those times, to paint so well she supported her husband and children. Beale usually painted portraits, so we saw many pictures of seventeenth-century notables in beautiful clothes. At one point, when Pippa showed a picture of the Countess of Somerset which Mary Beale had painted, Amber whispered, "Look at that blue. How did she get that?"

I shrugged. I had no idea, but I was beginning to think I had better find an art instructor for Amber. Perhaps she was happy with the instructor at her school. Mark and I were going to have to stay alert to give her opportunities. She was good at singing, riding, science, English, and now art. She had those talents. It would be up to us to be sure she had a chance to develop them. It was a daunting thought.

"That was cool," Amber said as we waiting outside the gymnasium in the sunshine.

Pippa arrived with one of the adults from the stage. "This is Professor Anderson. She's one of my instructors and came today to evaluate my presentation. It was an assignment."

The professor, a mid-forties woman, with a dramatic black cap of hair and long eyelashes, wore a shirt that floated over her capris.

She shook hands all around, including with Amber and waved. "I'm off. You did well, Pipa. Enjoy your weekend."

She left with a swish of draperies.

"Thank God," Pippa said. "She said I did well. Phew."

"You did do well," her mum said. "We were proud of you."

"Fascinating," I added. "I had no idea Mary Beale was so ahead of her time."

"She was amazing." Pippa was still enthusiastic.

"She painted mostly portraits?" Amber asked.

"Yes." Pippa bent down to talk to Amber. "There was more money in portraiture than landscapes, I expect, and she supported her family."

Pippa relaxed was Pippa effervescent. I had to interrupt to be heard.

"Is a vegetarian cafe all right?"

"What?" Pipa said. "For lunch? Sure. Is that okay with you. Amber?"

"Perfect," Amber said.

"It's The Spice Bank on High Street." I gave them the directions. "There's parking. See you there in fifteen minutes."

"Or there-abouts We are not as precise as you," Stella said.

I expect that my habit of punctuality sometimes irritated my friends, "Or there abouts," I agreed.

The tables were round and far enough apart from each other that we had some privacy. Amber and I were happily studying the menu when Pippa and Stella arrived. They were chattering like starlings.

Pippa told us more about Mary Beale and others of her era. I had no idea there were so many excellent women painting in the past. It was hard for them to get recognition, but Mary Beale's husband understood her abilities and acted as her office manager. He worked as well, but it was her talent that kept the family.

"Rachel Ruysch was another. Mary Beale lived in England; Rachel Ruysch lived in Holland. She was recognized as an important painter during her life time. She painted mostly flowers and doesn't interest me as much."

"You're staying home with me the weekend?" Stella asked her.

"Yes, until Sunday. Then, if you drive me to Alton, I'll catch the train back."

"We could go riding."

"I'd love that. Do you ride?" she asked Amber.

"I do. I take lessons at the Ashton Stables."

"Great. Maybe you can join us?"

Amber looked at me.

"That sounds like a wonderful way to spend the weekend. You might want to invite Stephanie."

She smiled. "I could do that."

I'd have to call Beth and invite Stephanie and make sure Beth knew I'd pay for it. Money was a bit tight in her house.

"Okay if we go and feed the ducks," Pippa asked her mother.

"Okay with you, Amber?"

"Yes. That'd be ace."

I nodded my permission, not that she was waiting for it, and watched them pick up the last of the naam bread and head out toward the piece of wild land behind the café where ducks hung out, sure of a handout from patrons.

"The constabulary was back to talk to me," Stella said the minute we were alone.

"David?"

"David and your loved one."

"Why?" I knew why, but I didn't think Stella did.

"I haven't a clue. I told them that my affair with Jordan was a long time ago. I wasn't interested in starting again, and I didn't make any arrangements to meet him."

"You didn't see him at all?"

"Of course I saw him. I rode at the stables he worked at, so he was there when I went to ride. I talked to him. We were friendly, just not intimate."

We had ordered another pot of tea and were sipping it as we talked.

"I told them that the last time I'd seen Jordan he was in good spirits. He was getting in a new horse. You know he bought and sold horses?'

"No. I didn't."

"I think that's how he afforded his life style. You know wining and dining woman, good cars, holidays."

"He made a commission on sales?"

"Yes. He had a good eye. A very good eye—and buyers trusted him."

"Did you sell Pansy through him?" Pansy was not her registered name, but it was what Stella called her. She was a smooth jumper but Stella had stopped competing in jumping events.

"No. He wanted me to. Said he had a buyer that would pay triple what I'd get anywhere else, but I had mind to sell it to a young lass who was just coming into serous competition. Pansy would help her get wins for the next four or five years at least. She needed Pansy, and she'd be good to her."

"So you didn't use Jordan for the sale."

"I explained it to him. That I didn't know his buyer and didn't know if Pansy would have a good home with her."

"How did he take it?"

"To tell you the truth he was miffed. I guess his commission must have been substantial. That was the end of our affair."

"He called it."

"Yes, I let him call it. It's easier that way. He acted like a child when he didn't get his commission. It's only money, but he didn't have my attitude to money. Like it's fine for what it can do, but you don't need pots of it."

Stella's attitude to money was cavalier, but Garman made so much she was never desperate. I'm not sure she had any idea of what it was like to budget, or do without so you could pay your rent, or to plan your grocery buying carefully, or walk instead of taking the bus because your pay cheque was days away.

"He didn't agree."

"He didn't, and you know he was petulant about it. Life's too short for that. So I bid him a fond farewell and moved on. Or, at least, I am planning on moving on. I haven't found a long-term replacement yet. Jordan and I resumed our friendship and passed the time of day civilly. I miss his sense of humor—and his gossip. He knew a lot."

"Such as?" I couldn't resist.

She thought for a moment. "Did you know Nigel was having an affair?"

"Nigel the vicar?" Helen Taylor had been right. She was sometimes right. She sat in that post office and picked up information like an international spy. The police should employ her. The trouble was, she didn't keep her information to herself, but spread it around.

"The very one. Vicar Whitney is having an affair with a clerk in the bookstore in Winchester. At least, that's the scuttlebutt. She is not aware he's married. Jordan saw him incredibly cozy with her in a pub in Winchester. He asked the barkeep who she was and got a nice dose of gossip about how they met every Friday night and had a room above the pub. Very romantic. Jordan thought it was funny,"

I was silent for a moment. It wouldn't have been funny for Joyce. Maybe she didn't care.

"You explained that to Mark and David?"

"Not about Nigel, but about Jordan and me, yes. I hope they're satisfied."

I didn't respond to that and changed the subject.

"Does Garman ever object to your affairs?"

"Not so far. He probably knows about them but never says a thing."

"He's not interested in you?"

She thought about it for a moment. "I wouldn't say he wasn't interested. We're civil, after all. He asks about my day, my friends, my activities. Occasionally, he comes to my equestrian events. His public face matters to him, so I trot about on his arm dressed to the nines whenever he needs me to. He's pretty easy to care-take without interfering in my life." She frowned. "He did object once, though."

"What happened?"

"It was when I was selling Pansy. I told him about the deal Jordan had for Pansy. He told me I was a fool not to take it. But he didn't interfere when I sold it to my friend. He just told me again I was financially stupid, but then Garman's whole life revolves around money—his money and other people's money that he manages. He sees almost everything in terms of pounds and pence."

"He didn't suspect you and Jordan's affair?" Garman wasn't stupid. He must have known.

"I don't think so. I did see him talking to Jordan at the stables once and in the village on The Street. They were friendly enough, so I doubt he had any idea. Or would even care."

"There is that. Why are you staying with him? The lifestyle?" In spite of her resolve to leave him the last time we talked, she was still dithering.

"I've stayed for the lifestyle and because it would upset the girls. But the girls are on their way to independence now. I'm still thinking of leaving"

Again. She's thinking of leaving again. I said nothing except, "Let me know if I can help." She was always thinking of leaving Garman. I had serious doubts that would ever happen. She was too comfortable.

Pippa and Amber returned, and we left the café, parting at our cars.

"Pippa is going to go to Paris when she graduates," Amber said as we were heading out of Alton.

"Is she?"

"Yes. She's going to join a team that investigates art fraud. Kind of like Dad. A detective but for art not people."

"I expect she'll be good at that."

"She's good at most things, I think."

I drove most of the way home in comfortable silence and the occasional snippets of conversation.

"Do you have plans for the rest of the day?" I asked her.

"Sephanie's coming over at four. She can stay for supper, right?"

"Certainly. What are we having?"

"What were you planning?"

"Is it my night?" I had a sudden fear that I had lost track of my schedule.

She reflected for a moment. "No. You did last night. So, it's Dad's."

"Right. You'd better use my mobile and text him. Let him know Stephanie's staying for supper. He'll be fine with it. It's just that he needs to know how many to feed."

She did that.

He got back to her in a few minutes.

"He says: *I'm picking up Chinese. Thanks for the heads up.*"

"He'll get enough for all. You know we always have leftovers anyway." I reassured her.

"True. It's funny, though we had a South Asian lunch and now we're going to have a Chinese dinner."

"I often have French or Italian on my tours."

"Then there's Caribbean and those open sandwiches. They're Scandinavian."

We spent the rest of our drive trying to come up with all the national cuisines we had tasted.

I took Gulliver for a walk to the river when we got home. Amber went to Stephanie's house to collect her. We met back at the house.

I fed Gulliver and started back on my tax return. The girls went to Amber's bedroom with a bowl of popcorn to keep them happy until the supper arrived.

The vegetable garden was still producing thanks to the attention of Peter Brown. I left the on-going tax work and harvested some cucumbers and carrots. We hadn't had frost yet and Peter didn't expect any for a few weeks, so we were still able to add the fresh veggies to our meals. I scrubbed the cucumbers and carrots and cut them into bite-size. Amber liked them raw.

Mark arrived with the hot food in many packages. We all ate with chopsticks, and it was a merry meal. Stephanie was a quiet girl but with a sense of humour. She appreciated the quips Amber and Mark traded and added a few of her own. The girls disappeared upstairs with all four fortune cookies.

Mark and I settled in the parlour with our tea. I told Mark about Amber's efforts to surprise us with her drawing of Gulliver.

"You said the right things."

"Yes, I think I did this time. It's a bit hit and miss, this parenting."

"It is. The job feels like that right now, as well"

Murder inquiries could be long and frustrating. "What have you learned?"

"I talked to Rose. She didn't use the flower cupboard. Her mother had arranged the flowers, and she didn't need to do anything but deliver them. But... if I wanted to know if there was anything missing from that cupboard to ask her mum because she sees everything."

"That's the truth."

"I got Helen to close the post office for fifteen minutes and hop across the street with me to view the flower cupboard."

"And?"

"And there is a knife missing."

"Ah! So it wasn't one of Stella's farrier knives or Leah's?"

"I can't be sure, but I'm going to act as if the knife came from the church cupboard. Helen said she would have known if it was not there earlier."

No doubt, she would have. "I'm glad. That let's Stella off your suspect list."

He was quiet for a moment. "She's not."

"What do you mean?"

"We searched Jordan's computer and found pictures of Stella on it."

I stared at him. "What kind of pictures?"

"Racey ones."

Uh oh, Stella. "Were the pictures dated?"

"They were and they were from early this year so nothing recent, but still they were only from this year. We have to talk to her again."

"You don't know if she knew about them or, if she did know, if she cared."

"True and it would be like Stella not to care, but she might care if Jordan threatened to show them to Garman."

I didn't have an answer to that. She liked her life with Garman. She might object to Jordan trying to disrupt it.

"I wouldn't pick Jordan as a blackmailer." I tried to find a reason why Stella wouldn't be involved.

"No evidence of it so far. But he wouldn't keep blackmailing records on his computer. We're checking his bank accounts to see if he got money outside his salary."

I remembered my conversation with Stella.

"He bought and sold horses for people, so he would have extra income from that. It might be substantial. Horses can sell for big prices. Especially show horses."

"I'll get Mira to check on prices, but roughly how much do you think they go for?"

"Millions, at times."

He was quiet. Then said, "I might have been missing a huge motive here."

CHAPTER SIXTEEN

Stephanie stayed overnight—Mark and I had heard the girls giggling late into the night—but she hustled back home after breakfast.

"My mom says I have to clean the upstairs bathroom before I can 'wander off'," she told me. Then we are going to Basingstoke."

I should think about a chore list for Amber. She needed to feel part of the household. Even though Rose came weekly, there was still recycling to sort, groceries to plan for, buy and put away, and a dog to be walked and brushed. I'd think of something.

Stella called and asked if Amber and I would like to join her and Pippa on a trail ride. I'd never been on one, so I was excited. Amber phoned Stephanie but she was already on here way to Basingstoke. Mark had left early to join David and Mira.

"I'll get changed." Amber headed to her room. Her new bedroom would be bigger. I wondered if she'd like twin beds so her friends could be more comfortable. The cot bed I had put in temporarily for company lacked springs or adequate padding.

We left Gulliver at home with promises of a walk later. The horses went too fast for Gulliver. He sent me a sidelong glance making me feel slightly guilty.

"We'll be back, and you will get a walk."

The driveway to the stables was lined with low-maintenance spreading junipers, but against the house in a small flower-bed dahlias bloomed in extravagant color. I wondered it that bit of beauty was nurtured by Joyleen. I didn't think it was something Leah would do.

We met Stella and Pippa at the stable's tack room. Stella and I presented our credit cards to Leah and paid for a two-hour ride.

"You won't need Joyleen to guide you because everyone is an accomplished rider but you, Claire, and they will watch out for you. Just follow the others. You'll be fine. Audrey knows what's she's doing."

It was humbling to accept that the horse was more accomplished that I was—but it was true.

Amber saddled her regular pony, Sadie. Stella wandered over to the horse box and petted the horse there.

"This is Jupiter. She belonged to Jordan, but he had a buyer for her., so she'll be leaving. She's dear. I have competed against her and always admired her. I didn't know her former owners were going to sell her, not that I would have offered the same as Jordan did. It was a little high but I'd pay that now. She's so good natured and so willing to work hard."

"Have you ridden her?"

"Once or twice when Jordan needed her exercised. I should ask Leah if I can ride her while she's keeping Jupiter here. I wonder who owns her now."

I managed to groom Audrey and saddle and bridle her. Amber did the same with Sadie. Stella and Pipa mounted horses that were much bigger and more energetic than ours. I watched in admiration as Stella turned her big, black gelding, Charger, in circles to control his exuberance.

"There's not a mean bone in his body," Stella said, patting Charger's neck when he calmed. "He's just excited. Let's go up on the ridge. It's beautiful there."

We agreed.

"Does everyone have water?" I asked.

We all had a cantle bag at the back of the saddle. I'd given Amber a small bottle of water and stowed my own there. I also had carrots for Audrey. There wasn't much room to bring supplies while trail riding, but I had my small camera stashed in my vest pocket. I hoped to get some good pictures of Amber to send to her grandparents.

Stella started in front of our line, but we soon let Pippa and Amber ride side by side in front of us and fell in side by side behind them. We rode along the bridle path between lofty beech and ash trees, then between farmer's fields where the hedgerows were ablaze with red hawthorn berries and orange hazel bushes. The horses easily climbed the hill behind the village and over into the next valley. We could see for miles: dark green and orange hedgerows delineating pale gold crops into squares and rectangles. In the far distance, huge ash and oak trees lined a small river.

"That must be Chawton that way," Pippa said, pointing to the west.

"I think so," I agreed. "Jane Austen's home."

Stella laughed. "For you, the country is laid out in a map of the homes of writers."

I smiled. "I suppose so." I did tend to think of places in the country as sites for mystery novels or residents of writers. I imagined writers, living and dead, standing in their settings, waving at me. The map would be covered in them. We were rich in writers.

I managed to get a picture of Amber on Sadie before we dismounted and fished out our water bottles. I should store pictures of Amber in a digital file and make her a yearly book from them.

"Jordan used to take us here," Pippa said, "Remember, Mum?"

Stella smiled. "I remember. He liked the view."

"He always checked the horses here. He'd go over everyone's tack to make sure the horses were comfortable. He really understood them." Pippa spoke as if she was providing a eulogy.

"I thought he was like that horse whisperer you see on the telly," Amber said. "He could talk to them, and listen to them."

"He had a lot of different horses," Pipa thought about it. "He seemed to have a new one he bought and then sold every few months. Some of them were beautiful. Do you remember Asteroid, Mum? That horse could run."

"I remember him. Jordan sold it to some rich woman from Russia, so he told me. I wondered it a woman could hold that horse, he was so strong and determined, but maybe she was too. I never rode him. Too much horse for me."

"I never rode any of those horses he had for sale. He said he sold Asteroid for two hundred thousand," Pippa said.

"Did he?" Stella snorted "Asteroid was a good horse—but not that good. I hope that Russian woman was happy."

"I'm sorry Jordan died," Amber said. "Somebody who's that special with horses should still be here."

We were silent for a moment, remembering Jordan.

Stella raised her water bottle. "Here's to Jordan. May he rest in peace." I glanced at her and saw that she was wiping away a few tears. She smiled at me and shrugged.

We all raised our water bottles. It seemed a little causal, but it was a spontaneous and respectful good bye to Jordan.

"I liked him," Stella said almost fiercely.

"Me too," both Pippa and Amber echoed.

From what I understood, most women liked him. I didn't say that. I was a little ashamed of the thought.

The bridle trail took us to a straight stretch where the girls in front urged their horses to canter.

"Try it," Stella said to me. "You just bring your left foot back and tap Audrey's side. That's her signal to canter. Relax into the saddle, and let Audrey do the work."

I slid my left foot back and tapped. Audrey started to moved more quickly and in seconds I was rocking with the horse in a slow canter.

"I'll keep pace with you," Stella said from somewhere on my right side. I didn't turn my head because I was concentrating on watching for low-hanging branches and avoiding anything that might appear in front of me.

"Relax," Stella shouted.

"I hear you. I hear you," I muttered and tried to breath deeply in order to relax my shoulders which were granite hard as I clutched the reins. Audrey kept up a steady rhythm and, after a few minutes, I found it fairly easy to stay glued to the saddle. I began to feel the joy of the speed and the connection to the horse. It was marvelous! The hedgerows flew by in a blur of color. Stella's horse thundered beside me; it's huge feet thumping the rhythm.

I laughed. No wonder Amber loved riding. Ahead, I could see the girls had stopped and were waiting by a gate. Right. Stopping. I should have asked about that.

I eased back on the reins. Audrey responded by slowing her canter, then changing in to a trot that sent me all over the saddle. I clutched the reins with one hand, grabbed her mane with the other, and held on.

"Heels down. Lean back. Pull back on the reins a little," Stella commanded from my right.

I did that and the trot, mercifully, changed to a walk. I readjusted my seat on the saddle.

"Well done." Stella praised me.

I wouldn't say bouncing around on the back of the horse was 'well done', but at least I hadn't fallen off, and I did stop her.

"How are you doing, Claire?" Pippa asked as we got closer. "Amber says it's your first trail ride."

I smiled at her. "It's glorious."

Both girls laughed. "It is at that," Pipa leaned down to open the gate. I'd have to learn to do that, open a gate from horseback.

We had one more stretch of open path where we could canter, and I managed the transition from a canter to a walk much better. It was easier when I knew what to expect.

I soaked in the bathtub when we got home as I suspected that, if I didn't, I would ache the next day. The house was quiet, the water warm, and I relaxed. My mind went back to our impromptu remembrance of Jordan at the viewpoint, then to the problem of who had killed him. I didn't think Stella cared enough about Jordan to have killed him. You must have to be driven with some kind of passion, need, or fear to kill another person. She'd been fond of him but not passionate. I doubt he was blackmailing her. Still, he had those racy pictures, so he might have been. Why didn't she tell me she'd had a fling with him recently? Maybe Jordan was blackmailing Garman: *Pay up or I'll publish pictures of your wife.*

While I could see that Garman would hate the scandal and humiliation of such publication, he'd hate parting with money even more and would likely choose not to pay. I'd mention it to Mark. Garman might have been paying blackmail—but not Stella.

Mark arrived home while Amber and I were constructing sandwiches: cheese for her, cheese and ham for Mark and me.

Stephanie arrived about two to join Mark and Amber in building a bee hive. According to Amber, honey is better for us than sugar, so we needed to build a home for those honey-producers. Mark read up on it and got some advice from the police dispatcher who, apparently, had raised bees for many years.

There was a local beekeepers' organization Mark had not yet had time to join, but he read their pamphlets and bought the necessary lumber and tools. Living with Mark had taught me that every new project required new tools. He and the two girls went to the back garden with their safety glasses, gloves, and a hammer for each.

"They make pink hammers for girls," Stephanie said, "but they aren't as good as the black ones."

"It makes you wonder about the people who make those, doesn't it?" Mark said. "Don't they think girls need good tools?"

There was a thoughtful silence.

I left them to their project and returned to my desk. The deadline for my taxes was October 31st. If I got them done this week, my accountant would have time to prepare them from my records.

The hive-builders stopped work at about five and came in for a drink and a snack.

"When is Amber going to get a mobile, Claire," Stephanie asked me.

I sensed an organized attack here.

"What are the rules about mobiles in your house?" I countered.

She chanted. "No mobile at the table. No mobile until after homework is done. Park the mobile at the downstairs charger when you go to bed. No taking it to bed with you."

Amber listened.

"Any more?" I asked.

"I can't take it to school."

Amber was surprised. "You can't? What if you get abducted coming home from school and you don't have a mobile?" She clearly expected to be able to take hers with her.

"I tried that with Mum. She said she'd take her chances."

"Where *can* you take it?"

"I've got it now." Stephanie held up her mobile. It rang.

We all laughed. Stephanie answered.

"Mum?"

She listened. "Okay. I'll ask."

"Mum wants to know if Amber can come over for movie night. We'll have popcorn," she said to Amber.

"May I?" Amber asked.

I approved of her grammar. I also approved of Beth, Stephanie's mum. "Sure. What time will you be home?"

"What time will she be home, Mum," Stephanie repeated into the mobile. Then, "One of the boys will escort her home at nine-thirty."

"How about I feed you now, and you trot over to Stephanie's about six."

Stephanie checked with her mother and all was agreed.

I hauled out the frozen stuffed chicken breast and chips I keep for occasions such as this and had it ready in thirty minutes They ate and departed.

Mark poked his head out of the parlour where he had been catching up on the rugby tournament.

"All quiet here?"

"It is."

"Those girls can talk." He ambled into the kitchen and hugged me. We enjoyed that for a few minutes, then I put out our dinner. The same menu as the girl's, although I'd taken the time to make a salad and pour some New Zealand Sauvignon Blanc.

"How was your ride?" he asked as we ate.

"Loved it." I told him all about it.

"I should try it." Mark looked a little wistful.

"You really should, but I don't suppose you have much time for something new."

"No, probably not." He shrugged. Work came first most of the time.

"Stella mentioned something you should know." This was going to interest him.

"About horses?"

"About horses and Jordan." I told Mark about the sale of the horse for two hundred thousand. "Stella doesn't believe it was worth that."

"You mentioned this before. I'm looking into it."

"What did you find?"

"If the selling price was inflated there is one good reason for that?"

"What?" Aside from greed.

"Money laundering."

I hadn't thought about that, but I did now. "A person has ill-gotten gains and wants to be able to admit to having that much money, so they pay a great deal for a horse, then their money is legitimate because it is a hard asset."

"That's right." He finished his wine and set the glass back on the table. He leaned forward, expecting me to understand the importance of what he was saying.

"The value of the horse will go up simply because someone paid a lot of money for it." I guessed.

"Right again."

We were both quiet for a few minutes. I was considering if Jordan had been part of a money laundering scheme.

Mark gathered our dishes. "I've invited Andy and David here tonight. Are you through at your desk?"

It was hard for me to concentrate, especially on taxes, when another conversation was going on in the same room.

"For now."

Andy and David arrived about seven-thirty.

"Sorry to drag you out on a Saturday," Mark said as he ushered them into the kitchen. "but I just want to talk about a couple of things. Do you have the composite file, Dave?"

Andy had passed on the composite file to David, as he was on another case now and only here as a favor to Mark.

"I do." He held up his tablet.

"Good. Now, Claire has some information."

I repeated my story about the horse.

"Stella also told me that Jordan had offered to sell Pansy, her last horse, for triple what she could get locally. She preferred to sell it to someone she knew, as she gets enormously attached to her horses. Jordan was upset with her because he said he could make a good commission on it. She did sell it privately to a friend, so he didn't get the commission. But he was promising an astronomical price."

Andy grunted. "It sounds like Stella wasn't in on it."

"I don't think she even suspected it. Still doesn't." I said.

"You said he bought and sold many horses. If he was buying and selling horses regularly, there might be big money involved here."

"Where would he keep them? How would he make the transfer?" David asked.

"At the stables," I said.

Daivd peered at his notes. "Leah, the stable owner. She must have known."

Mark was more cautious. "She would have known he bought and sold horses, but not necessarily that he was moving horses for criminals who wanted to launder money. She might not have had any idea of the prices he was asking, and he might not be laundering money, just making a huge profit."

Mark's ideas stimulated me.

"How would Jordan get the buyers? How would he have contact with the rich and criminal? I bet he selected the horses to buy. He was well-connected in the equestrian competition world. People buy new horses all the time as they advance in the competitions. Jordan would know who wanted to sell a horse, or buy a new one, but the people he knew in the equestrian world would not have the kind of money to buy a new horse at inflated prices, or very few of them would."

I spoke more quickly as ideas tumbled around in my mind. "If someone else found the buyers and put them in touch with Jordan, then all he had to do was arrange the sale, take his commission, and the horse moved to a new stable. After a few deals like that, the word would go out that Jordan knew some rich buyers, and he would be contacted by people wanting to sell."

David was spell-bound as if I was telling him a story. "We could search his computer to see if there are any records of transactions."

"It isn't illegal," Andy said. "I mean it isn't illegal to buy a horse for a great deal of money. The buyer could just say he was gambling on improved performance."

"He could. But if we knew who it was, we might be able to get the tax department to check if he had reported earning that much money."

"Unless he or she was from out of country," David said.

"Depending on the country. We get good cooperation from some countries and not so good from others," Andy told him.

"Even so," Mark said. "We are less interested in the money laundering itself than money laundering as a motive for murder. We need to know who was arranging to contact the buyer and who was arranging the transfer of money."

"Did Jordan pay out a commission to anyone," Andy asked. "After all, the one who arranged the deal would want to be paid. Either the buyer paid him or her directly or Jordan did."

Mark spoke to David. "Get Mira on Jordan's computer first thing on Monday."

"I've got the boys' football games tomorrow or, I'd do it," Andy said.

"The joys of being single," David said. "I can do it in the morning, after church, as I'm singing a solo, and before my rugby game which is late on Sunday afternoon. I'll have a few hours. I'll look at the computer."

Mark glanced over at me. "I'm building beehives. But I'll be here. Drop by if you find anything and have time."

"Will do." David stood and gathered his papers and tablet. He smiled at me. "Thanks, Claire. That was good thinking on your part. Money laundering. Who would have thought it in our sleepy village?"

I remembered the malice and brutality that sometimes occurred here but didn't argue with him. He'd find out soon enough that while most people here were good, kind souls, we did have the wicked.

CHAPTER SEVENTEEN

On Sunday morning we went to church. This was not my habit, but as Amber was now singing in the choir, we had to attend. She looked impressive in her red choir robes with white collar, one of twelve singers. She would get respect there because she had inherited her dad's musical genes and sang beautifully. I wasn't sure her commitment to the choir would last, but I hoped she would stay in it until Christmas. Christmas music was always a joy to hear and to sing.

That meant Mark and I or at least one of us, had to be in the congregation every Sunday. Church attendance hasn't been high on my list of preferred activities, Mark and I weren't even married in church, but in my garden with a commissioner officiating. Nigel might have been offended by that because he seemed aloof and a bit disdainful of us. Joyce wasn't offended as she attended our reception and gave us a soup tureen. I remembered that because I wondered then and still wonder if I'll ever use it.

I watched Nigel during the service. He seemed aloof to everyone as if he was gracing us with his presence. It was hard to believe he had any passions especially one for a clerk in Oxford. He was a man out of time and would have fitted in better in the 1920s when the clergy were important in a village and had authority. Now, he took umbrage at many behaviors. Joyce had told me that he resented people looking at their mobiles in church. Granted it was rude, but people will do it, so it's a waste of energy to get angry about it. The church had changed since the last century, and he needed to change with it. St. Hilda's was still the social hub of the village, gathering us together in times of celebration and sorrow. He had a role, more as a social worker than a priest. I didn't like him in either role.

"Stephanie sings alto," Amber told us on the way home. "I sing soprano so we can do a duet, Mrs. Fotheringham-Whitley says."

"That will be a treat," Mark said seriously. It would be.

We arrived home to find Dierdre and Michael with the two kids and two dogs on our doorstep.

"It's the last Sunday of good weather for a while. Neither of the kids had a game so we decided to come for a visit. We can leave and drive to the shore if you are busy."

I kissed her cheek. "Come in. Good to see you. Let the dogs out in the garden."

"Will do."

I turned and gave Michael a hug. He smiled and his blue eyes lit. "Claire. How is it going?"

Michael really wanted to know.

"So far. So good," I said, knowing he was asking how Mark and I were managing with Amber. "You're welcome here today. It's good for us and good for Amber to know she has cousins."

We moved toward the back garden where we could hear Amber explaining the construction of the bee hives to Josh and Kala. Her voice was just discernible above the yapping of the excited dogs as they greeted each other. In a few minutes, the dogs had settled into furious digging in the sandbox and Mark and Amber were allocating jobs that were going to make the completion of the bee hive much more likely today.

Deidre and I went into the kitchen and found sodas, coffee, tea, cake, and biscuits for all and some dog toys. I threw the toys into the sand box while Deidre set out the food on the wooden picnic table. She and I took our drinks—coffee for me, tea for Deidre—under the Bramley apple tree. We sat back and watched all the activity with no desire to be part of it.

"How is the murder inquiry going?" Deidre asked.

I thought about all the information I couldn't tell her: Jordan's horse sales, Joyce's affair with him, Stella's affair with him.

"They're gathering information on wills, finances, affairs, last sightings, and still trying to find his mobile."

"All important, especially the mobile. How's it working out for you and Mark sharing parenting duties?"

"It's working …just. I'm not sure how we will manage long-term."

She shrugged. "Mark really needs to be free to move around the country and so do you."

"I know, but it might not be best for Amber."

"Don't give up your work. It's important to you."

"What did you do to accommodate the kids?" I was out of the country when Josh and Kala were small.

"We both went on point seven-five hours and hired a nanny. Now we both work full time, and they stay alone for an hour before one of us gets home. We do a lot of schedule-meshing."

I watched Mark and Amber happily chatting with my family and wondered how we could maintain bonding if both of us were away.

"Don't worry about it now," Deidre advised. "How are the plans for the house coming?"

"We're making notes and collecting ideas. Come on in, and I'll show you."

Deidre and I pored over the rough plans for about twenty minutes then decided to order pizza for the family.

"We're going to collect the pizza," I called to Mark.

He grinned and waved a hammer at me.

"Pizza!" The kids echoed.

"No pineapple for me," Josh said.

"No anchovies, Mum," Kala said.

"I'll take everything except meat," Amber called.

We'd already called in the order, as we had known their preferences. No need of the reminder.

When we returned, the hives were finished. We parked the pizzas in the warming oven and went to inspect the hives.

"Very cool," I praised the builders.

Amber demonstrated how she and Mark would remove the trays. "They're called supers," she informed me. "They slide in and out."

It was ingenious. "Now all you need is bees."

"Soon," Mark promised.

Mark had positioned the hives where they would get sunlight and some rain but well away from our picnic table. I approved. We adjourned to the kitchen where Deidre and I distributed the pizza and sodas. Mark put on the tea. When we had finished the pizza, I cleaned off the table and Mark spread out the house plans. The dogs had taken care of any crumbs on the floor.

"Here's where my room will be," Amber pointed, full of enthusiasm.

"And what's that?" Kala asked.

"That's my new bathroom."

Kala turned to Deidre. "Fab! Mom, why can't I have my own bathroom?"

Deidre shrugged. "Josh will be at uni in three years, then we won't need another bathroom."

Kala was silent for a moment. "That's forever"

I laughed and rolled up the house plans. "Why don't you go into the parlour and put a taped game show on the telly. You can see if you can come up with the answers before the contestants."

They ran into the parlour and soon we heard raucous calls accompanied by barking dogs It was bedlam, and I loved it.

Laughter, affection, noisy interaction. Lovely. On the day I'd heard that Amber was coming, I hadn't anticipated the joy she'd bring.

Mark unrolled the plans again, and we four adults had a serious look at them.

"Add a laundry chute from the upper floor to the utility room if you can," Deidre said.

I peered at the plans. "Good idea."

"We could fit it in here," Mark pointed.

"Or here," Michel suggested.

About one-thirty, the doorbell blasted out its harsh ring.

"When are you going to replace that?" Deidre complained.

I would likely never replace it.

Mark opened the door to David Penberthy. The noise level from the parlour increased.

Michael recognized an official visit and stood. "Claire, do you have keys for next door? We could take the kids over there and look around."

"I do, and I know Patrick wouldn't mind." I fetched the keys while Mark introduced David. In five minutes, the dogs were in the back garden and my family, including Amber, were next door. Our side of the house was quiet.

David powered up his notebook and clicked onto a page of notes.

"I searched Jordan's finances. He's was doing quite well out of his horse-trading business. He had a tidy sum about £500,000 saved and invested in conservative stocks and bonds. I checked out the horse business in detail. He had a list of the horses, their names, their appearance as in color and distinctive markings, their passport numbers if they were imported at any time, age, sire and dam, country of origin, and any registration information. The names of the sellers are there, but not the names of the buyers, except for one from Yorkshire which, although there is no name, has a mobile number."

"What would that mean?" I asked.

Mark waited for a moment, but David didn't offer any explanation. Mark spoke. "That one exception where he noted the mobile number might mean it was an unusual sale. Anything strike you as odd about that sale?"

"One thing. He has three columns of numbers. There was no number in the third column for the Yorkshire sale."

Mark was quiet for a moment. "It could mean that he routinely didn't want anyone to find out who he sold to, although in the world of horses, I'd think people would know. This Yorkshire sale was an exception of some kind."

"A different kind of sale?" I asked.

"Perhaps. He could be buying horses and selling them to one broker who resold to others, but this one sale was not to that buyer."

I pondered that. "The regular buyer might be someone who was jacking up the price even further and hiding income from the tax department." Her Majesty's Revenue and Customs, particularly the tax department, was on my mind these days.

"Possibly," Mark said. He turned to David. "Have you found his mobile yet?"

"Mira's still looking. She's a bit of a ferret." His voice held some admiration. Perhaps, Mira was becoming more valuable.

"Get the name and address of the Yorkshire buyer from the mobile company. Try Vodafon. If they don't have it try EE and O2".

"That'll have to be tomorrow. I'll get Mira on it then."

"That'll do. I don't want to warn this Yorkshire buyer that we are interested in him, so don't ring him. We'll pay him, or her, a visit."

David grinned, probably anticipating some excitement.

"Keep an open mind. He may be honest. Does Jordan say how much he paid for the horse?"

"Yes. Seems reasonable. Here's what's interesting, gov,"

David said. "Except for the Yorkshire sale, he doesn't give the name of the buyer, just a code of some kind. Every buyer has a code and the price. Actually, three prices: the price he bought it for; the price he sold it for, and another price."

I was fascinated with codes. "Let me see."

He glanced at Mark who nodded, then David passed me his notes. I stared at the combination of numbers and letters. When I was about fourteen, a friend and I used to create codes to use in notes we passed in class. All you had to do to break a code was find the pattern.

"How much did he sell the horse for?"

"About twenty-five percent more. "That was his profit. He'd have to pay transport and stable fees out of that, so it would not be exorbitant."

"It's relative to the selling price," I said. "What is the price in the last column?"

"Roughly twenty percent of the sales price."

The three of us stared at the figures in David's notebook.

"If he bought it for fifty thousand," I said which is what Stella said she and Garman paid for her last horse, "and sold it seventy-five thousand. Minus his expenses which leaves him with a profit of about ten thousand on each horse. That's a nice profit."

There was silence. Then Mark said. "True. But it's not money laundering."

I stared at the figures and at the codes. "What if this number in front of the code which is the same for everyone but the Yorkshire one, is the code for one buyer who sells the horse on for an outrageous profit, like a million more."

"You mean a broker buys from Jordan, inflates the price by say a million and sells it to a criminal?"

"I was thinking that."

"Now *that* would be money laundering," Mark said. "And I bet Jordan knew it was happening. He supplied the horses, took a good profit, and passed the horse to the broker who dealt with the criminal buyers."

"That really opens up the field of suspects, doesn't it?' I asked. "I mean if Jordan was finding horses for criminals to buy and launder money, it was no doubt criminals who killed him."

"Perhaps," Mark said, "but why?"

David said, "If they had a good thing going with Jordan, why would they kill him?"

"He was trying to get more money out of them, or blackmail them," Mark offered.

"You wouldn't think he'd try either of those things," I said. "He wasn't stupid. Besides, according to this spread sheet, he was only taking a profit on a legitimate increase in price, not on millions."

"Not stupid, but he might have been greedy," David said.

"Or he might have been trying to stop," I said. "And the seller above him didn't like that."

Mark and David were quiet for a moment considering the motives.

"Anything else of interest on his computer?" Mark asked.

"That broker really interests me," David said. "He's likely the one who is adding a million or so to the price of the horse, and selling it to some criminal off shore. The buyer pays the inflated price, gets the horse with its passport as an asset with it's inflated value. Likely the broker returns most of the money, keeping back a say ten percent broker's fee so the broker makes a hundred thousand on each sale."

"Now *that's* profitable money laundering," Mark said.

David concurred. "Just so."

"We need to find Jordan's bank accounts," Mark said. "If he made just twenty percent profit, he wasn't money laundering, but if he partnered in this inflated sale price then he was. If he sold even four horses a year and has been doing this for years, he must be worth a lot of money. He might have another bank account. Who inherits?"

"Mira didn't find a will in his flat, but Garman Bennett's name was on a small address book she found."

"He might be his lawyer then," I said. "Garman does law work for a lot of the horse people Stella knows."

"David, you get a copy of the will on Monday. I'll get over to the stables and ask Leah for her records. She must know how many horses went through her stables."

"Jordan must have paid something for stabling," I said. "Her accounts would show that."

"I'd better get forensic involved with this, especially for those codes. They have a dedicated accountant. We could use her."

"And maybe touch base with the Integrated Gang Unit?" David suggested.

Mark grimaced. "If I have to. Those sods are so territorial."

David started to gather his papers. "Let me copy that code," I said. "I'd like to puzzle over it."

"Help yourself." He handed me the tablet. I copied five codes onto my mobile notebook. It would be fun to tease at them. I might even find the pattern.

"There is one horse at the stables that Stella said Jordan had a buyer for, but it was still there on Saturday when we were there."

"I'll check on it," David said.

David got to the front door before he was almost bowled over by the kids as they swarmed up the stairs. They laughed and smoothly avoided him, running through the house to the back garden. The dogs barked; the kids shouted and laughed.

"I do hope you're finished," Derdre said, coming in behind them.

"Just leaving," David assured her and slipped through the front door.

"Good timing," I reassured her.

"That house is going to make a huge difference to your happiness,' Deidre said.

I brightened. "What do you think?"

"I think you need to have your own study."

I agreed. We chattered as we walked back to the kitchen. Deidre took my mind off the horse-trading activity that seemed to be taking place at the stables, a place I visited a couple of times a week, and a place where my precious step-daughter spent as much time as she could.

I interrupted Deidre to say "If Jordan's death centered around the riding stables, should I keep Amber away from there?"

She stared at me. "Jordan died in church. Are you going to keep her out of church?"

I shook my head. My sister, the practical one.

CHAPTER EIGHTEEN

Deidre and her family left about half four. Amber announced she was going to Stephanie's to help paint their shed. Mark kissed me briefly and headed out to his office. He wanted to get his requisitions to the forensic department and the Integrated Gang Unit written and sent. I took Gulliver for a short walk down to the river and back. A short walk was all he could manage after his exhausting morning with the kids and Deidre's two dogs.

I heard the bells from the church calling for Evensong. I like that service. No sermon, just music, so I dropped Gulliver off at home and slipped into a pew near the back.

Joyce led the choir into the pews at the side of the nave. There were about twenty in the adult choir, a large number for such a small village. I would like to get back to singing but perhaps not in the church choir. I usually sang with the community choir which had started again in September. I missed it and might join in after Christmas when they would begin rehearsals for the *Pirates of Penzance*.

This evening, Joyce's choir sang a movement from Bach's mass in B minor, the Kyrie. It was lovely. After the choir, our organist Anthony Michael played a baroque piece I didn't recognize. The organ is a good one and the sonorous, uplifting music took me out of my worries into a kind of meditative state.

Nigel's nasal drone intoning the lesson brought me back to reality. I returned to my worries. It was difficult to understand how millions of pounds could disappear into an accounting of income and expenses. Jordan's Excel page showed a clear income-expenses and profit statement. The third column of numbers didn't belong on that page.

That's what bothered me about the statement. There was no record of expenses to put against that third column. It was as though it has been added for some reason, but it was not really part of the statement.

Nigel stopped talking and gave us his blessing. The choir sang their blessing and we stood to leave. I waited until Joyce left the dressing room and complimented her on the beautiful rendition of Bach.

"Oh, thank you. How kind of you to tell me. I'm glad you enjoyed it."

I noticed she looked pale and had dark smudges under her eyes.

"Would you like to come to my house for tea," I said impulsively. *Oh crikey. Did I just invite a murderer to my house?* That was unlikely.

"I'd like that. Nigel is going to visit his mother, and I begged off, so I don't even have to tell him where I am going."

I didn't comment. She seemed relieved to be avoiding him and her house for a time.

I fussed with the tea, using the floral china mugs we'd received at our wedding. They weren't something Mark and I were comfortable with, but they suited Joyce. I found some cherry loaf I'd bought from Helen Taylor, fetched the linen napkins, and set the repast on the table in the parlour.

Joyce had settled on the sofa with Gulliver on her lap.

"Gulliver," I said. "Down." Joyce wouldn't be able to drink tea or eat with Gulliver on her lap.

He rolled his eyes at me with disbelief, but got down and trotted over to his bed.

"He's a dear."

"He is," I said and poured her tea. "Cream? Sugar?"

"No, nothing, thank you." Joyce sipped slowly. "This is lovely. It's so peaceful here."

It was a good thing she hadn't come over a few hours earlier.

"Where is your daughter?" She glanced around as if expecting Amber to suddenly appear.

"She's at Beth Blackford's place. Stephanie is her friend."

"Oh, yes, nice family. Stephanie's a good alto. Amber has a lovely voice as well."

I agreed, and we sat in silence for a few moments then Joyce said, "I'm going to leave Nigel this weekend. Please, don't tell him, or he will hit me, and I might lose my resolve."

My tea cup stayed suspended; I was frozen. *Hit her?* Wife battering. I had never suspected that.

"I won't," I said firmly. Flashes of memory from long ago lit my mind: my dad cuffing me on the side of the head, Adam raising his fists, threatening me, and sometimes smacking me on my face, then following it up with another to the other side. I shuddered.

"No. Definitely, I won't. You have to get away."

"I am not staying to be the recipient of any more violence. He's always sorry. and he always does it again. I have had very good advice from a women's shelter. I'm on the board there, so Nigel never suspected I was looking for help for myself. He wanted to become part of that board himself. He wanted to supervise me at all times, but he was convinced by the rules that there were to be no men, even vicars, at the shelter, so I went there without him."

"Good for you, Joyce. I can't stand Nigel, and I didn't know he was hitting you. Do you want some brandy in that tea?"

She grinned. It made a huge difference. I could see how pretty she was when her eyes shone with humor.

"No, thanks. The tea's just right."

"What are your plans?" It sounded as though she had arranged an escape route.

"The shelter in Alton has set me up with another shelter quite a distance away. I'll stay there for a few weeks while I get my lawyer to serve divorce papers on Nigel and receive more counseling. From there I will contact my lover. He's a retired doctor and has bought a new bungalow for us at the seaside. I will be happy." She was now almost fierce.

"Wonderful,' I said. A new lover? I had no idea Joyce had a new lover. What happened to Jordan? I had to ask. "How long ago did you break up with Jordan."

"You knew about that?"

"Just recently," I said.

"About six months ago. He was a dear man. He was the one who gave me the courage to think about leaving Nigel. I hadn't expected anyone like Jordan to happen to me. The affair was a revelation. I knew Jordan was a man who went from woman to woman, so I didn't expect it to last. I'll always be grateful to Jordan." Jordan seemed to have an extraordinary ability to leave his lovers happy.

I worried that Mark and his team would put the wrong interpretation on Joyce's departure to the shelter. "Call the police station when you get to the new shelter and let them know why you left. Give them your email. You don't want them to think you have disappeared because of the murder."

She looked stricken. "I hadn't thought of that."

"They'll be understanding, as long as they can communicate with you."

"Oh, my word." She put her cup down. "I need to think of so many details."

"I have some good news for you, at least I think it's good news."

"What?"

"Did you know Nigel has a girlfriend?"

Joyce was astounded. "No! Really." She grinned. "That's fabulous. I'll tell my lawyer. Who is she? Here in the village?"

"No. She lives in Winchester."

"What a hypocrite. To think of how righteous he was about Jordan."

"He knew about Jordan?" Mark didn't think he had.

"He did and made me pay." For a moment she looked grim. I wondered if Nigel had made Jordan pay with his life. Had Joyce ever considered Nigel might have killed Jordan?

"This time he's not going to spoil my life." She leaned back in her chair for a moment. "A girlfriend. Lovely." She finished her tea.

"More?"

She held out her cup, and I filled it.

"Do you need any money for this move? I can give you some." Dreams and plans were all very well, but a woman needed to be practical.

"How nice of you to offer. I don't think do. I have saved some, but I knew I might be dead before I saved enough, so I'm going now with what I have. My parents have money, but I don't want to involve them as Nigel will frighten them. I can go to my parents in a month or two if I must."

I supposed she meant if her retired doctor rescinded her invitation, or he died, or one of them got ill or any number of fateful occurrences.

"I've stayed for years with Nigel because I was afraid I wouldn't be able to make my own money, but I've researched on line, and I will get a small subsidy as a victim of domestic abuse. I know my parents will give me money, but I'd rather not ask. They gave me a settlement when I married. There isn't much left of it. Nigel used it to buy a new car and furniture for the house. I'll be fine, in time. I only need to look after myself for a few months while I make sure my relationship with Peter is solid. I have no intention of going from the frying pan to the fire."

I knew what kind of courage it took to leave Nigel.

"I left an abusive relationship some time ago," I said. "Some of the plans I made were practical. Do you have a separate bank account from Nigel?"

"Now, I do. I have saved £300 which will help me out for the first week."

"You'll need more than that. Give me your email, and I'll transfer you enough to get by for a couple of weeks."

Joyce blinked. "That's generous of you."

"I've been in situation remember. Women unite here." I remembered with every cell in my body the fear of violence and the way it paralyzed you.

She smiled and gave me her address. I suppose she viewed it as a small loan. I typed it into my contact list.

"Give me a minute." I logged onto my savings account where I kept extra money.

"There. I put two thousand pounds into your account." I felt confident it would help. This was going to make a difference to her.

"Two thousand! Oh, you shouldn't have. That's amazing. That gives me all kinds of choice."

"That's the idea."

"But can you afford it? Your have a new daughter, more expenses, and I hear you are buying the Stonnings house." She leaned forward, concerned for me.

"I can afford it," I said. "I don't want repayment. Consider it a gift. Help out someone else when you can, and congratulations on your bravery."

I wanted to say: *get a good solicitor, get your half of the house and contents, be sure you are safe* but giving her money didn't entitle me to run her life.

Joyce cried a little, then left for home. I hoped she would escape from Nigel safely. If he had killed Jordan, would he kill Joyce?

I was exhausted. That much emotion drained me. I snapped on Gulliver's leash and headed out the door. We had a quick walk around the cricket pitch and back home. Gulliver joined me on the sofa where I sank gratefully into a nap.

CHAPTER NINETEEN

Monday morning after both Mark and Amber had left the house, I took Gulliver for his walk, fed him his breakfast, and settled my accounts for my last tour. Last week's bookkeeping was all about last year's taxes. Today, I had to update my accounts ready for next year's taxes. While it's always a chore, I have to keep good records or the end of the year is a nightmare of figures and lost receipts. I also like to ensure that the tours are profitable, so need to see the expenses and income set out on my Excel sheet. The last tour was only six days, so it wasn't as profitable as the fortnight tours.

I hadn't planned or advertised for my next tour. This was the first time I wasn't working on a second tour before I finished a first. I wasn't sure how to manage my time and keep Amber feeling secure. She made herself secure in many ways: she was reasonably diligent around her studies; she had at least one friend; she had healthy outdoor activities. Even her vegetarianism, while a little inconvenient for us, was no doubt good for her, but I worried. I worried the trauma of loosing her mother and coming to an entirely new family was going to be more than she could handle. I didn't know how to help her with that. I'd rely on Max-the-Wise-Advisor. I sent daily mental thanks to Amber's late mother and to her grandmother for their care and wisdom in raising her, but she was only ten-years-old. Someone should be home with her at night to see she made it to her riding and her choir, and to reassure her she hadn't been left without love and support.

Meanwhile, I had to attend to my business. How could we manage both? It was a problem I was no where near solving. I planned a fortnight tour and trusted we would work out the details of Amber-care.

I would like to take guests to the Orkney and Shetland Isles. Ann Cleeves set many of her books there. Marsali Taylor's Shetland Sailing Mysteries might not be as well-known to North American readers, but I could recommend those who sign up for the tour read them before they come. Alana Knight had a mystery set on the Orkney Isle. I could research and see if I could find more. The archeological sites there would keep tourists intrigued for days. The more I thought about the northern Scottish isles, the more excited I became about them. I would plan, then talk to Mark—and Amber. She would have an opinion and perhaps even a solution. It would have to be in the spring. Winter is grim that far north.

It was noon before I finished planning the rough draft of the Shetland and Orkney Isle tour. I felt a glow of satisfaction as I imagined the places we would see and the history we would learn. I loved my tour business.

Mark wouldn't be home at noon; he rarely stopped for lunch. Amber got a hot meal at school, at one of the few schools that still provided hot lunches. Bless Hampshire with its affluent residents who happily paid for the convenience of the catered lunches.

I let Gulliver out into the garden and wandered around, deadheading roses and admiring the growing chrysanthemums. They would be blooming soon and still be blooming on Guy Fawkes Day.

Deirdre called.

"I have an hour off between appointments," she said. "I've been thinking about your new house plans. Make sure you add cupboards. Those Victorians never installed enough cupboards. Take advantage of the space under the stairs, and any odd walls like indents where you could put a cupboard or a stack of drawers."

Deidre is nine years younger, but she has the oldest sibling attitude—dictatorial. On the other hand, she often has good ideas.

"Sounds smart," I said. "Perhaps I can get them to add cupboards to this part of the house."

"Hey! Why don't you renovate your side at the same time?"

My brain froze for a second. "That's huge."

"Yes, true. Maybe too much to take on." She said that reluctantly as if she had envisioned a massive make-over of both houses.

I dissuaded her. "I could consider a few things like cupboards over here, but I like the kitchen and the parlour we have, and I love the bathroom and bedroom."

"Right. Just the Stonning side then."

We chatted a few more minutes, then she left me for her next appointment.

I made myself a bacon and tomato sandwich, feeling a little guilty at having bacon in the house, when I got a call from Arthur Greenwood my solicitor.

"Come in when you can, Claire. I have the papers for you to sign."

"The house?"

"Yes, the house. The Stonning's signed early so you can close the deal today."

I almost yelped with excitement. "I'll be right over."

Arthur was in Alton, so I loaded Gulliver into the van with me and drove to Arthur's office. I parked in the Lady Place Car Park and walked with Gulliver to Arthur's office on Cross and Pillory Lane. I imagined, in centuries gone by, the pillory was where justice was executed for all to see, the poor convicted person sitting or standing with their head and hands in the wooden locks.

The square brick building had been modernized and had an impressive penthouse and a lift. Gulliver was suspicious of the lift. He stopped and sniffed the open door.

"Come on, Gulliver."

He planted his bottom on the tile floor and stared at me, his head cocked as if listening for further instructions. I held the door open with one hand and fished a treat from my pocket with the hand that held the leash. "Come on, sweetie."

For a treat, Gulliver would do almost anything. He trotted in. I petted him and praised him while the door closed. Arthur's office was on the top floor. The windows on every side gave a stunning view of the surrounding country. I was always impressed with it when I came to consult with Arthur and also wondered how much of my money went into maintaining such lavish offices. Still, his fees didn't seem out of line, and I trusted him. Maybe he had private income as I did.

"Congratulations," he said as he ushered me into his office. "Hello Gulliver." He went to his desk, Gulliver tugging at the lead to accompany him. Gulliver knew where Arthur kept the dog treats. When Gulliver had been fed, Arthur turned the file on his desk so I could read it.

"As you wanted. The house is in your name."

"I have left it to Mark should I die first. It isn't that I don't want him to have it."

"I know. I advised you to own it outright because it is also your office and you can deduct part of the expenses of the house against your income."

Mark had agreed to this. That meant I paid the property taxes. We shared the rest of the expenses.

"As you also wanted, I applied to have the titles of each house amalgamated so it becomes one house. That may take some time."

"All right." I read the sales agreement, noted the price was as agreed, and signed the document.

"I'd hand over the keys at this moment," Arthur said, "but you already have them."

I grinned. "I do, and I can't wait to renovate."

"Rather you than me," Arthur said. "It can be a headache." He reminded me of his brother Thomas who was a rose-growing friend of mine, but he was shorter and thinner. I knew he had two teen-aged daughters and his wife was a local nurse, but I didn't know the family well.

I smiled. "I suppose the actual renovation may be difficult, but the planning is pure fun."

He smiled in return. "Enjoy it."

I was in a festive mood as I left him. I didn't have time to visit Mark at the station. He'd be busy, and it was on the east side of Alton and not convenient. I needed to be home by half three. Amber would love to know the house was ours. We could celebrate. I stopped at the bakery and bought a chocolate cake. That was special, then made a brief stop at the wine merchant's and drove home with a bottle of Pol Roger Vintage brut. It was celebratory without being outrageously expensive.

"We got the house," I informed Amber as she came in the front door.

"I thought we already had it," she said.

"We had a contract, but now we have the title."

"So cool. It's really ours?" She dropped her books and petted Gulliver.

"It really is. I bought a cake and a bottle of champagne. We'll have a party tonight with your dad and celebrate."

"So cool. Let's make lasagna. Vegetarian?"

"Of course, vegetarian. You change and come down and chop the vegetables. I'll get the pasta boiling so we can put it is the oven."

"Text dad. He should try to be home for supper."

"I'll do that." I started toward the kitchen, then remembered I was going to direct her attention the hall table. "There's some mail for you." I pointed to the small table.

"Oh." She picked up the envelope. "Grandma."

Her grandmother wrote her once a week. Gulliver sniffed at the envelope.

"She sent a card again. This one's got a robin on it."

I smiled. I liked Freya, and I was happy she kept in contact with Amber.

Amber tore open the envelope. "You know, Grandma has a drawer full of cards like this. She sends them to all her friends. She doesn't text." Bits of the envelope floated to the floor. Gulliver sniffed at them.

"Well, it works for the two of you because you don't have a mobile."

Amber sent me a sharp look. "Yet."

"Yet" I agreed.

I sent a glance at the floor. She gathered her books and the pieces of the envelope from the floor and wandered toward the stairs, reading her message with Gulliver following her. She stopped at the bottom of the stairs, turned, and lowered the card. "She wants to come and stay. Is that all right?"

"Of course. When?"

"Tomorrow?"

She read the card again. "She says she has to come to London to see a specialist about her eyes. She says it's just normal cataracts, but she needs to check them out, so she'd like to take the train here and arrive tomorrow. She will stay at a hotel." Amber sounded worried. "There isn't a hotel in village."

"Ah," I held up my hand. "We've just acquired a new house that has two bedrooms. Let's get one ready for her. I'll call her and invite her."

Amber dropped her card and flew into my arms. "Oh, thank you, Claire. I love Grandma!" Gulliver, always ready to join in pranced beside us.

I hugged her back and laughed. "We have a lot to do. First, you change, then you get the vegetables ready, then we'll go over to the other side of our new house and check out the accommodations. How's that?"

"Great."

"Do you have ay homework?"

She glanced back. "How about I skip it?"

I considered that. "This time, skip it. I'll write an excuse note."

She dashed upstairs.

While she was changing, I rang Freya.

"I can only stay for a night, lass." She said. "Those specialist don't give you time to plan, they don't. Just yesterday mornin' her girl called to book me in. Shocking it is."

I agreed it was.

"It's just these pesky cataracts. I have to take the appointment or I will be a long time waiting for another."

"We'd love to have you. We'll get your bedroom ready here. We have room; you don't need a hotel."

"Really now? That's reet lovely."

"We're looking forward to seeing you. I hope you can stay the whole day. I'll let Amber take the day off school, so you can spend it with her."

"What about her studies?"

"You know, Freya, she could probably teach the class."

She laughed. "If it's na too much trouble, I'll just be off on the train to Alton, isn't it?"

"It is." I arranged to pick her up at the station and bring her home for supper. I'd have to make another celebratory supper as we would all be excited to see her.

Amber danced around me. "Grandma's coming. Grandma's coming." It was wonderful to see her so happy.

"Help me get her room ready."

We picked out some bed linen from my bedroom closet as well as some bath salts, soap, and towels. Amber and I were laden when we went next door to make up the bed. Gulliver danced around our feet. I'd arranged for Patrick and Rita to leave the bed in the guest room. Everything else would be removed by next week.

Mark did manage to get home for a six o'clock dinner. Amber and I had put out the second-best china, and napkins as well as some pink roses in a pretty vase. Mark and I had a glass of champagne and Amber had a taste. We'd finished the chocolate cake and had the rough plans spread out on the table when the doorbell clashed and clattered.

"I'll go," I said.

I didn't know who to expect, but definitely it wasn't Nigel—especially Nigel in a flaming temper.

"Where's my wife! How dare you hide her!" He was as tall as I was, but seemed bigger because his arm was raised, his fist clenched, and his fair hair, usually carefully combed back was hanging in disarray over his face. He was wild. My stomach clenched. I started to breathe faster.

"No. She's not here." What was I supposed to say to a distraught man? *Pay attention, Claire. Think of all those online courses you took on handling distraught tourists.* My mind went blank.

"She said you'd shown her the way to a better life. A better life! I didn't know she meant that was without me until she left. I came home from town, and she was gone. You know where she is. Tell me!" He moved within striking distance. He was capable of hitting me. He'd hit Joyce, and he was supposed to love her.

"Mark," I said. I didn't think I'd managed more than a whisper, but I heard him tell Amber to stay in the kitchen and keep Gulliver with her, then he was behind me.

"You want to put that arm down before I break it," he said quietly, "and charge you with attempted assault."

Nigel froze. He stared at Mark, then at his raised arm. He lowered it.

"My wife's gone," he said more quietly now.

"Has she?" Mark said.

"She left me a note. She said Claire gave her money."

"Claire is generous," Mark agreed. His voice was calm. It seemed to make Nigel calmer.

"Why would she do that? As long as Joyce didn't have any money she couldn't leave." His voice rose again. "Claire's interfering between and husband and wife. She's no right to do that."

There was a short silence. I knew Mark was putting together Nigel's threats to me, his temper, the possibility of violence Joyce had probably endured, and her flight.

"So your wife leaves you, likely because you're a violent sod, and you come to my house to threaten my wife because you're upset. What does that make you?" Mark's voice rose. Now, he was getting angry. The calm police officer was being superseded by the furious husband. I backed away. In any physical fight with Nigel, Mark was likely to win. He needed me out of the way. It wasn't going to come to that, though. Nigel was almost babbling.

"I'm sorry. I'm so sorry. I'm upset. Joyce can really upset me. I didn't scare you, did I, Claire?" He craned his neck to see past Mark. Mark stepped to the side to block him.

Nigel straightened and stared at Mark. He froze.

"Listen, Nigel," Mark said. "I'm going to walk you home, and you're going to stay there. You are not going to bother my wife in any way at any time, or you will find yourself in the local cell while I find enough charges to keep you there. Do you understand?"

Nigel sighed. "Yes. Yes. Sorry."

Mark took Nigel by the upper arm and turned him toward the street. He looked back at me. "Twenty minutes," he said.

I half-smiled and retreated to the hall and shut the door. I turned to find Amber facing me with a knife in her hand. Gulliver was sitting at the kitchen door behind her.

"Has he gone?" Amber said, her voice trembled a little.

"He's gone."

She dropped the knife. "He was going to hit you."

"Yes, he was—but he didn't." I opened my arms, and she ran to me.

She hugged me fiercely. "I am not going to lose you, too."

"Not a chance," I said and hugged her back.

She sniffed and stepped back, wiping the tears from her face with her sleeve. "He was scary."

I stooped and picked up the knife she'd dropped. "You're pretty scary too. You were coming to help."

Gulliver came into the hall and licked my hand.

"Well," she thought for a moment "We're family, right?"

"Indeed we are."

I put my arm around her shoulders and pulled her to me, nudging her toward kitchen. It felt natural. For the first time, it felt entirely natural. "So my intrepid warrior, what were you planning?"

"Are you making fun of me?" She eyed me suspiciously.

"Only a little bit because I am so relieved we're both all right. I truly admire your courage."

She smiled. "You were brave, too. You stood up to him."

"Truthfully, my sweet, I was shocked frozen and couldn't think or move. Sorry. I wasn't quite the brave heart you thought."

"You didn't run."

"Couldn't move."

We both laughed.

"What will happen now?"

"Now, your dad will take Nigel home, calm him down, and call a friend or an elder in the church to come and stay with him."

"Babysit him."

"More or less," I agreed, "and then leave him. I doubt Nigel will ever do something like that again."

"He's violent, though. Maybe he killed Jordan."

I considered that idea. "Maybe. Your dad will find out."

Amber stood. "Cocoa?" she asked.

"Good idea. I've gone off champagne for the moment." I'd let her take care of me. It would help.

She bustled around then brought two mugs of cocoa to the table.

"Did you really give Mrs. Fotheringham-Whitley money so she could leave?"

"She was leaving anyway. I just gave her money to make the leaving more comfortable and to give her more choices."

"Do you have a lot of money?"

"I do."

"My mum said that a girl should always have her own money."

"Your mum was right."

"I miss my mum. She worked a lot, but she always listened, you know?"

"My mum did too."

"Oh. Your mum is dead too, isn't she?"

"Yes, she is"

Amber reached out and took my hand. "It hurts, doesn't it?"

I nodded, taking comfort from her concern.

"Will it stop?'

I reflected on sorrow. "It gets easier, so you don't suddenly find yourself remembering her and crying in the middle of a shop."

Amber laughed. "Yeah, that happens."

"But you'll always have that hurt," I said. "It …softens somehow, but it's there."

There were tears in her eyes. "When I heard that idiot at the door, I was scared. And then I thought, 'He's not going to kill my new mum. No way.' So I got the knife."

I didn't know what to say. She was going to defend me. Part of me felt almost overwhelmed with gratitude that she would care that much. Another part was relieved she didn't get into the mix. She might have been the one that was hurt.

"Thank you, love. You are a warrior. I don't know what your dad would say about that. Maybe you should ask him what the most effective action would have been."

"For next time?"

"Oh, my word! There better never be a next time!"

She laughed. Gulliver poked his head up, and Amber gathered him onto her lap. He licked her face.

She didn't really expect something like this to happen again, but I remembered the times I'd been in danger both because of Mark's investigations and because of my own. I had Amber to consider now. Still, I couldn't have predicted Joyce would tell Nigel I'd given her money or that Nigel would react the way he did. If I could do it over again, I'd still give her money.

CHAPTER TWENTY

Mark found us still at the kitchen table when he arrived home. "How is he?" I asked.

"Embarrassed," Mark said. He reached out and held Amber's hand. "How are you?"

"I'm good. He didn't threaten me. It's Claire he threatened." She stared at her dad with disapproval. He looked blank for a moment, then his eyes lit with understanding. He took my hand.

"And how are you, my love?"

I reached for Amber's other hand. "I'm fine." We sat holding hands in a circle like a group of infant school children playing *Ring Around the Rosie*.

Mark sighed. "Any of that cocoa for me?"

"I'll make some," Amber said.

We disentangled.

I was still processing Nigel's weird behavior. "What did Nigel have to say for himself."

Mark waited until Amber returned with the cocoa. "Amber, what Nigel was doing here was a big-person problem. You shouldn't have to deal with an adult problem."

She started to protest. He held up his hand. "But since you were involved, I will tell you some things. All right?"

She was quiet.

"All right?" he repeated.

"Only some things?"

"That's right. Only some things." He made no more explanation.

"All right," she agreed.

"You have to keep this confidential. No discussing it with Stephanie, except what you witnessed yourself. No talking about our ideas around this."

That was quite a distinction for a ten-year-old to make. I hoped Mark wouldn't tell her too much.

He sipped his cocoa. "Ah. Thanks for this."

"Tell me, dad. What was the matter with the vicar?" She was serious, her brown eyes wide.

"He was upset that his wife left him."

"I got that," she said impatiently.

"He blamed Claire. "

"I got that, too."

"He thought he was too important, too necessary to his wife for her to leave."

"Even if she wanted to? Like didn't he get it that she didn't like him?"

"I don't think so."

"I guess he wasn't kind to her."

"That's exactly right," Mark said. "He was unkind and sarcastic. He thought because he kept her without any money, she would stay with him."

"Claire said she was leaving him anyway."

Mark looked at me for an explanation.

"She's set up an escape route with a women's shelter," I said.

"Good for her," Mark approved.

"That means I won't sing in the choir, doesn't it? Mrs. Fotheringham-Whitney was the conductor."

I hadn't thought of that. It might take some time to get a replacement for all that Joyce did in the church. Nigel might leave. There was going to be consequences at the church to her leaving.

"For a while, anyway," I told her. "The church will sort it out eventually."

"Will the vicar come back here?" Amber spoke quietly. "He's scary."

"No," Mark said. "He's very sorry and offered his apologies to you both. He won't be back."

There was a hard edge to Mark's voice. I noticed it, and I expect Amber did as well. I wondered what else Mark had threatened him with if he so much as glanced our way.

Amber yawned. Mark put his cocoa down. "Here. I'll escort you to bed."

Amber yawned again. "All right. Gulliver, come."

Gulliver peeped out from under the table where he had been hiding, hoping for crumbs.

Amber put her hand in Mark's as they climbed the stairs. Mark was back in ten minutes.

"Out like a light," he said and dumped his cold cocoa into the sink.

Amber was up early in the morning, making herself a protein shake when I arrived in the kitchen. It was something she had shared with her mother, and I encouraged her to continue the habit, although I didn't want to drink it myself. I could drink the one with blueberries mixed in it, but anything else tasted like medicine.

"Can I cut some flowers for Grandma's room?"

"May I and yes, you may. Don't take the big bronze chrysanthemums. Peter Brown is growing those for the fall fair." Correcting her grammar was automatic. I'm not sure if I was channeling my mother who taught me to speak correctly, or I was harkening back to my days of teaching English to executives in America, but I'd better restrain that habit. It could be annoying.

"The ones near the back fence?"

"That's right." I found a bowl and some dry cereal. I dished stewed apricots over it and added milk. I loaded the French press with Seattle's Best coffee and sat at the table.

"I can cut any other flowers?"

Was that too broad a permission? "Pretty much. What do you have in mind?"

"Some of the roses, some of those white flowers by the door."

"Sweet box. Yes you can have some of that. There's some white heather by the walk that might still be in bloom."

"What can I use for greenery?"

"Perhaps the laurel?" I pointed out the window.

She rinsed her glass, stashed it in the dishwasher, and headed outside with a pair of secateurs and Gulliver.

I checked Freya's room later. It was as welcoming as we could make it. Amber had set out a new bar of rose-scented soap, some bath crystals, clean towels, and a welcome card she'd made, as well as the flowers which sat in a cut-glass bowl on a dresser. I called the school to make Amber's absence excuse.

"Mrs. Taylor saw the vicar at your house last night and said he seemed upset. Has that affected Amber?" Isobel Cameron asked.

The village missed very little. "No. The vicar was here, and he was upset, but Mark took him home and calmed him down."

"Really?"

"His wife has left him." The village would know by noon today if Mrs. Taylor had anything to say about it. I might as well let Isobel know. "Amber's absence is to allow her to go with me to meet her grandmother who is coming to visit. I think it best if they have a day together."

"Oh, yes. She talks about her grandma. She lived with her for short time."

"That's right."

"I agree. It will be good for her to take some time with her grandmother. We will see Amber tomorrow?'

I promised I'd send her to school. Amber collected Gulliver, and we headed for Alton and Freya's nine-thirty train.

Amber dashed into Freya's arms as if she had been afraid she'd never see her again. She was only ten. She couldn't measure time the way adults did. She might have been afraid to tell us how much she missed her grandmother.

"Claire, luv. Reet grand to see you. There, there," she said to Amber as she hugged Amber. "Now, pet, let me have a proper gander at ya." She held Amber away from her and gazed into her eyes. Then she hugged her again.

"Ah, you're happy just. Now where's this mutt of yours?"

Amber shot me a sideways look. "He's not mine alone, Grandma. We share him."

"But," I put in, "he prefers Amber and sleeps on her bed now."

"There's a dog with good taste," Freya said.

I laughed. "He's in the car. You'll see him in minutes."

Amber sat in the back with Freya and Gulliver while I drove the short ride home like a chauffer to persons of importance. Amber chattered about Gulliver and how wonderful he was and how she was riding Sadie who had problems moving from a trot to a canter and how she wanted her own horse.

"I know you'd be good to any animal, Amber, me darlin', and would get up early before school to muck out the stables and exercise the dear one and after school to groom the horse and feed it. You're a responsible one."

Amber was silent. The work involved in owning a horse was just coming home to her. I mentally thanked Freya.

"Here we are," I said as I pulled up in front of the house. "Amber can take you to you inside."

Freya was determined to be cheerful and supportive of our domestic life. She must miss Amber badly, but it wasn't possible for her to have her granddaughter close, and she was determined to support us. I was lucky. She could have resented me and Mark and even Fate for making it too difficult to keep Amber.

Amber took Freya to her room then brought her back to the kitchen for tea. Amber made it, and I absented myself to my desk in the parlour, so they could have a private natter, and I could get on with tweaking the plans for my next tour. I had to determine the date and put it up on my web site.

Mark came home for lunch. I made ham sandwiches with chutney and cheese for Amber.

"What's this Amber's ben tell' me about the vicar?" A wazzock, is he?" Freya asked him.

"No," Mark said. "Not crazy but upset. His wife left him."

"Sounded right narky with it."

I agreed. "He was, but he's gone now and has calmed down."

"Is Amber in danger 'cause of your work?" Freya asked Mark.

Mark hesitated.

I answered. "The vicar was here because of something I'd done," I said. "I gave his wife, Joyce, some money so her leaving would be more comfortable, and so she'd have more choices. The vicar did not take that kindly."

"Oh." Freya was quiet for a moment. "Hmm. I don't like it. Not you giving the woman money. That was generous. But that the vicar found out about it."

"That bothered me. I didn't think Joyce would tell him."

She grunted a little. "You can't always tell what will happened when you stir the pot, as it were."

We were all silent. I expected Freya to bring up Jordan's murder, but Amber might not have told her.

"So, tell me about this new house." She changed the subject.

We were still talking about closets and sinks when Mark left for work.

After lunch I left Amber and Freya poring over the house plans and returned to working on my Shetland tour. Before I started, I took a few minutes to work on the code I'd received from Mark. It wasn't sophisticated. His forensic team would get it quickly. As far as I could tell, it was a list of names: Princess Patricia, Cumberland Archer, Majestic Magic. They sounded like horses. All the names had the letter B in front of them. I sent my discovery to Mark via text.

At three-thirty Amber left to collect Stephanie. Freya and I had a cuppa in the kitchen.

"She's happy," Freya said.

"I think so. She misses her mother, of course, but not all the time."

"That sorrow never leaves. My Brittany was a marvel."

"Tell me about her," I encouraged.

"She was full of life. Curious, always curious. Good at her studies always. It was so cruel for death to take her so young. When you see those crooked politicians smarming their way through life as healthy as an ox and then my sparkling, good daughter dying so young, you do give up on any kind of fairness in this world. She was a solid woman. Morally solid, you know? But independent."

"She never told Mark she was pregnant."

"Nah. I tried to convince her he had a right to know, but she said he wasn't ready to be a dad, and she wouldn't tie him down."

She hadn't given Mark any choice. "That was kind, but perhaps not wise."

She snorted. "Na kind so much. She just didn't want to share Amber. When she knew she was dying, she recognized his rights fast enough."

"We're happy to have Amber. She's a dear." I tried to comfort her because I was sure this visit was intended to be an investigation of Amber's situation.

"I can see that, love. But it's difficult. You have your job. I hadn't realized it took so much time away from home."

I was quiet, thinking about the challenge before us. "It does, but we will adjust and work out who stays with Amber. Mark is going to work from home more."

Freya watched me for a moment. "Well, you're young enough and energetic enough to deal with it, I guess."

I was young relative to her, but I didn't consider fifty-two young.

Amber arrived with Stephanie in riding togs, and we all headed out to the stables where the girls had a scheduled riding lesson. We left Gulliver behind in the house.

I had cancelled my lesson for today, so I could stay with Freya. We watched the two girls learn how to move through a prescribed course. Joyleen was teaching them, standing in the center of the paddock, giving them encouragement and directions.

"Amber's a beautiful little rider," Freya said. I felt a warm glow. Amber was such a pleasure to watch. I had no idea stepmothers and grandmas could be so bonded over our mutual love of a child. *You'll feel maternal occasionally,* Max had told me. *Just enjoy it, and don't worry when you don't feel that way.* It was a new experience and a bit overwhelming. I agreed with Freya that Amber was a good rider, swallowed, trying to cope with this new sensation, and looked for something to distract myself.

I saw two horses being led toward a far barn. They were beautiful bays. The sunlight shone on their coats giving the warm brown an almost red sheen.

Leah came out. I introduced her to Freya.

"Lovely little rider, your granddaughter," Leah said. "She could compete if she has the drive."

"Aye. I suppose," Freya said. "It depends on what captures her interest. Her instructor seems competent."

"My daughter," Leah said and smiled.

"You seem a lot more cheerful today," I ventured.

Her smiled broadened into a grin. "I am. I definitely am. Joyleen is going to the equestrian health course at the uni.

She'll live here betimes in Jordan's old apartment. I am so pleased she's settled."

I smiled in return, but I was thinking rapidly. Leah had had financial problems. Now she was giving up an income source, Jordan's apartment, plus she was paying university fees.

"Did your ship come in?"

"You could say that. Mr. Bennett sent over a copy of Jordan's will. Jordan left me a chunk of money, but the rest goes to Joyleen."

I stared at her, "Joyleen?"

Leah bit her lip as if punishing herself for loose talk.

"His daughter?" I guessed.

"Yes." Her voice was low, but I heard her.

"It was good that he recognized her."

"At last." She picked up energy. "He could have told her earlier. He refused to let me tell her. He said he'd leave if I did. Joyleen's a little confused and angry that he didn't tell her himself. We both are. But happy that he's making her dreams possible just like a good father should."

That was why Jordan had never enlisted Joyleen as one of his girlfriends. I'd wondered about that. "I'm happy for you both."

"Thanks. We can't access the money until after the inquest and, of course, Mark's lot need to find the murderer, so the courts are sure neither Joyleen nor I was the killer. But we're guilt-free, so I hope they get on with it and solve it soon."

"I'm sure they will," I said, conscious that Freya was taking in every word.

"Murder?" Freya said when Leah has left us.

I should tell her about Jordan's death. She had a right to be concerned about Amber's proximity to murder. "The riding instructor was killed."

"Where?"

"In the church, actually."

"The church!' Freya was scandalized. "Did Amber see it?"

"No." I said. "She knows about it, and we've talked about it, but she didn't see the body."

"Thanks be." She as quiet for a moment, her eyes following Amber's course in the riding ring. "I hadn't thought of murder, but then that's what Mark does, isn't it? Solves murder cases."

"Yes."

"Hmmph. I'm going to have to wrap my mind around that."

While she was thinking about the effects of Mark's work on Amber, I puzzled over the knowledge that Joyleen was Jordan's daughter. Why wouldn't he have told her?

People's motivations were inexplicable. Perhaps at first, he didn't know about her, then when he did, he arranged to work where he could keep an eye on her and be ready to help if needed. It was more than some fathers did but much less than most. He might even help her more now that he was dead. I shuddered a little. I was not going let that be my epitaph.

Freya was still quiet as we waited for the girls to finish their lesson by grooming their horses.

Leah and Joyleen had not known Jordan had left them money, so they hadn't any motive to kill him. In fact, Leah would have considered the loss of Jordan a blow to her business. Jordan had certainly angered or threatened someone. I wondered if he was blackmailing Nigel. If Jordan knew Nigel had a mistress, would he have blackmailed him? Possibly. That didn't mean Nigel murdered Jordan to stop the blackmail. It was a thought. Mark needed to check Nigel's alibi with the girlfriend.

CHAPTER TWENTY-ONE

Freya accompanied Amber to Stephanie's house to meet the Blackford family. She would approve of that warm, busy, noisy family. Mark arrived home with David in tow.

"There's too many people right now at the nick. We're looking for some quiet."

I suspected they were avoiding the pushy Mira again and gestured to the parlour.

"We'll take the kitchen table," Mark said and spread out papers on the tabletop.

Gulliver sniffed David's boots, gave them an exploratory lick, then turned back to his mat by the garden door.

I set out tea for the three of us while I asked questions. "Did you find the vicar's girlfriend?"

"Mira did," David said.

"Did the girlfriend give Nigel an alibi?"

"She did." David sounded glum. Nigel was now a suspect who had slipped off the list.

"Who is she?"

"A little rabbit of a woman, according to Mira, who works at the Communications and Engagement office of the Bishop of Winchester as a secretary." David read off a report.

Stella had told me she was a bookstore clerk. I'd have to remember Stella's gossip wasn't always accurate.

"Mira checked with Miss Sylvia Phillips. She said she'd cooked a 'nice' dinner for Nigel, and he stayed until about one in the morning. Mira said she cried through her whole statement."

"Not a lot of empathy seeping out of that report," Mark said.

"Somebody's going to have to talk to Mira." David looked up from the papers.

Mark sighed. "I'll do it."

"This Slyvia Phillips sounds like a solid witness in spite of the crying," I said.

"She does. We'll check with her neighbors and workmates."

"You might want to go carefully at the workplace. I remember they had an upset at the bishop's office. He had to resign over something to do with finances and the Isle of Jersey."

The two men stared at me. I shrugged. "I don't really know the details."

"But the Isle of Jersey," Mark was incredulous and momentarily distracted from his suspect list. "What's that to do with Winchester?"

"I agree, the Channel Islands are a long way from Winchester, but The Isle of Jersey is in the Bishop of Winchester's territory, or, at least, it was. We're talking about British bishops' bureaucracy here. Anything is possible."

"I had such a good theory for Nigel as the killer," David said. "Jordan was blackmailing him over the girlfriend, and he lost his rag."

"It's not going to fly," Mark said.

"No." David agreed reluctantly. "Can we eliminate Joyce?"

I was startled. "Joyce? I don't think Joyce would kill Jordan. "

David consulted his notes again. "By her own admission, she'd been dumped by Jordan."

"Yes, but she's found someone else. Much more suitable and reliable."

"What's this?" Mark said. "That's not in the notes."

"She told me she's going to take some time to carefully consider him before she moves in. Sorry. I thought you knew."

"We'd better check that. I'll send Mira, but I'll talk to Mira first, so she doesn't cause offence. We'll need the name and address of the new lover. If that checks out, we move her toward the bottom of the list."

David spoke up in Mira's defense. "She did a good job on tracking down that Yorkshire buyer."

I remembered that horse that Jordan sold to a buyer in Yorkshire. "Who was it?" I asked.

"A farmer, a Garrison Wood, who was selling his daughter's horse. She had gone to uni and hadn't ridden for a couple of years. He was pleased with the amount he got. Said it was more than he had expected but not a lot more."

"So legitimate then?"

"I think so," David said. "He's not a suspect. Seemed straightforward. He'll send us a copy of his bill of sale."

"Just tying up a loose end." Mark agreed.

I topped up our tea mugs with hot tea from the pot. "Who else have you eliminated?"

Mark checked his notebook. "Tony Michel was playing the organ and went straight to the pub after. He wouldn't have had time to clamber down the stairs to the front of the church stab Jordan and get to the pub. It's a near thing, but Mira couldn't manage to make it fit the times. She did a good job testing that."

Mark read from his notes. "Leah and her daughter Joyleen were both teaching and have witnesses to attest to them being at the stables at the crucial time. Mira found a witness who saw Rose Taylor at the cemetery, but the witness was certain Rose never entered the church."

"Who do you have left?" I asked.

"Stella, Garman, Jordan's new girlfriend if she exists and we can find her, any creditors Jordan might have, any criminals he might have known."

Stella. I didn't want Stella on their list.

"What have you learned about money laundering using horses?" I asked. "It seems to me that if Jordan was going to report the money laundering or in some way disrupt it, many people with a great deal of money would want him silenced. They would be much more likely to kill to protect their business than Stella would. She doesn't take her lovers seriously. Never has."

There was a short silence.

"We dropped the ball on that. Too busy with practical details and didn't stop to consider our speculations about money laundering might be correct." He shuffled the papers. "Here's the forensic accounting report." He read it quickly. "The summary's at the bottom. It says Jordan's accounts show a reasonable commission on the sale of twelve horses last year. No evidence of money laundering."

I ruminated on that. "If Jordan wasn't doing anything illegal, maybe nothing illegal was going on. Or maybe someone else was running a game."

"Have they figured out the codes" David asked.

Mark glanced at the paperwork. "Not yet. They've only had them a day." He turned to me. "Claire did, though. She translated the codes she had to the names of horses with the letter B in front of each one."

David held out his hand. I went into the parlour and got the paper on which I'd worked out the codes. "Give forensics this."

"Thanks." He glanced at it, then tucked it into his notebook. "B? Bob, Bill, Baldy?"

We stared at each other.

"It might not be a name," I said. "It might be an area, or a town."

We were silent. No one had any idea what it might represent. It was too broad. If it represented a last name: Badger, Bennett, Barclay. That was my name. Anyone could be suspected. There were a lot of people whose names started with B.

Mark reported "I contacted the Integrated Gang Unit, but no one has gotten back to me." Mark looked at David. "What about the will?"

"I got it?" David pulled out a bundle of papers. "He leaves most of his assets to his daughter, Joyleen Headly."

Leah had told me that.

Mark reached for the papers and started to photograph them with his mobile. He did it rapidly.

"How do you do it so fast?" I asked.

He held his mobile so I could see the face. "See this icon? You send the first photo, then press the icon, and it will automatically send all the others in turn until you press it again."

"Clever."

He finished recording the will. David took the papers back.

"He had quite a bit put by. He left some to Leah Headley and to a cousin. His horses he left to Joyleen. The solicitor is his executor."

"Garman Bennett?"

"That's right."

"He'll do a good job. He's fusty but intelligent. Just what you need in a solicitor," Mark said. "Garman is still a suspect, but we don't have a motive for him. He says he was out in his car testing it because it was making an odd sound and instead of taking a lunch break, he drove around. He took the car into the garage the next day, so I expect he's telling the truth."

"He is fussy about his cars," I agreed.

"We'll see if we can find someone who saw him on the road. Lots of checking still to do."

"Who do you like for the murder?"

"An unnamed criminal at this point. I like the money laundering theory; I just can't fit it to anyone." He clicked off his tablet.

"Passion. Greed. Fear." I said. "Strong motivations all."

"We'd better get back. I need to speak to Mira." Mark didn't like having to point out behaviour problems to his staff.

"Good luck with that," David said as they left.

I took out the ingredients for supper and began to assemble a cottage pie. I'd had a half hour to myself when Stella burst into the kitchen via the back door.

"Those gits! They suspect me of murdering Jordan. Me? I couldn't be bothered. They've been to the house twice. Garman's furious."

"Make a salad while you're talking. I have Amber's grandmother here for dinner."

"Will do," Stella agreed and opened the door of the fridge.

I fried the mince, added the onions and the spices, a few sliced carrots and peas, and let it all cook for a few minutes. I fried a cup of vegetables separately from the meat and put them in a small ramekin for Amber. Then I added tomato sauce and water to both and poured the mince mixture into a casserole pottery dish, a wedding present from Helen Taylor. I talked to Stella as I mixed the scone mixture for the tops: flour, baking power, butter, salt, and milk. I spread the mixture over the mince mixture and Amber's small ramekin and put both in the hot oven.

"Why is Garman so angry?" I asked as I washed up the utensils I'd used.

"He hates having anyone 'invading his house' as he puts it."

"Does he have something to hide?"

Stella was quiet for a moment. Her fingers which had been gathering grated carrot stilled. Then she recommenced her salad making and her talking. "He might, you know. I need to find out what's gong on in his life. I <u>am</u> going to leave him, and I need to know just what our financial position is. I have no intention of leaving poor. He may have another family for all I know."

"Do you really believe that?"

"No. But you can tell a man's life by his ledgers, Garman is always saying that, so I need to have a look at his accounting ledgers."

"Aren't they on his computer? How will you access the files?"

I shook out a tablecloth and spread it over the table. I set out the knives and forks while Stella put the newly constructed salad on the table. She sat and watched me as I finished putting the plates and glasses in place.

"I wish he'd mumbled it, so I heard it once. I'm quick at memorizing. I just need to hear it once, and I'd remember it."

She did have a phenomenal memory. It came of memorizing scripts, I expect.

"I can guess it if I try harder" she said. "Garman isn't very imaginative. I *hope* I can figure it out, or we won't get far."

What did she mean 'we won't get far'.

"I hear your daughter and Freya coming. I'll leave, but how about coming to my place tomorrow night. Garman in going to town to see his clients in the afternoon and his mother in the evening. He'll stay over."

Garman did that once a month. Stella enjoyed the break from him.

"I'll check to be sure Mark's home to stay with Amber, but that sounds good. I hope we find enough money so you can live well."

Amber and Freya were at the door as she was leaving.

"I plan on it." She kissed Amber's cheek, shook Freya's hand, and was gone. I meant to ask her about her recent affair with Jordan. Those racy pictures worried me, but I didn't get a chance. I'd ask her tomorrow.

CHAPTER TWENTY-TWO

In the morning, Amber kissed her grandmother goodbye and headed out to school. I helped Freya into my van, gave Gulliver the 'up' command, closed the door behind him, and drove to the station.

"I miss the lass mightily," Freya told me as she gathered her bags, preparing to board the train. "She's been a bright spot in our lives. We wander around like lost fledglings now, although she's the one who's fledged."

"We'll do our best," I said.

"I know that, hen. She's in a good place. You don't mind if I visit? Me and Granddad?"

I smiled. "Love to have you." I don't remember my grandparents, and I'd lost my mum years ago. "We could do with some relatives."

Gulliver poked his head between the seats and stared at her. She reached over and patted him. "He's good for our Amber."

I remembered the times when I had a touch of resentment that Gulliver preferred Amber—but just a small touch. Love doesn't divide, it expands, I told myself. Gulliver could love us both.

"Yes, he's good for her, and she's good to him," I agreed.

We were early so remained sitting in the car.

"I have something to tell ya, luv," Freya said.

I thought about the medical appointments so casually announced as the reason for this visit.

"You are ill?" I asked.

"Not me, luv. I am down here for my eyes, but it's granddad, he's failing."

They had been married a long time. It must be hard to know that. "I'm sorry."

"Aye. Thanks. He's not dying at the moment, but his memory's failing, and they tell me I have to make plans for him as it will get worse—and pretty smartly."

I reached out and took her hand. "I am so sorry." I didn't know what to say or do. "It must be dreadful."

"That it is. When I first heard that young doctor give the verdict I wanted to reach up to the heavens and grab whatever power that be and shake him for the unfairness of it all. My George who is a good man and has been a good man all his life! What kind of god lets this happen?"

I squeezed her hand, and she patted mine.

"I got over that right smartly. It didn't do anyone any good. But I'm sorrowful, no question."

We sat in silence for a moment. The enormity of such a diagnosis, the changes it had and would have on Freya and George's lives must be overwhelming.

"That's why you couldn't keep Amber."

"That's why, luv, and the fact that we *are* old."

The train was due any minute. Freya opened her door. "I'm not sure what we will do but selling the house will be one of the decisions I have to mull over. I can't keep it without George."

"I'm so sorry, Freya," I reached for her hand again. She grasped mine, squeezed it, and stepped away. "Thank ye. You look after our girl, now."

"I will." I had made that promise to myself, and now I made it to Freya.

I stayed until the train pulled out then returned home, thinking about the drastic changes Freya was facing.

My Shetland tour was almost in order. I had two more hotels to check on before I put the description and booking arrangements up on my website.

Rose was in the house when we returned. Gulliver cocked his ear at the sound of the Hoover upstairs. He padded to the bottom of the stairs but didn't go up. Rose didn't want him interfering with the Hoover. I returned to my computer and was concentrating on comparing prices of different hotels when Rose appeared with a cup of coffee.

"Oh, thanks, Rose. I guess I should stop for a few minutes." If I stayed hunched over the computer for hours without a break, my shoulders ached.

"I hear the police can't find the killer of Jordan Cooper. That's nasty, that is."

I agreed. It was nasty.

"Do they have any clues?' She knew I wouldn't tell her anything, but she always asked. She probably hoped I'd get careless and let something slip. I might if I was distracted or tired or not paying attention. If she wanted me in that state, she shouldn't have brought me coffee.

"Not that I can say."

She nodded as if confirming her own ideas. "They say Joyce Fotheringham-Whitney has left town. I'd heard she'd been more than friendly with Jordan. Did her husband find out? Did she kill him?"

It's always wise to give Rose something to glom onto so she doesn't go too far into fantasy. "She was upset certainly. She felt she needed some time away. The police agreed. She wasn't being restrained by the constabulary."

"Oh." Rose pondered on the information for a moment. "So, it's someone else."

Before she could dive into blaming another resident of our village I rushed into speech. "I have to get back to my computer, Rose. Thanks for the coffee."

She took that direction and left me.

As if Rose had conjured her up, an email pinged onto my screen from Joyce.

Settled in the shelter. Feeling much better. Thanks for everything. Will be in touch. Love, Joyce.

That was a relief. I still didn't know where she was, but I did know she was safe from Nigel.

The next email was from Stella.

Garman is out tonight. Having his monthly meeting with his big accounts and staying in London with his mother.

I had a mental picture of Garman having a meeting with giant ledger books, but I know Stella meant the luminaries of big companies who employed Garman.

Come over after the moppet is in bed. 9ish? And we'll investigate.

I answered. *Yes, if Mark can stay home. I'll get back to you.*

Mark agreed to stay home after Amber was in bed. Gulliver had gone up with Amber, and when I peeked in, they were both asleep.

"See you about midnight" I told Mark as I kissed him goodbye.

"Enjoy Stella. She's always good value."

I hadn't told him we were going to break into Garman's accounts. Mark was fussy about legalities.

Stella had poured a glass of cabernet sauvignon for each of us and put out some biscuits to nibble on. We settled in Garman's office, an oak-paneled room with drab pictures on the wall and dark, heavy drapes covering the windows. Stella turned on the desk lamp.

"I hate this room. It's as stuffy and old-fashioned as Garman." I was likely going to hear a lot of Garman's faults tonight.

"Before you start, Stella. I need to know something."

"What?"

"You said it was years since you had an affair with Jordan."

"It was years."

"No recent connection?"

She was still. "Oh, that."

"Tell me about it."

"It was just a one-time slip. Garman was away; Jordan was feeling badly about losing Joyce. I happened to find him at the stables one night when we were both down. It was just a comforting thing. Neither of us wanted it to continue."

"You'd better tell Mark. He already knows."

"Oh shit! He always thinks I'm a bad influence on you, and this will cinch it."

I was surprised. "No, he doesn't. He says you're good value."

"He does?"

"Truly."

"Oh." She sighed. "I guess I'll tell him then."

She took a sip of wine, set the glass beside her and moved to the computer. She sat in front of the computer, indicating I should sit on the chair beside her. I sipped wine while she clicked it on.

The first direction on the screen was a demand for the password.

"Do you know it?" I asked.

"Garman's so predictable. It's got to be his mother's name."

She clicked on 'show', so I could see her attempts. "Doris is her first name but that's too short and too easy to guess, so there has to be some numbers. Maybe her birth date. June 19th."

Stella typed 'Doris0619'.

Access denied.

"Hmm" Stella concentrated and wrote "Danvers0619".

The screen cleared and we were in.

Stella was jubilant. "Bingo!"

"Her name Doris Danvers?" I asked.

"That was her maiden name."

"That's an easy password."

"Agreed, but to be fair, few people would know her maiden name or her birthday. Now, quiet. I have to find the files I need."

She scrolled down an impressive list of folders. She stopped at *Finances: Household*. She paused there. I read the list: Finances: Investments A, Finances: Investments J, Finances: Investments S, Finances: Summary C.

"We're going to be here all night checking out all those investments."

"Then we'd better get started," Stella said. "We have to do it tonight. It's another month before I'll get a chance like this. Can you take notes?"

"For sure." I found a pen and some printer paper and prepared to record the information Stela found.

"No point in starting with the household bills and payouts. That wouldn't show where he got money from or how much he has. Let's start with Finances A."

She pulled up an Excel file that showed a list of stocks and bonds.

"I should print this off," Stella said.

"You print it off, and I'll take a picture with my mobile. That way we'll have two sources of information." I pulled out my mobile.

"Good idea, and it will be much faster than writing it down. Look at all these stocks" She was quiet for a minute, reading intently. "My Word! The total is two-million-five-hundred-thousand-six-hundred and forty-five pounds! I had no idea he made that much money, or that he had invested it. No wonder he could buy me a horse every few years."

We clicked through the pages of stocks as the printer whirred and gave us copies. Stella studied the names of the stocks. I took a picture of each page.

"Send those pages to yourself," Stella said. "I'd feel better knowing there is a copy somewhere else. If you lose your mobile those pages will appear on your computer at home, won't they?"

"Yes." I sent them to my computer. "It's synched."

We stared at the amounts.

"You are going to get a comfortable divorcé," I said.

Stella smiled. "I didn't expect to be this comfortable." She clicked out of a file and opened the Finances: Investments J. We studied the page trying to make sense of it.

"This is an income-expenses statement," I said. "See the top part is money in, the bottom part is expenses or money out and the very bottom is the balance."

Stella scrolled down.

"The balance is three million." Stella said. She stared at me "This is scary. What's Garman doing to make this much money?"

"Nothing legal." My tone was grim. I didn't like what we were discovering.

She went back to the top of the file, and we read the income list. There were lists of letters and numbers.

"It's a code," Stella said.

I recognize a couple of those." They were the same as the code I'd taken from Mark. "Those are the names of horses." B must have been for Bennett, Garman's last name.

"He sold them for astronomical amounts."

"Assuming the rest of them are horses, he was selling horses. Let's look at the expenses."

The same codes were there with a ten percent commission which left a huge balance. Garman was making enormous profits.

"Print it," I said. Mark would want to see this. I took a picture and sent it to myself.

"Let's do the next one," I said.

Stella clicked on Finances: Investments S.

The same codes for the horses appeared with the purchase price listed beside their names. The next column was headed Commission 10%. Even ten percent gave a grand total of two million. That must have been Garman's commission.

Stella dutifully printed off a copy, and I took a snap and, again, sent it to myself.

The final Finances Investment C file was an income-expense statement. It showed the commission from the earlier page of over two million as income. The expenses were the cost of initially buying the horses at a much lower price and a commission to Jordan. That total was taken away from the Garman's commission. The give him still a balance of over two million.

This time when I took the picture I sent it to Mark.

"Your husband," I said grimly to Stella, "is money laundering. He's buying horses at one price, jacking it up by astronomical amounts and selling it to crime lords. That's who wants to do this."

She took a deep breath and focussed on the spread sheet. "How do you know this isn't legitimate?"

"Look at the numbers, Stella. No one is going to pay that amount for a horse that previously cost far, far less. The last buyer wants to clean up dirty money. An expensive horse with a legitimate bill of sale will allow him or her to show expensive real assets. The buyer now has real assets as well as the money which Garman returned to him or her. See this column. It's the amount returned to the buyer, still leaving Garman with that two million as he didn't factor in that over-the-top price in his balance sheet. He can use the same money to buy another horse. Essentially Garman is selling bills of sale for his ten percent commission."

"This is dodgy," she said.

"It is," I agreed.

"Totally illegal, right?"

"Totally illegal." That was enough for Mark to apply for a search warrant. I didn't suggest that to Stella. She had enough information to absorb right now. She hadn't bargained on betraying her husband to the police.

We were quiet. "If he gets caught, he'll be broke." She was going to understand quickly that he *was* going to get caught because I was going to report him.

"Possibly." This was a huge scam. I clicked another shot of the last spread sheet and sent it to Mark. I was concentrating on texting him an explanation when I heard Stella gasp. I looked up.

Graman stood at the door. His eyes snapped. His face was taunt. He was furious.

CHAPTER TWENTY-THREE

We froze for a second. Garman was going to hit one of us or both.

"Why aren't you at your mother's?" Stella demanded.

Even in anger, the habits of the marriage prevailed. She demanded; he answered.

"She's not home tonight. She's gone to Aunt Barbara's. They're going to the flower show."

"I forgot about that." Stella said.

I managed to text. *Garman here. Come.*

Garman walked further into the room and checked the screen. Stella hadn't clicked it off.

"I see," he said.

He held out his hand for my mobile. I shut it off. He couldn't get into it without my fingerprint. I hesitated but saw the determination in Garman's eyes. He'd take it from me if I didn't hand it over. I passed it to him. He slipped it into his suit jacket pocket.

"I told you not to use my computer," Garman said.

"I can see why," Stella snapped. "You are running some kind of crazy scheme, making money off horses. Horses! I expect you just sell them to anyone and never concern yourself with finding a good fit, the right owner."

"I am very, very angry with you Stella."

She spit back. "I'm furious with you. You're a right prat! How could you use horses in such a scam? Do you know how the new owners will treat them? Do you know if they'll be cared for or just run until they die of exhaustion. Did you check to make sure for the new owners were responsible people?"

It wasn't the scam that upset Stella. It was the fate of the horses.

"Of course not," Garman said. "It's business. I'm not sentimental."

"You're hardly human," Stella was almost shouting. "You haven't got an emotion under that robot shell. All you worry about is making money!"

"You spend it. You can't complain."

"Well, I am."

Garman half-smiled. For some reason that sent chills down my spine. He was so calm, so reasonable, so determined.

Stella must have picked up on that. "What are you going to do now?"

"I was going to pick up my computer and a few clothes and leave the country."

"Running out on me, are you?"

"I wasn't planning on taking you with me, no. I thought you'd leave with one of your many toy boys."

Stella's face flushed, but she controlled herself and said nothing.

Why would he leave the country? Money-laundering was a white-collar crime. He could fuss about and delay the courts for years. He'd only need to flee the country if he'd committed a heinous crime, like murder. Murder was his reason for running.

Without thinking, I said it out loud. "You killed Jordan."

Garman cocked his head and stared at me. "Clever, aren't you? I never could see why you befriended Stella You are much smarter."

"Stella's smart." I defended her.

He shrugged. "Not smart enough. There is no way you two are going to stop me. You are not going to alert that busy inspector of yours until I'm long gone." He reached over and shut off the computer. "I'm not going to kill you. Not purposefully, anyway. You should be rescued before you die—unless help doesn't come in time. I'll call in the fire. The brigade should respond quickly. I won't set that in motion immediately, though. I need two hours." He was planning aloud. I didn't like his plans.

"You're going to set fire to the house?" Stella was incredulous. "What are you thinking?"

"I'm thinking of destroying evidence. There is nothing like a hot fire to rub out ledgers and computer files. As for killing you? I might, and I might not. You can sit in the cellar and worry about that as I have to set fire to the house. Worrying about that will leave you sweating in fear and give me some satisfaction."

Garman pulled a knife from his pocket and gestured with it towards the door. "To the cellar. I've heard enough from you."

Stella looked from the knife to Garman's face. What she saw there convinced her to move toward the door. I followed her. Mark would come, but Garman could kill us before Mark arrived.

"Was Jordan a part of it?" Stella demanded as she passed Garman. "How could he? He loved his horses."

"No. Stupid man. He bought horses for me. He knew I was inflating the price when I sold them, but he didn't know by how much. He found out because one of my buyers contacted him directly. Then, he knew what I was doing."

"Was he blackmailing you?"

"No. Again, he was foolish. He had the same scruples about the fate of the horses you do. He was going to stop me, to report me to the HM Revenue. No department of justice can touch the ruthlessness of the tax department. I'd lose everything."

He wasn't afraid of the justice system but the tax system. That was impressive. The justice system was concerned with...well... justice. The tax department didn't care. They were ruthless.

"So you killed him?"

"Let's just say his death was convenient for me."

He spoke conversationally as he herded us toward the kitchen and the cellar door. "It gives me food for thought, though. I could knife you and start a fire. You know assassins do it all the time. They drive by, shoot someone, and torch their own car, so there is no evidence left that they were involved. I could stash your bodies in the cellar and torch the place as I leave. No one will miss you for days, Stella. You don't do anything that requires you to show up. As for Claire, if Mark knows you're here, he will expect you home about midnight. You and Stella often chatter for hours. I have time."

We slowed our steps and almost shuffled to the basement. Would he really kill Stella? If he killed Stella, he'd also kill me. He'd leave no witnesses.

"Why do this, Garman?' Stella sounded more puzzled then fearful.

"Because I'm tired of never having enough money. You barely make enough to feed your horses, and I want the kind of life my customers have. I can get it, too. I spend time with men who are rich and who have power. Some of them have several wives at the same time. That attracts me, but it takes money. Lots of it."

"You have lots of it." I said, thinking of the totals I'd seen on those spread sheets.

"I have, and I'm going to keep it."

"You could let us go, Garman," Stella said. "Give me some of that money, and I'll get a divorce. You'd have tons of money left."

"Ah, I might have been able to work out something with you because your idea of honesty is self-serving. But Claire is another matter. She's is more principled. Her honesty is more universal. She'd let that officer-husband of hers know."

I stumbled against Stella and cut off her response. I knew she was going to say that I already had. She couldn't say that. That would put pressure on Garman to act quickly. I didn't want that. Time was our friend.

"Oof," Stella said and glared at me. I glared back. She blinked. I could almost see her brain working.

"Down the stairs," Garman said. I grasped the handrail—I didn't trust Garman not to shove us down the stairs—and followed Stella down into a large, dry cellar. Stacks of wine lined one wall. The windows were high and narrow. Garman glanced around. "Sit." He gestured with the knife to the two hard chairs beside a small table. A tasting table for the wine, I assumed. We sat. I moved my chair a little so that he couldn't attack us both at once. One of us would have a chance of surviving.

"No wifi down here. I will leave your mobile upstairs, Claire, because you no doubt have a GPS locator on it. I'll wipe my fingerprints off it."

I felt my shoulders relax and my knees turn weak with relief. He wasn't planning on killing us. At least, not at the moment.

He turned to Stella. "Look after the girls."

"Oh, look after the girls," she mimicked. "Turning your back on them too, are you"

He shrugged. "I'll have a new life." He turned and bounded up the stairs, slamming the cellar door. He had moved quickly and took us by surprise. We heard his steps overhead. He must be collecting his computer and documents from his study. He was a man of numbers and vast amounts of reports. He would likely take the time to pick up reports—unless he was going to burn them all. It would make sense for him to burn the house and everything in it. Maybe leaving the girls without a parent would hold him back.

He'd need his passport and some clothes. We might have a half hour before he put a match to the house—if that was his plan. Where was Mark?

"You know, Stella, his nasty nature and talk of fire makes me nervous. Would he torch this place with us in it?"

"No, of course not." She was quiet for a moment, then said, "Still, I don't think I know him well enough to say that with any confidence. He did tell me to look after the girls. That sounds as though he was planning on leaving me alive." She sounded dubious.

I had a vision of smoke seeping under the cellar door to asphyxiate us before the fire could reach us. But then fire could move so fast it could engulf us before we could consider how to fight it or escape from it. I shuddered. I wasn't going to stay here. I stood and wandered around the cellar. I eyed the window and dragged the chair over positioning it directly underneath.

"This won't get me high enough. You're taller. Do you think you could fit through that window if you got up there?" I asked her.

She scrutinized the window then her curves. "I couldn't."

I looked at my lack of curves. "Maybe I could."

She searched around the room until she found two loaded cases of wine. She pushed them over the floor to a position under the window. "These are heavy enough to make a stable platform. Let's put the chair on the crates."

We did that, and I managed to climb up and reach the window. I unlocked the window and pushed. It didn't move. It was a casement window. A nail driven into the side was preventing it from opening.

"I need some sort of implement to pry this nail out."

Stella prowled around the room and rummaged in a drawer.

"How about a corkscrew?" She handed it up.

I worked away at that nail digging into the wood surrounding it until it was loose and I could pry it out. Occasionally, we heard Garman's footsteps. He wouldn't stay in the house long. I didn't trust him to leave without starting a fire. He was fiercely angry at Stella. I clenched my teeth together. I was not going to die in a fire.

The window opened into the back garden. There was about a three-foot drop to the pebbles below. I glanced back into the room and found Stella examining a bottle of wine.

"This is an excellent year. "Would you care for a glass of merlot?"

I smiled. "Later. I'm going out now. I'll come back and unlock the cellar, but I'll get a constable to come with me. I don't want to run into Garman."

"Good idea. Preferably an armed constable."

"Right." The window was just wide enough and high enough for me to slip through— perhaps. It was hard to judge. I took a deep breath, let it out, and shoved. A man's hand reached for mine. For a second, I feared it was Garman and froze. I looked down to see Mark's face close to mine. The relief was immense.

"Need a hand?"

"Finally!' I said.

I squirmed; he pulled; and I was out, balanced on the widow sill.

"Stella?" he said.

"She can't fit through there. We had to get out. Garman might set a fire. He has a knife. He put us in the cellar."

"I figured something of the kind since you didn't answer my calls."

"Who's with Amber?"

"Rose and Gulliver."

I struggled the rest of the way, and dropped into Mark's arms. He kissed me briefly.

"Run through the garden, to the gate and into the squad car. All right?"

"All right."

I turned to call down to Stella.

"Don't," Mark said quickly and quietly.

"Oh, yes, of course. You don't want to alert Garman." My brains must be scrambled. Fear can do that.

I scurried through the garden, to the gate and the squad car as directed. A female office was driving. Mira. Mark had her come on this raid, but he didn't want her in a position to cause him trouble. Another squad car was there. Cst. Witten was standing by it; his broad shoulders were reassuring. Andy met Mark, and they entered the house together.

Mira and I watched the front door.

"He shouldn't be in there without more backup," Mira muttered.

"He has backup." There were three of them.

"Not enough. He's got Sergeant Forsyth who isn't even on this case any more."

My sudden fear subsided, leaving me angry. Mark probably called Andy because he couldn't get hold of David. Andy lived close by and his husband Bruce could mind the kids. Good choice. Andy was experienced. Mira was not.

"What's wrong with you? Andy is great backup. Bertie's got muscle. Did you think you'd be better?"

She started to speak, but I interrupted.

"Look at yourself! You're complaining because you aren't inside, part of the team. Why is that, do you suppose?" Why didn't she look at her personality: rigid, uncompromising.

Then I was ashamed of myself. She was contributing to solving this case and doing her best. She was young, ambitious, and not personally involved here. She couldn't view this rescue operation the way I did.

"Sorry," I mumbled.

She didn't answer, just maintained an angry silence.

Oh, well. We weren't going to be friends.

In ten minutes, Mark came out pushing a handcuffed Garman in front of him. Andy and Bertie followed. I jumped out of the squad car and watched Andy and Bertie put Garman, who hadn't said a word, into the back seat of the second squad car. They'd take him to the station.

I met Mark. "Can we get Stella?"

"Let's do that." He stopped to ask Mira to wait.

Stella was sitting at the top of the cellar stairs, drinking that fabulous wine.

"I have two glasses," she said when we opened the door. "Oh, here's Mark, the rescuer of confined maidens or perhaps not maidens. Matrons. How lovely to see you. I was expecting smoke, you see and you are much more welcome. There's another glass in the cupboard. Claire, you said you'd have a glass of wine." Her voice sounded brittle as if she had drunk too much and was trying to act sober, or she was afraid she'd fall to pieces and was talking to keep from wailing.

"I did promise," I said to Mark.

"Have a quick one then. But, Stella, don't drink more than one, as I still have to get a statement from you."

"I'll drink just enough to calm my nerves."

I slid a glance at the bottle. She hadn't drunk much before we arrived.

We solemnly toasted. Mark didn't drink but watched us with some amusement.

"Here's to Garman, wherever he may end up," Stella said and looked at Mark. "In prison?"

"Quite likely," he agreed.

"May he stay there—a long way from me."

We drank.

CHAPTER TWENTY-FOUR

Stella and I each dictated a statement and signed it at the station. Superintendent Addison had climbed out of bed to attend. My first thought was that she didn't trust her staff, including Mark, to take correct statements; then I tried to be fair. Mark couldn't take my statement because he was my husband. It was possible the super wanted to be sure the case against Garman was tight.

"She's as teasy as an adder," David warned us when we arrived at the station. I was expecting a difficult time, but it was only long, not acrimonious. It was two hours before the superintendent was satisfied, and we were allowed to go home. Mark drove us first to Stella's place where we walked to her door.

"Will you be all right? You could stay in our new spare room," I said.

"I'll be fine. It was Garman who killed Jordan, so there isn't any murderous maniac roaming around." She gasped a little as she spoke, perhaps just now realizing she'd been living with that murderous maniac.

Mark reassured her. "We'll keep him on unlawful confinement and threats charges until we can get the evidence we need to charge him with money laundering and possibly the murder of Jordan."

"Do you have his computer," Stella asked as she punched in the code on the door pad.

"We do."

"That's good. He always writes down everything. You should find your evidence." She walked into the house, then turned back to face us in the doorway. "Do you think I'll be poor when you find all his money?" she asked Mark.

Mark considered her situation for a moment. "The Crown can't take your house from you, so you will at least have that."

"Oh, good to know." She kissed him on the cheek then did the same to me. "Good night, my friends."

"Come over tomorrow," I said, worried that she might be depressed, despondent or reckless.

"Yes, tomorrow," she sighed.

That sigh checked my sympathy. Stella was getting all the drama she could out of the situation.

"Stella," I warned.

"All right. I'm fine, really."

Perhaps she was. It would be a relief to her to have Garman in jail. I worried about her, though.

"Do you think Stella will be all right?" I asked Mark as we drove home.

"Stella will always be all right," he said.

I wasn't so sure. She was brash on the outside and vulnerable in her core. The exact opposite of Joyce now I thought about it. Joyce was soft on the outside but steel inside.

Mark parked in front of our house.

"We are going to have to give Rose some information," I warned Mark as we got out of the car, "in return for responding to your call for a sitter."

"Hmmph," he grunted. But he did tell Rose a little about the evening. I heard him start on the abridged story as I climbed the stairs to check on Amber.

Gulliver lifted his head then lay it back on bed beside Amber. She looked angelic, her dark, curly hair spread on the pillow, one hand on Gulliver, the other lying on a book. I removed the book and kissed her good night. She didn't stir.

I had a bath and finally got a little warmer. I rubbed arnica on the bruises on my ribs and shoulders, impressed there by that tight window. I donned my warm pyjamas and a dressing gown. It wasn't cold out, but I felt cold. Mark had returned from driving Rose home and had tea on when I went downstairs

We settled on the easy chairs at the end of the kitchen. I munched chocolate biscuits and offered some to Mark.

"Just what I need. Carbohydrates. Amber all right?"

"Sleeping."

"Good." He let a deep breath. "Are you all right?"

"I am." I did a fast mental inventory. The notion of fire had terrified me. I managed to stay calm now with just the occasional shudder. "What's going to happen to Garman?"

"If we can get the evidence we need—and I think we will if he kept records of everything—then he should get a long prison sentence."

"What about proving Jordan's murder?"

"That will be harder, but since we're pretty sure it was Garman who killed him, we'll find the evidence. He had the motive and the opportunity. We're hoping we'll find Jordan's mobile in Garman's study or his work office."

"Didn't you get a location from the service provider?"

"No yet. They are more bureaucratic than the government and take an age to execute a simple request. We'll get him, though."

Mark was confident of his case because he knew Garman's fussy personality and his penchant for writing down everything. Garman was going to be convicted by his own habits.

The house was quiet. Peaceful. Stella's house would not be so calm. Her family had been blown apart, the husband and father no longer reliable. Garman hadn't been a nonentity. The girls had relied on him to support their education and their ambitions. And he had done so. *Don't give him too much credit, Claire. He could well afford it.* Now that support would drop away. Stella was going be her daughters' refuge and their solace as well as their banker. How would that change her? She might not realize how strong she could be. I had faith she'd manage to keep a home where her girls felt supported. I wondered how Amber would take the arrest of Garman.

Amber showed up at breakfast. "Gym today." She indicated her bulging rucksack.

"Volleyball?" I guessed.

"Volleyball." She agreed. "What happened last night? Gulliver kept turning around in bed."

I told her. She forgot to eat her toast she was so enthralled.

"The cellar? Mr. Bennett locked you in the cellar?"

"He did, but your dad came and arrested him."

"Mr. Bennet's in jail?"

"He is."

She snapped off a piece of toast and chewed on it. "You really live, Claire. Locked in the cellar. Why?"

I gave her a brief version of why.

"Hmm. He was something in the church, wasn't he?"

"The treasurer."

"The treasurer. Was he taking money from the church?"

"I don't think so, but the police will check."

"They'll get forensic accountants. Dad told me about them."

"No doubt," I agreed.

"It's interesting living here," Amber said. "But I miss Grandma and Granddad."

"I know you do."

"I was thinking. You know, we're going to have more room. Could Grandma and Granddad come and live with us? They could look after me when you and dad are away, and we could look after them because they're getting old."

I stared at her. She had an amazingly good idea there.

"That sounds like an excellent plan. We can talk about it." They might not live with us; they might prefer their own house close by; or they might come to stay for weeks at a time and return to Yorkshire. I'd talk to Freya. With George's progressing dementia, it might be just Freya with us and George in a care home.

"Great," she said.

I handed her the lunch tickets. The school provided a hot lunch, but she needed to have tickets for it. "Enjoy your day. Remember, don't talk about what happened last night."

"Ta." She pocketed her ticket. "The vicar's in a knot and the treasurer's in jail and the choir conductor has disappeared. There isn't going to be any choir this week, is there?"

"Highly unlikely," I said. "But the church will get another choir leader."

"And another vicar?"

"Quite possibly. If your choir doesn't reassemble soon you could join the community choir."

She was thoughtful. "I'll talk to Stephanie. Maybe we'll join the musical theatre. That sounds like more fun."

Gulliver accepted the last bit of crust Amber fed him and followed her to the door. From now until Amber arrived back home, Gulliver was my dog. I was lucky to have both a daughter and a dog.

Stella came over in the afternoon.

"I told the girls," she said as she sat at my kitchen table.

"How did they take it?"

"With near hysterics, but I got them calmed down. Louisa wasn't surprised. She said her dad had a computer for a brain and no emotions, so she didn't expect him to be totally honest. She was surprised he was associating with criminals, though. She thought he'd be too fastidious. Pippa was the worst. But she's the youngest, and she takes everything with drama."

I didn't say it, but Stella smiled. "I know: the acorn doesn't fall far from the tree. We understand each other. She'll need about three more wild phone calls and a visit home, and then she'll get back to her life."

"What about their uni fees?"

"I have enough for that. I'll not be able to buy another horse for some time, though. That grieves me."

We were silent. Stella's horse was to her what Gulliver was to me. I glanced at Gulliver sleeping on the rug near the door. I couldn't stand to give him up.

"Do you want a loan?"

She grinned. "Ah, to have your fortune. No, I will get another horse, just not yet. My solicitor said I would be able to keep the house and its contents, as Mark said. But all that lovely millions Garman had accumulated in stocks and bonds will go to the Crown."

"Don't pine for it. You'd never have seen any of it anyway."

"True, Garman would have kept it all. I'll sell the house when the Crown finally lets me—probably in two years—and move into something smaller that doesn't take so much money to keep in good repair."

She sounded surprisingly practical. She must realize that she had relied on Garman to bail her out of any bad decision. Now she was on her own.

Just when I decided she was emotionally stable and practical, she started to cry. Huge tear drops overflowed and ran down her cheeks.

I patted her shoulders and passed her some tissues.

"You know, Claire, when I think of Garman he seems to be disintegrating, like a man you see through a rainy window. I expect it's my image of him or my understanding of him that's disintegrating. I thought all those fussy OCD accounting traits showed steadfastness and reliability, but they were used to create a fraudulent life. I thought he was so...so... respectable! He had his position in the church, in the town. That's all melted away. I don't like what's left."

I held her hand while she cried. "I'm crying for the brave dream I had of our modern, workable marriage. What a sham. I don't know anything," she moaned.

"You couldn't have known. You had what appeared to be a good life."

"I had the trappings of a good life; I didn't have the substance." She stopped crying, wiped her eyes with her tissue, and sniffed. She sat up straight, checked her mascara in a small mirror she had on a keychain, patted her hair in place, and let out a huge sigh. "Have you got any scotch?"

I didn't think she'd cry again.

Later that afternoon Gulliver and I walked through the village to the river. Gulliver patrolled the bank looking in vain for a duck.

"They're hiding or sleeping, Gulliver." I had no idea where the ducks were. In another stream or river, perhaps. I threw Gulliver a stick, and he chased that for a few minutes.

Amber had a good solution to our child care problem I'd talk to Mark and, if he approved, talk to Freya and George. They might not be ready to move, but they might. They loved Amber, too. Freya might think of some way of helping us with child care that I hadn't considered.

I called Gulliver and we made our way along the footpath to the village. I gazed at the rooftops, the crooked streets, and the stone buildings. Ashton-on-Tinch had been a village for seven hundred years. It would be shaken by Garman's acts and his effect on the church, but the community strength would flow back as it had done for hundreds of years and surround us all in village concern. Stella would survive. She might grieve for lost dreams and plans. She had married with the same sense of possibilities that most of us do, and that marriage had shattered around her. She would shake off the problems and details that the break of trust had thrown at her and manage them one by one. She would do it with only a few days of mourning, I was sure. She'd make plans and work toward them. No doubt, she'd drag me into some of them.

"Come, Gulliver." I snapped the leash on his collar—I didn't trust him not to run in front of a lorry—and started through the village to home. I ruminated on the notion of change. Change was part of all our lives. Stella wasn't the only one who had to adapt. It was a though the gods had picked up the village, shaken it like a kaleidoscope and set it back in place, leaving Nigel and Joyce, Stella and Garman, Leah and Joyleen and the rest of us with a new view of our lives

The villagers weren't the only ones who had changed. I thought back to when Amber first arrived. She'd been the newcomer who had cautiously felt her way into our household until she was confident enough to assert herself. Mark and I were lucky that she was kind and tolerant of our awkward parenting skills. We had come quite a way from those first days traveling toward a tight family unit. So far, it was a surprisingly satisfying journey, if frustrating at times. I expected Amber would have some challenging experiences in store for us. I found I was smiling at that thought. Teenager years were coming up. What a roller coaster that could be—thrilling, exciting, terrifying. Mark and I would be scrambling to give her wise counsel and good choices while keeping our equilibrium on that wild ride. I was still smiling. It would be worth it.

ABOUT THE AUTHOR

© Duke Morse

Emma Dakin lives in Gibsons on the Sunshine Coast of British Columbia. She writes fiction—traditional, *The British Book Tour Mysteries*, and historical mysteries, *Murder in Vancouver - 1886*,—and non-fiction. Her memoir *Always Pack a Candle: A Nurse in the Cariboo-Chilcotin* was a finalist in the Lieutenant Governor's History Award and winner of the BC Historical Society Award as well as a BC Arts Council Award. The sequel *Always on Call* was a finalist for the BC and Yukon Book Prizes Bill Duthie Award. But she keeps returning to her favorite genre, traditional mysteries. She travels to Britain to villages, towns and cities she features in her books, meets people who live there and eats in the elegant restaurants—all in the name of research. Her love of the British countryside and villages and her addiction to reading traditional mysteries keep her writing about characters who live and work in those villages. She enjoys those characters and trusts you will as well.

www.ingramcontent.com/pod-product-compliance
Lightning Source LLC
LaVergne TN
LVHW031538060526
838200LV00056B/4555